Brushed OFF

M. LEE MUSGRAVE

Black Rose Writing | Texas

ISBN: 978-1-68433-649-4
PUBLISHED BY BLACK ROSE WRITING
www.blackrosewriting.com

Printed in the United States of America
Suggested Retail Price (SRP) $17.95

Brushed Off is printed in Garamond

*As a planet-friendly publisher, Black Rose Writing does its best to eliminate
unnecessary waste to reduce paper usage and energy costs, while never
compromising the reading experience. As a result, the final word count vs. page count
may not meet common expectations.

As an artist and author, during my many decades within the art community I have met and worked with a vast array of engaging individuals. I am especially thankful to those who enthusiastically encouraged and championed my creative efforts. They have all been very kind and patient. Among those helping with this project are long-time acquaintances Bob Hicks, who edited the first draft and Jorge Barragan, who rectified the Spanish dialog --- and both of whom, despite their busy schedules, took time to suggest ideas that helped make this project unique and a joy to write. I honor and value their friendship.

Brushed OFF

CHAPTER ONE

It was a placid November night, the kind that lulls me into thinking I should stay in Los Angeles despite my misgivings about the dissonant appeal of its sanguine façade and the schizophrenic nature of its mixed blessings.

I had been standing on the deck, gazing at the empty beach through a veil of Cerulean moonlight, when a leisurely scent of sea air began teasing my nostrils and thoughts. Should I return to my easel and the sly seductive aroma of fresh paint or continue studying the ripples of light skipping along waves at the edge of the dark Pacific?

I never really did decide for as I stood there quietly musing, a metallic mauve colored Mercedes s560, with its lights off and making a low guttural sound, drifted into the cul-de-sac.

I strained to see through the aberrant ochre glow glaring from the nearby street lamp, but little of the 560's alluring form was visible and even less of its shadowed driver. My eyes drifted back along the subtle curves of the umber sand dunes, beyond the slithering concrete bike path, toward the open sea while my mind fondled recurrent timeworn thoughts of moving north.

I was feeling tired, but my sleepy left eye still managed to catch the 560's gentle quiver as it sidled forward. It seemed to be on automatic pilot as if its occupant set it to obey the no-parking sign.

The city had recently installed a new kind of yellowy-orange sodium-vapor bulb in the street lamps of Ocean Park, supposedly easier on the eyes, but to me they made the night and the scene seem abnormal. Before I could tilt my head for a closer look, the car's dawdling journey cut short. A burning cigarette flew from the driver's window, cool blue halogen headlights cracked the murky darkness, and the revving engine lifted the front of that sleek marvel of engineering as it sling-shot out of the cul-de-sac with sweet ease.

By the time it reached the corner it must have been doing sixty or more. Even after it was out of view I could still hear it charging like wind rushing through a narrow canyon. My blood woke up and surged while my right ear rang and my pulse warned me metal and glass were about to be redesigned. But erie tire shrieks broke the moment followed only by a bewildering silence filling the sullen night. Undoubtedly the stop sign at Neilson Way had fulfilled its intended purpose, or so I supposed as an abrupt breeze rustled the dry fronds of the palms. I quickly retreated back into my cocoon, where bright studio lights seemed as though they could burn away all trace of gloomy thoughts germinating in the back of my mind. But, it was futile. The pulsating colors filling the canvas before me only heighten my sense of anticipation. Seeds of conjecture were sprouting and fabricating scenarios. Why would anyone with such classy wheels be dilly-dallying around Ocean Park at this hour?

"Only fools and lost tourists wander around this neighborhood at night," I whispered to myself.

My mind felt a strange rejuvenation, but my eyes were still drooping like the jowls of an old hound dog. Perhaps it was a sloshed executive from Brentwood trying to dilute his inebriated blood with some sea air before sneaking home to a trophy wife in an over mortgaged mansion. No doubt he'd been drinking to soothe out a tough day trying to earn enough to keep them both and tootling around in a silky 560 made it all seem doable.

"No, no, it must have been a wired teen out joy riding pop's wheels while pop was out of town. Yeah, that's it, no problem. Forget it." I said out loud, as if that would put an end to any further fantasies.

Fumbling for my favorite faux Budz-chacom chew-toy pipe, I settled down into my aging and threadbare La-Z-Boy. I was intent on giving my full attention to the problem I'd been working on all day ... should the conjugated yellow scalene be another color or perhaps its shape is not quite right? Should I scumble it or keep it clean and crisp? The more I stared at it, the more it slapped me back.

I bit down hard on the briar and leaned forward, determined to regain control over the commanding image. My eyes cried for relief. Metamorphosis took control and they succumbed to a timeless trance where yellow became lavender.

I turned away quickly, tensing every muscle at the back of my skull. My eyes opened again and focused on the white fridge in the kitchen nook. There was a brief pleasant moment as the inclined side of the unequal sided arrowhead darted in and landed in a deep hue of Thalo green. It hung on the fridge door as if magnetized. I craned my head longingly toward the stairs leading to the bedroom loft. The shape surged forward again, leaping up each gray step, getting lighter and lighter in value as it ascended into the cool darkness above.

"O.K. this time I'll fix you; I'll focus on the shadows and you'll disappear."

I think that's what I muttered in my drowsy stupor.

CHAPTER 2

The back of my neck was in a knot. My right arm didn't seem to work and in the distance I could hear wet sandpaper scraping the end of my nose. My eyes peeked through slits to the sight of a long pink tongue surrounded by pearly white fangs while hot, smelly, dog chow coated breath invaded my lungs.

"Duie stop! Yeah, yeah I like you too, but it's too early."

The words stopped, as if my mouth were glued shut while my eyes seemed permanently focused on the studio ceiling. At such an angle the black jacketed track lights resemble one-eyed ravens witnessing my resurrection. Beyond them the skylight framed a clear blue sky filled with circling white gulls.

The image made me contemplate setting aside the abstract celestial landscape I'd been working on for most of the past 24 hours and redirecting my energy toward completing the California Artists Log video whose deadline was still looming on the top of my to-do list. CALog is a public television series I host and it is my bread and butter while my own painting career is in, shall we say, transition. It's a challenging position to be in, a real balancing act between being a gracious TV host who has to hold in reserve his personal feelings about much of the LA art scene and redirecting my own personal lexicon of contemporary landscape painting. The first requires a high level of repartee and the other a deep seated commitment to meaningful visual exploration.

A little bit of self-analysis always seems like time well spent, but at the moment my mind was still muddled maybe even befuddled.

Duchamp's barking and scratching at the sliding glass door sent my thoughts of doing anything further into never-never land. I was still too lethargic to force my mouth to function and Duie wasn't listening anyway. He wanted outside to give a goldenrod shower to the nearest mound of pristine pearl white beach sand and to deliver his gruff good morning vocals to the local wing set. His joy at charging them into panicky flight each dawn has always been relentless. Ah, the simple life but, then again, to envy is to waste ones desire. Time to get up.

Deciding to forego the comforts of my bed for the tortures of the antiquated, spring-sprung La-Z-Boy was not a choice I could recall, but there was no denying I had made it and every joint of my body was complaining. Duie wanted to do his business outside and I certainly needed to be reborn, so there was no getting past it. It was time to rise and shine or at least shimmer a bit.

After a slow, careful shave and a speedy, nippy shower Duie and I headed for our race-walking along the freshly raked beach. Ocean Park beach always looks surreal on Thursday mornings. At the crack of dawn huge motorized monsters arrange every grain of sand into neat orderly rows. When you stand on the pier and scan the sprawling shore it looks as if the City Council decided to help the World Food Council by turning the area into a farm. But in reality, the mechanical raking is done to make the beach look tidy and unsoiled so the weekend onslaught of tourists will feel welcomed and at ease.

Race-walking is a long-distance discipline within the sport of athletics. Although it is a foot race, it is different from running in that one foot must appear to be in contact with the ground at all times. I do it only for exercise, not sport.

With Duie doing the scouting in front, we followed our usual loop; north along the bike path to the pier, beside the pier pilings to the water, alongside it to the city line and back by way of The Promenade. Some mornings, when painting seems like a dead-end street or editing on the latest CALog doesn't seem Emmy-bound, we'll go all the way to the Venice Pier or even to the marina. But this was a regular day, so I was set for my final duel with the Garcinia yellow scalene and to finish editing my long overdue CALog video.

While watching out for small bits of glass and globs of who-knows-what in the wet sand, as well as admiring Duie's determination to bite each incoming wave, I realized there was more activity than usual for the morning hour over toward the nearby aging business buildings. I was already tired of race-walking anyway, so I shortened the loop and headed over. The area is very eclectic, both in architecture and people. There are sparkling new two story California light and space homes standing next to old 50s era wood bungalows and a few nondescript gray industrial buildings, plus even a couple of office and storefront complexes, the kind most often referred to as *architorture*. The commotion was on the west side of the second industrial building near the entrance to artist Brice Peregrine's studio.

The gathered early morning beach crowd seemed excited yet strangely aghast. The thought occurred to me perhaps a street artist had left another four-letter graffiti epistle on the exterior of Brice's studio. The last one had been extremely insulting to him and you could still see a ghost image of it under the gray paint hastily slapped over it. As I got closer, no new graffiti was in sight so I scanned the swarm of joggers, strollers, and assorted exercise enthusiasts and spotted old Mac sitting on the curb near the front. He's the unofficial street gleaner around the hood and lives in the alley beneath some outside stairs. Gesturing for Duie to stay by my side, I approached the elderly man.

"Kind of early for you, isn't it Mac?"

His hand rose slowly to mop his leathery face as he lifted his head while shaking his shoulders and straining to focus his watery blood-shot eyes. He spoke in a low, sadly earnest manner. "He was always good to me. You know, one of the few who would share like you do."

Even with the more than usual layers of dirt on his face, it was obvious he was distraught. He had spoken more words in one sentence than I had ever heard him utter before.

"Do you mean Brice? Did something happen?" I said.

Apprehensively I sat down beside him on the awkward-concrete. Mac dropped his hand and looked directly at me. Perhaps for the first time I noticed how aged he really was.

"I was passing by, you know, working the street, looking for little favors people leave for me. You know. Like you do."

His voice became more somber as he fondled the buttons of his multi-stained khaki shirt.

Embarrassment rushed across my face. The most I had ever given him was the tattered Macintosh he had worn for the past two years. He is never seen without it. In fact, that's why everyone calls him Mac. None of us ever bothered to ask him his real name. It was a way to be friendly without causing discomfort or getting too involved.

Shamed, I stood up. A strange brew of anxiety and curiosity steered me through the small group near the door and straight into Brice's studio. Duie rushed in behind me as my olfactory receptors signaled something peculiar wafting from inside. It was a bizarre mixture of proverbial paint fumes and a grotesque unrecognizable spice. Duie even sneezed fitfully.

Brice was never a tidy artist, but a quick glance revealed the normal casualness of his studio was now in complete chaos. A strong feeling I was intruding crawled up my back.

"Who does he think he is?" someone behind me uttered. I wanted to respond, but somehow I knew my voice was not the one I needed to hear.

Paintings were thrown everywhere. Many with broken stretcher bars and holes clobbered through them. The scene looked as though a small tornado had come through the open skylight, had a kick-boxer fit, and left without disturbing anything else in the neighborhood. Every quart-sized canister of paint Brice owned had been opened and its contents generously distributed–into a Pollock-like camouflage that covered everything.

"Surely Mac didn't do this?" I whispered to Duie as he instinctively leaned against my leg. "No, Brice maybe, but not Mac."

Every artist goes a little wacko once in a while. Maybe Brice was dueling with a yellow scalene and things got out of hand. My notion was answered before I could exhale.

Beyond the turned over easel, sticking out from behind more broken paintings were two aged Teva sandals dappled with a rainbow of paint splatters. The heels were together, the toes akimbo. I froze in place as Duie tiptoed toward them with his neck stretched and nostrils flared.

As I stepped carefully around the disquieting pile, trying not to disturb even the smallest fallen brush or blob of paint I saw a mass of oozing gunk. It was Brice, on his back. His arms were at his side and his face was covered in thick, gooey globs of Hooker's Green.

He looked exhausted, as though he'd copulated with every painting he ever sired. Even though the pile of canvases, paint canisters, and brushes covering him was a mess, for one sharp yet fleeting moment it impacted my visual cortex as if the scene was an intentional edifice.

My eyes focused on his contorted mouth. It was open and overflowing with an ugly mixture of paint and dark red blood. In the middle was a smidgen of gold. It's very familiar blunted form was instantly recognizable. I bent down for a closer look. I was right. It-was the handle end of a number 15 size brush. You could still read the manufacturer's gold colored code number peeking through a smear of greenish red-stained paint.

Hoping Brice might take a big gasp of air if I removed it, I reached my hand forward and instantly felt a stout vise grip my shoulder.

"Don't," a voice of authority said.

It was Cisco. I stood straight up, perhaps a little too quickly for I felt a sharp twinge of vertigo. I call him Cisco. His–real name is Francisco Rivas, police Detective Rivas.

"You know better than that," he said.

I suddenly felt weary as the colors surrounding us swirled like the merry-go-round at the pier and the vise moved to grip my arm. I could even hear the faint tinny sound of mechanical music as if it were far off in the distance or at least buried deep within my memory.

Cisco's focused stare at my anesthetized face caused the illusory music to quickly fade and the circling kaleidoscope to resume its previous resting place. I began to feel lucid again, but my frame of vision felt shaken and quirky.

"Go outside, Sketchy," he said in an almost inaudible voice. "And take Duie with you."

With faded breath, I uttered, "He may still have a chance."

Cisco glowered at me again, gestured toward the door and put his hands on his hips, revealing his badge and gun. The move was an obvious signal for me to leave. I did.

The pitch of the roof in the low winter sun was still shrouding the front of the studio in tints and tones of a dirty achromatic grey and the multi-colored mob of lookie-loos grew as if in anticipation of a street busker performance. But Blue-bulls pushed them back across the street into the light while stringing a bright honey-orange ribbon to protect the dead from the living. The move suggest the prospect of even more entertainment. A punkish voice hidden in the crowd sang out, "What's the cost of admission?"

I wanted to retort 'demise', but speaking seemed even more out of place than ever and besides, I was moving in the opposite direction as I scanned the area for Mac. With him not in sight and Duie close to my heels, walking became difficult somehow. My feet seemed to have gained weight and oxygen was even harder to swallow for the odor of death and caustic paint was lodged deep in my throat. All of which made me wonder what Brice could possibly have done to cause such rage to explode all over him.

Growing up first in a New York public housing tenement and then in the east side of Santa Monica's Pico barrio, I'd smelt death many times and though it had been a while, I didn't remember it being so pungent. Perhaps my olfactory nerves had been coated with too much sea air since I'd managed to acquire digs right on the beach in Ocean Park.

As flashbacks of the CALog I'd made of Brice a couple years ago screened at the back of my eyes, I found myself in the alley right in front of Mac's little hovel.

He was there, all curled up in a sort of fetal position surrounded by grungy cardboard walls and reeking unkempt blankets. He should have stayed in bed, for the tranquility of his small refuge was about to be overrun by bulls. Well-meaning blue uniformed bulls with polished badges and combat style shoes, but hardnosed bull's nonetheless.

Trying hard not to be too intrusive, I sat down next to him. As CALog host I'd learned to do that with some degree of grace.

Mac leaned up against the wall and frowned at a stain of green paint on his greasy soiled pant leg. "He had it all. Now he has even less than I."

It was a calm, smooth, baritone voice. Not like the Mac I had heard minutes before. The next moment of silence seemed endless, but it actually died a quick death. At least it wasn't a violent one. In fact, it was rejuvenating. Mac sat up straight. He was clear-eyed and somehow bigger, even regal-looking, which made me recall old films of King John, hiding out with Robin Hood, waiting for the right moment to disclose his true identity.

Mac has large, muscular hands, his gray speckled beard outlines a firm jaw and frames a straight, broad nose that leads up to full, flat, amber eyes topped by a continuous thick eyebrow and deep creases across a wide forehead. I wondered what he used to do for a living. As I studied him an entirely new perception of the man formed in my mind, along with a desire to sketch a quick portrait of him.

"This sort of thing isn't new to you, is it?" I said.

"I used to be in Local 93. You know, down at the San Pedro docks. Night foreman. Everyone called me Eclipse because I did my best work at night," he said in a sort of half laugh. "I've seen a lot of men start the day off in good health and end up."

He let it hang there as he reached down and petted Duie, who was tilting toward him.

"Often the voiceless speak loudest about humans and our private anxieties and sympathies. Don't they fella?" he said quietly.

Duie's tail began gently waging as he stared directly into Mac's pale eyes.

"Can I use your place to clean-up? You know, a shower and shave. I don't want to be treated like a bum when they come to question me."

I was stunned as Mac lifted me up by one arm and began to move us both. We walked hurriedly out of the alley and up Appian Way toward my place. His stride was almost too much for me: I felt like Duie tagging behind his master. Duie looked even more surprised as he endeavored to match the tempo of our pace.

No wonder I had given our self-anointed leader my old Macintosh. Unconsciously I must have realized he looked much like the bear-of-a-trail guide who had given it to me while we were hiking in a sudden rain storm along the Klickitat River in the Cascade Mountains of Washington during my last escape from smog, heat and sirens.

"What happened to that slow shuffle you're famous for?"

He didn't answer as I stammered with halting breadth. His course of action was set and he was right, we weren't lost souls. We had things to do, places to go, people to meet. People to meet, Cisco would surely be looking for us.

"Some tall pines, rippling water and quiet vistas would have made for a better morning," I said under my breath.

"What?" asked Mac with a sharp crack to his voice.

It was my turn not to respond. Besides the surgery scar on the back of my neck was beginning to pulsate more than normal and that was not a good thing.

CHAPTER 3

Detective Francisco Javier Rivas is only 37, but his receding hair and hard demeanor had always made him seem much older than I. He was a homie who had shaken his Chicano gang days in the Pico barrio and made good. We had gone through college together and even hung out as buds when he first joined the force, but hadn't spoken much since he became a Homicide Detective and especially in the past couple of years. Now his unmarked car was parked across the street from my front door. Unmarked huh, all police detectives drive the same model dark gun metal selenite grey Dodge Charger with oversized, strong looking tires and old fashioned spotlights mounted above the side-mirrors. They make you think of the FBI and gangster movies, and definitely radiate bad news more than the sporty-looking white and blue jobs the guys on the beat drive. At least their wheels make them seem more like the surf patrol.

As I peeked out my front door peephole Cisco just sat there, staring at my house. Reluctantly, it seemed to me, he got out of his car, walked across the street and gave the door a slight thump. I waited a moment, thinking maybe he would leave. No, he thwacked the door harder. I opened it, but neither of us moved or spoke. Unexpectedly, DeWain appeared on his super-sized skateboard.

"Here's ur paper Mr. Terra. Ho's ur painting goin', uh?"

Before I could answer DeWain whizzed past as his skinny ebony arm catapulted the L.A. Times right between Cisco and me, landing it next to a dozen other editions on the studio floor. Almost as though he knew it would end up right there anyway.

I subscribe to both the Times and the Santa Monica Sentinel even though I spend more time reading their websites than their print editions. I like the idea of having a newspaper delivered each morning; plus a free press is the backbone of our democracy. And anyway, I always have uses for newsprint in the studio.

The wake of the flying paper log caused Cisco to hastily step inside and impulsively reach his arms out. To my surprise I greeted him with a mirror image, but our manly embrace ended self-consciously as we both turned away avoiding any eye contact. He walked into the studio and I waved to DeWain as I stepped inside and closed the door.

"I see you're still trying to make those quirky-looking space age landscapes," Cisco said a little too quickly.

"Yeah, and I'm pretty successful at it, too."

I was bullshitting. I hadn't sold a painting since last spring.

"My last show, over at the Balladeer Gallery, was a big hit."

Another lie, damn it.

"Didn't they go broke, owner returned to Europe or something?" he stated in a more slowed cadence. It had been a long time since I'd seen his casual side.

"Some family problem, back in the old country, I think."

Actually they simply ran out of money and got fed up with LA. 'That's it James, no more art double speak.' I said to myself. This is Cisco, not some collector from Trousdale. Keep it straight and up front and change the subject. "I suppose you're looking for Mac?"

"Mac, who's he? He got something to do with this case?"

"He found the body. You know, first person on the scene and all that."

"Oh him. No, we know all about him. We don't need anything from him."

Mac was still upstairs using my facilities, preparing for his big moment. How could I tell him it came and went quicker than he scrubbed the grime from his brow? With Cisco in the house I hoped he wouldn't reveal his presence.

"It's good to see you, man. One of us had to take the initiative."

The words rushed from my mouth easier than I had expected. Perhaps it was because I had rehearsed them often.

"I am here on business." He paused and turned to face me. "But it's good to see you too, Sketchy."

He turned back toward my drawing table, picked up a sketch book and leafed through the pages, pausing to study a doodle here and there. I had forgotten how much he always seemed mystified by the drawings I'd make while we sat in boring lecture classes or strolled the streets together in our youth. When he raised his head I felt compelled to put the focus on him.

"I hear lots of good things about you. Word on the street is you're the best man in the department."

I was actually smiling now. It felt good.

"Catrina tells me you only work north of Wilshire cases now, society stuff, right?"

"What do you mean Catrina told you'? Are you on her again?"

He was obviously perturbed. His sienna face had taken on a decidedly crimson undertone.

Hoping to squelch the fire, I said: "No, no, we bumped into each other at the club, that's all."

"Uh-huh, just make sure that's the only kind of bumping you do with her. My little sister doesn't need you foolin' with her again!"

The way he had emphasized the name Catrina caused the aneurism on the back of my neck to twist a little. A moment of strained silence pervaded the studio, but was instantly overshadowed by a clamor. Cisco's eyes darted toward the stairs as his head crooked back. We both heard the shower running and I could tell by his raised eyebrows he thought it was occupied by a woman. I wasn't sure how to inform him it was Mac. Cisco returned to perusing another sketch book.

Shortly, the sound of loud water drops began to pommel through the ceiling, the kind created when you step out of the shower and leave it running. Their thunderous drone filled the space between us with an air of unnecessary tension. Damn plumbing.

Cisco seemed anxious, but when Duie rushed in through the opened sliding glass door and ran right to him instinctively he reached down and petted him all over.

"Te acuerdas de tu viejo amigo Cisco?" he said.

If I'm not mistaken that means something about remembering an old friend. Cisco held his hands together and Duie jumped on them and did a flip which was only natural since it was Cisco who had taught him the trick. There were patches of dried green paint on Duie's feet and the tip of his wiggling tail. No doubt he'd got into it at Brice's studio. Its effect on Cisco was noticeable as he endeavored to wipe it off with one of my grubby studio rags.

Gesturing toward the ceiling, he said, "Look, this is tough on both of us and I don't want to interrupt your private life. Let's take this one step at a time." His deep official detective voice had returned.

"O.K., how can I help?"

The offer blurted out of me with an apprehensive sense of alliance. Cisco paused and smiled unexpectedly before speaking in a clear, concise manner.

"Do you know of anyone who will be happy Peregrine is dead?"

"Someone who doesn't like graffiti art?"

It wasn't meant to be a joke, but as I thought about it, it could be true. After all, a lot of galleries still refused to show it and the business owners around this neighborhood hate it.

"Don't give me any of your art double talk, this is serious. A man, an artist has been killed."

"Right, well maybe it was some punks. You know Brice never did try to fit in down here and besides, he's had trouble with the gangs before."

"Why's that?"

"He doesn't, I mean he didn't always use generic graffiti. Often he'd copy what he saw on the walls and the gangs don't like it when you steal their thunder. You know that."

"Punks maybe, but how many of them drive a Mercedes s560 coupe?" Cisco said with sharp focused satisfaction.

It seems one had been seen parked near Brice's studio during the night. Metallic mauve streaks and yellow scalenes rushed back into my consciousness. I think I told him everything I could remember about the car, but thumbing through my disconnected brain cells seemed as slow as an old dial-up connection. Perhaps it was because of those obnoxious fumes I'd inhaled

"Well, check around with your arty friends and see if anything off color pops." He scoffed as the shower noise ended abruptly, causing him to hasten toward the front door.

"Making those art videos for television must open a lot of doors and keep you connected to what's going on behind the scenes in the art crowd," he said hurriedly. "Any info you can gather that will push me in the right direction would be greatly appreciated and let me know if you remember anything else about the 560."

Wow, I don't think I've ever heard Cisco speak so, well, mature before. We shook hands and I shut the door in a stupor as I watched one of my best jackets coming down the stairs. Mac had out done himself. How could I tell him he was inessential? I decided we needed a drink. It was barely 8:30am. I decided some hearty Kefir and a toasted blueberry bagel would do the trick. The priceless look on Mac's face when I suggested it kept a grin on mine throughout the day.

CHAPTER 4

It was First Thursday, a good time to get out and see what the art crowd was saying about the tragically gaudy ending to Brice's life and prosaic, not so colorful career. Most of the Westside galleries open new exhibits in the evening, so I got dressed in my usual opening fare. Dark gray slacks, black ankle boots, an electric blue tailored shirt and my favorite deep blue Geox coat. I was set, at least on the outside.

I drove over to the alley at the back of the Verge Gallery. There were always vacant parking spaces next door behind the offices of the Ocean Park Heating & Air Conditioning Company off Colorado Avenue. It was around 7pm when I pulled my old wheels into a spot labeled "President ONLY". I wondered what it would feel like to work for a small firm who always seemed to have more business than it could handle. The thought of doing a 9 to 5'er, Monday through Friday, swept the thought clean away.

It was dark in the alley when I turned off the car and stepped out especially since there were no new street lamps about. I heard voices coming from behind the dumpsters at the far end of the building, so I pondered which way to go. The long way, down the full length of the alley or in the direction of the sound of muffled conversation? I was feeling good and after all I was on a mission. I chose the short trek just beyond the dumpsters.

Near the end of the gallery building about at the middle of the block-is a narrow passageway that runs alongside the building and comes out right in front of the galleries. As I turned past the dumpsters to enter it I almost tripped over a crouching figure.

"Que suerte!" The figure said.

He was right, I was lucky, because I managed to keep my balance and not step on any of the three day laborers huddled in the shadows. They were passing time playing catch penny with nickels and dimes. Empty bottles of Dos Equis XX rested on the lid of the dumpster nearest their game. I made a gesture of apology and stepped through the middle as quickly as I could. Their clothes were darker than they, soiled from endless hours of toiling at the dirty jobs no one else wanted to do in the better homes and gardens of LA's Westside.

Their faces wore mixed expressions of stiff pride and humility. I wondered if their families, probably south of the border, knew the depths of their sacrifice. They were probably waiting for the free food the galleries often give away to the homeless after an opening reception. The heavy pong of urine ended my musing.

I wasn't sure how large a crowd would be at this opening for the primary way contemporary art has been presented to the public for the past century or so has been changing of late with the advent of the digital era. The dominant position of the 'solo exhibit', where an artist has spent a year or more creating a body of new artworks to debut, advertise, be assessed by critics and offered for sale is fast eroding. There are few mega-opening nights anymore because dealers don't necessarily need a large brick and mortar gallery nowadays. If they can finance a booth at a few major international art fairs each year and have a strong presence online and in social media they can do as much business as they did in a 'real' gallery without the endless need to fund lease payments, salaried staff and assorted other continuously increasing expenses. In fact, many traditional dealers have told me they are doing more than 75% of their business from connections made at fairs and online. This is why there are fewer exhibitions annually at their galleries and why they leave them up for longer stretches of time.

The art world is simply adapting to new technology, new collecting patterns, and new demands by its evolving audience. The only reason traditional opening receptions like the one I was walking toward are still relevant is because the general public and new collectors alike want to meet the artists, like to hear them talk about their work and like to see how genuine they are. All of which requires face to face contact more than only images and text on a computer screen. That level of interaction is what spurs the development of long term collectors. Plus, without exhibitions there would be no critical reviews and though they are more prevalent than ever since the arrival of the web there are far few of them in newspapers and magazines, which really limits the general public's accidental exposure to thinking about art.

For me, art is still very much a person to person experience that thrives on direct contact far more than texting, blogging or tweeting. Nothing is eternal, but I hope brick and mortar galleries remain at least through the tenure of my life, I thought as I approached the bright lights streaming from the front of the galleries near the end of the passageway.

As I stepped out of the shadows and turned left my eyes were momentarily blinded by the glare and glitz of men in tailored suits escorting women draped in the latest California casual haute couture parading everywhere. Nickels and dimes wouldn't pay for even one stitch of their ensembles. This was definitely a social affair. I wasn't even sure who the exhibiting artist was and it was an overflow crowd for the Verge Gallery, especially considering how slow gallery business had been again this season.

'Maybe the recession is over and no one told me. Maybe, but I doubt it,' I mused to myself. More likely the size of the crowd reflected that this gallery represented Brice. Maybe they'll get the rights to represent his estate I supposed, but one thing was for sure, there wouldn't be any hors d'oeuvres or snack handouts left over from this reception. It was a full-house affair.

Surrounding the entrance was a clique of young graduate art students. You can always identify them: they dress in only one color, black. Their prime objective is to somehow make a connection with anyone willing to look at their artwork.

It was hard to see what the exhibit consisted of. The space was wall to wall with socialites, nouveau-riche executives and the usual assortment of opening gadflies. However, sprinkled here and there were a few up-and-coming collectors and at least two adjunct critics. I then realized no one was even looking at the exhibit. It was a real fanny-bumper, with each mini group actively engaged in private, yet public, natter about Brice. It seemed like some kind of unofficial wake for the death of a middle-aged established artist rather than an opening reception for a young emerging one.

As I was deciding on which faction to horn in on, I heard air-kissing sounds behind me. I turned to see Dr. Brian Mazor escorting his wife Camille through a trio of young want-to-be studs. The couple looked just like the photo of them I saw on the society page of the Times' website a few days earlier. As I recall, they were being nominated for membership in the Homely Hills Country Club after having moved to L.A. from Boston.

"Get a life," said the doctor.

His ashen gray looking jowls turned purplish under his aging skin when he growled.

"Yeah, I bet you get a new life every night, Pops," said the lead want-to-be.

The young stud tasted the perfumed air and sized up Camille's sexy taut thighs while she ignored him and the crowd pretended to be only mildly concerned. I decided to make a move.

"Dr. Mazor, I'm James Terra. It's nice to finally meet you."

I was putting on my best face, my gracious CALog host face. The want-to-be took one look at me and realized he wasn't making the kind of points he needed. He moved away with a modest gesture of repentance, one of the few perks I enjoy as a recognized art community insider. I gave him an easy smile.

"Are you with the gallery?" Mazor said through his teeth, which seemed as drawn and wan as the rest of him.

"No, but I would be happy to introduce you to Christy ..."

Camille interrupted my gesture, put out her hand and smiled all over me.

"I've heard of you. You're an artist and host of those PBS video log things. They talked about you in my class. Your nickname is Sketchy, isn't it?"

She purred beautifully.

"Yes, uhm what class? You're not an art student are you?"

"I'm studying with Nellie Myerhoff," she said.

Her level of pride with that declaration was noticeable to everyone within earshot. I really liked the way Camille moved her charming mouth.

Nellie isn't an art teacher at all, but rather an elderly social maven who coaches young trophy wives how to fit into the Westside charity fundraising circle which requires some basic knowledge of the LA art scene.

"How is Nell? I haven't seen her since her son died. Some printing accident, as I recall."

Raised eye brows and a look of distain slithered across Dr. Mazor's face as our budding conversation was overpowered by the undefined accent of David Bernkopf. An egotistical artist of small stature and structure. His red hair and waxy complexion fought with his metrosexual three-piece suit as he pontificated to a group off to our right.

"Peregrine was inept. The most impressive thing he ever accomplished was to get himself murdered, 15 minutes of unmerited attention," he said while squinting his mouth and fingering his right earring.

Visions of Brice coated in green paint flitted before me. I could feel myself getting incensed. I mean, after all, Brice was dead. Maybe he wasn't a great artist, but he certainly didn't deserve to be dumped on by this dingle-berry.

"You know, David, a little humility might win you more friends." I said firmly.

"Friends! You're always going on about such dung. Why don't you stick to your TV gig and let the rest of us do the real creating. James Terra, salt of the earth, what rot".

His air of complete self-gratification was enough to make me want to barf, spit or at least squelch all the acid out of him, but I was determined to control my need. Besides, losing my temper wasn't good for my health.

"If you weren't so blinded by the neoclassical badge you wear on your forehead, maybe, you'd see more than your own reflection."

I wasn't sure what the hell that meant, but I said it with resolve anyway and David looked like he had never heard those particular words used together in one sentence before. Neither had I, but I recognized how once spoken a small affront can spiral into aggressive impulses and cause one to lose all self-control.

Wine glass in hand, he angrily lunged toward me. As I stepped aside, his body momentum caused him to trip over the tip of my boot. He looked surprised as he slammed into a sculpture stand, breaking the wine glass and cutting his hand as he slide to the floor, holding the back of his head with his free hand.

I was ready for him to bound back up. But he seemed to linger on the floor, staring at the maze of shoes surrounding him. When he finally arose, the look of anger on his flushed face had changed to a strange mix of know-it-all satisfaction and inexplicable glee. He stared once more at the crowd, then into my eyes with a look of brotherhood all artists recognize, took the handkerchief from his breast pocket, calmly wrapped it around his bleeding hand and waved to the crowd as he sauntered out of the gallery seemingly happy with himself. His behavior caused me to think he had probably imbibed drugs with the wine.

I started to call out to him, but realized the sculpture stand was still wobbling and its crystal treasure was ready to attempt flight. As I stood there staring at it I could see its beveled glass figure eight form in smithereens and it hadn't even fallen yet. Why couldn't I move? Maybe I imagined it would look better rearranged. Everyone gasped as it leaped into the air, especially the featured artist who had created it and was standing just beyond its reach.

The gleaming form's maiden voyage was short. Trophy wife Nicole Volkov scooped it up from mid-air with ease and cradled it in her arms like a newborn. A communal sigh of relief flowed from the crowd and swaddled all. The sculpture certainly looked improved as Nicole stood there with her chest protruding through its negative spaces.

"Now I understand this piece."

It was a juvenile thing for me to say, but Nicole showed she liked it by smiling seductively. I wanted to continue my courting, but her husband, Patterson, stepped between us, took the sculpture from her and tossed it to me. I gulped as I pulled it from mid-air and stood there looking dumb while he promenaded her out the door. Everyone seemed to be waiting for my second act, but I didn't have one. The embarrassed featured artist seemed totally perplexed and dumbfounded by it all.

"I'm glad someone had the guts to shut David up," said Gallery Director Christy as she took the sculpture and returned it to its place of honor while smiling at the artist, who hadn't moved an inch from his spot of honor.

It felt good to be rescued. Christy gestured for her assistant to stand next to the newly installed sculpture.

"Thanks Christy, but I wasn't trying to be heroic. I simply forgot how short a fuse David has."

"Yeah, well he's been more explosive than usual lately."

"Why's that?"

"Oh, the Art Council spurned his grant application again," she said sarcastically. "And he needs the money."

"I see. Who did they select?"

She smiled broadly. "A real woman, of course."

A gentle wave of laughter rippled across the room and everyone seemed to relax. I took a slow look around for Camille and her dour husband, but they had left too, so I considered slipping quietly out as well. As I turned toward the door, Christy took hold of my arm and walked me to her office near the rear of the gallery.

"Was it something I said," I uttered softly as I inhaled deeply.

"Ah no, well yes, it was several things you've said over the years," she said with sincerity.

"Well, you know Christy, I'm not a critic and CALog is not a pulpit or lectern. I'm more of an art sleuth. I ask questions and pursue answers," I replied.

"Right, and that's exactly why I want to encourage you to do another Log about Brice. One that would cover more of his entire history. His early work and his rock 'n roll stage, not only his graffiti paintings that you featured last time."

I'd seen Christy this way often, especially when she was in the heat of a sales pitch. This is why so many artists were always trying to get her to represent them. She has the ability to make each artist's work seem vital, a rare quality in a gallery director.

"Well, right now the station and the producers have asked me to not do more than one show per artist. That said though, they may be willing to consider doing a special show highlighting the artists who have passed on since we started the series," I said as sympathetic as I could considering we were standing in the middle of the opening reception for an entirely different artist.

She looked down at the floor and said, "Mmm."

"And I'm certain they wouldn't want me to do anything related to Brice until the police have found his murderer," I whispered.

"Yeah, I can understand that," she replied stoically. "You're a good guy James and I know you'll make the right decision for me and Brice, bless his soul."

"Do you know of anyone who will be happy he is dead?" I asked with Cisco's words echoing at the back of my mind.

She scanned me with a cocked eye. "If you mean beyond the local gangs I'd have to give that some thought, but obviously, David comes to mind. I mean classic and graffiti don't mix well."

"Right, OK, only wondering. Don't you think maybe you should get back to taking care of the living right now, I mean you've got a gallery full of art lovers waiting for you."

I gave her a hug. "We'll talk about Brice another time, I promise."

It was turning 9:00 pm as I headed out of the gallery toward the passageway that led back to my car. I wondered if I'd encounter the three catch penny players again, but as I reached the dumpsters they were nowhere in sight. The invisibility of L.A.'s domestic laborers has always fascinated me. Their daily grind maintains mansion after mansion and business palaces galore, but very little of that plenteousness reaches them. The only time anyone seems to pay attention to them is when the leaf blower or vacuum cleaner or some other atrocious tool they're using makes a racket. Their hard work is essential to the wellbeing of the community and they deserve much more than they get in return.

To get that depressing thought from my mind, I turned on my favorite satellite radio blues station and drove down the dark alley, striving to avoid an endless parade of pot holes while bouncing my brain to the beat of Jelly Jelly.

"Green, green who's got the green, green paint everywhere. Fifteen minutes of gooey glory."

As the song ended the familiar feeling of an impending question inched up my spine. What was that look on David's face about? It seemed almost as though he discovered a diamond imbedded in the floor, or maybe spotted a potential buyer for one of his neoclassical gold leafed paintings. No, that can't be right. If it had been either of those things he would have stayed there instead of darting out quickly. He was on the floor and staring at, at, uhm, at shoes and ankles?

As I drove down Colorado toward the twinkling pier lights I didn't really feel as though I had garnered anything useful for Cisco, but I did feel it was time to head home where at least Duie would be happy to see me return so early.

CHAPTER 5

The morning was clear and crisp with a cool breeze blowing in off the San Gabriel Mountains to the northeast, making the events of the previous twenty-four hours seem surreal. Not wanting anything to destroy even the thought of such natural perfection, I spent most of the day in the studio painting. Denying myself the outdoors has been my way of reminding myself there are lots of nice days like this in LA even in winter, so why not get one more painting finished. But by late afternoon I couldn't resist any longer. Duie and I headed out the door and onto the beach.

The sky looked like rippled glass as a brunt orange sun arched for a dive into Thalo blue and Duie chased white gulls. I am a sensualist and a surrealist, and the natural beauty was so fulfilling I closed my eyes and just stood there. Slowly, one by one, all sounds faded away. The unruffled cool mountain air mixed with the salty sea breeze, caressed the nearby palms and circulated all about me. I felt fortunate and serene.

"This is the LA I love," I said to Duie. "And unfortunately so do millions of others, damn it."

Two startled tourists hurried past us, wearing matching graphic tank tops emblazoned with a big red heart and a silhouette of swaying palm trees. A man speaking loud to his dog will intimidate anybody, especially on a deserted beach in LA as evening shadows begin to encroach.

As I stood there trying to enjoy a tranquil moment of reverie a curious, yet familiar, wiggling feeling in my left side seemed far, far away, but persistent. Finally it overpowered my state of bliss and brought me back to consciousness.

"I knew I'd find you here."

The kiss was warm and sweet, and went deep into the center of my chest. I knew it was Nicole without even waiting for my eyes to verify it.

"Let's go over to the club and get a bite to eat." I said enthusiastically.

"Food, I make you think of food." She pouted.

"No, but I haven't eaten all day and you brought me back to reality." I said.

"Damn you James, can't you ever be romantic?"

It wasn't a question, and there was only one way to stop it from becoming a debate. I lifted her into the air and we kissed again. My air, the air of my private happiness. We twirled and twirled again and then fell onto the warm sand.

"Come on, let's go." I said.

My stomach growled a little too loudly as she tilted her head, snuggled her lean firm body against me and looked up through the top of her eyes and long dark lashes. It was a pose I had seen a thousand times before and loved every time. I was focused on her lips, waiting to watch them massage my mind.

"You know I'd go anywhere with you, but not tonight. Patterson is giving a speech at the monthly International Businessmen's Dinner and I have to play the dutiful wife."

My mouth puckered up and mimicked hers. "International Businessmen's Dinner. When are you going to leave that dinosaur and move in with me?"

She said in a whisper mated gently with the velvety air, "Don't start, please."

Shrugging I took her hand and we walked along the water's edge a short distance to a small knoll of sand. As we sat down to watch Mother Nature turn off the blood orange light in the sky, Duie ran to us with a small twig in his mouth and began retching. A piece of bark was stuck in his throat, but after choking briefly he managed to expel it.

"It said in today's Art-eNews Brice was found that way," she said quietly.

"What do you mean?"

She shivered and spoke in a faded manner "With a stick jammed down his throat."

"It was a paint brush. A number 15."

A look of astonishment gripped her face. "How do you know?"

"I was there."

"What?"

I took the twig away from Duie and threw it beyond the surf. Its disappearance into the dark waters didn't seem to bother him as he scoffed at it.

"You were at Brice's?" Nicole said with a little too much wonder.

"Duie and I were jogging by, that's all."

I wanted to gush the whole event out like an excitable teenager, but the reverberated vision of Brice's opened mouth saved me from slipping into adolescence.

"Do you know of anyone who really hated Brice's work?"

The solemn tone of my voice seemed to return Nicole to maturity as well.

"Well I wasn't crazy about it myself, but it doesn't mean I'd kill him. After all who would for such a reason?" She said.

"Well, someone did."

"You know Nellie was talking about this the other day."

"Nell Meyerhoff? What did she say?" I asked.

"She was talking about how some people are really bothered by contemporary art. In fact, the new girl in our group, Camille Mazor, may be very disturbed by it."

"Then why is she in the group?"

"Oh, she inherited a big collection from her Aunt. You know old lady Wagner."

"Harriet Wagner? It's been some time since I heard anything about her."

"That's because she died last spring, right around the time you disappeared for a couple weeks."

Her eyebrows raised and her eyes glared at me, but I just smiled and chose not to respond.

"Apparently she kept adding to her collection right up until a few years ago. A real eccentric," she continued with a little too much sarcasm.

"And what do you mean, you were 'jogging', I've never seen you run to anything."

I ignored that question too.

Harriet Wagner had been a major player in the art world. Her stately Beverly Hills home was filled with some of the best paintings ever created on the West Coast. She always seemed to know which artists were going to be hot before there was even any smoke. She had an eye, as they say, plus she was a good-looking woman. So much so, some even suggested she never paid for a single painting, with money, that is. She never seemed to like my work, though, and I hadn't even been aware she'd been ill.

"What does Camille Mazor do?" I said.

"Do! She doesn't do anything, darling. She's married to a doctor. A psychiatrist from Boston and I'm sure she has enough to do keeping him content. They were at the opening last night. Don't you remember? You did speak to them."

"Don't remind me. Damn, that whole thing was stupid, wasn't it? You made some good moves though." I said as I snuggled her breast against me.

"It serves David right. What did he think he was going to achieve, anyway? You would have flattened him. No wonder he ran away, the little scallywag." She snuggled me back.

"Well it was stupid, anyway. I hope his hand isn't cut too bad."

"To hear him tell it, he can paint with his toes, so let him suffer for a while."

"You like to see artists suffer, don't you? That's why you keep me on a short leash."

"Don't give me that. You like to give me a little pain once in a while too."

I couldn't resist. I rolled over on top of her, kissed those welcoming lips, rolled again and slapped her hip hard. It felt so good, I did it again.

"See what I mean?" She said coyly as she rubbed her hip.

Her kisses were hotter now and I wanted to spank her again, but she was on her feet before I opened my eyes.

"Look at this, you've made a real mess of my hair and I just had it done for the dinner," she said. She headed toward her car as she dusted beach sand from her pants and wrestled with her hair.

"I'll phone you tomorrow," I said as I waved.

Nicole always seemed like the right woman for me, but she would never give up Patterson's money, so I never had to worry about not being able to offer her a secure future or a future of any sort.

As I laid on the sandy knoll feeling weightless while listening to the soft lapping waves and watching the circling gulls turn into stars I left myself behind, lifting higher and higher into the dark blue night sky. The silver wisp glistened and gathered around me and I was smiling at myself.

Suddenly, I chill gripped my core. My feet turned numb and I began to fall, faster and faster as air rushed past my ears becoming louder and louder. I sensed I was going to hit the rocks just as a wave of cold sea water slapped me awake. My clothes were wringing wet. Duie smiled at me from his dry perch just out of reach of the incoming tide.

It was time to go home. Friday night on Ocean Park beach or any of the beaches in LA is not a safe place to doze anymore. Only a couple of weeks earlier, on another romantic evening, the beach turned deadly for a man who was killed as he rushed to aid a young couple who were being bullied by three punks. He was pronounced dead at the scene from a small-caliber bullet to the heart. Police still have no leads to follow. About all they can do is add the senseless shooting to their bulging files.

LA has always had a Jekyll & Hyde kind of personality. A lament threading just beneath its sunny surface and now the disease has spread right to its rim, like broken glass lying in wait in the sand. Putting an end to another of my favorite diversions, quiet midnight walks on the beach.

CHAPTER 6

As I foraged around my impracticable kitchen nook, looking for something clean to drink from, I noticed the foggy morning winter light made the white canvas on the easel look grey and the yellow scalene orange. I liked it so I walked to the easel and opened a canister of Cadmium orange. Duie, prancing at my feet, had a brush between his teeth so I took it and scooped up some paint. As I extended the brush toward the scalene my hand stopped in mid-air. Grey and orange, those were the colors of Mazor's tie. I wondered if the morning light would make him look different too. I picked up my cell, googled Dr. Mazor, and found his office number. As I hit dial I felt like a kid about to play a risky adult game. I hit speaker button.

"Dr. Mazors' office, Ms. Struthers speaking."

"Hello, this is James Terra. Would it be possible to see Dr. Mazor this morning?"

"Are you a client of Doctor? Your name is not on Doctor's client list?"

"Uh, well no, but I'm a friend of Nell Meyerhoff's and I met the doctor the other night."

"I see. Please hold for a moment, Mr. Terra, and I will speak with Doctor."

Nell's name will open most doors in Beverly Hills and I was sure it would get Mazors' attention, even on a Saturday morning.

"Doctor can see you at eleven Mr. Terra."

"Right, where is the office located?"

"In the Beverly Palms Building, just off Wilshire."

"Thank you Ms. Struthers."

It wasn't natural for me to be so polite, but I can't seem to help it when I know I'm about to tell someone a pack of lies. My parents could always tell when I was lying because I'd stop speaking properly and begin fracturing my gab with slang.

No doubt I thought it made me sound adult. Being in the art game had taught me to turn the scenario around.

Wilshire Boulevard is LA. If you start at its east end, near the heart of the city, the buildings are old and filled with a mix of generations struggling to comprehend the American dream. It then passes through Korea Town, where huge merchant signs slap you into acknowledging they are here too. The west end leads into Santa Monica and is lined with swaying palms that stop at the very edge of the country on a bluff where seniors while away hours watching the sun set on the forever young beach crowd. In the middle it passes through the surreal hills of Beverly and Westwood. Most of the multitude in Los Angeles aspire to live in that stretch, but the nearest they ever come to taking up residence in the 90210 zip code area is a leisurely drive down Wilshire Boulevard.

The valet at the Beverly Palms Building must have thought I was making a delivery when I leaned out the window of my dated wheels and said "Dr. Mazor?" He directed me around the back to the loading zone. Free parking was fine with me.

The lobby was fitted out with plush emerald green carpet, polished brass and a jungle of tropical plants. I thought of Rousseau, especially when I spotted an imitation tiger skin sofa near the elevator. Mazors' office was listed as on the top floor. I took a deep breath, stepped in and pressed the cloud nine button. I was going to have to pretend my mind was trying to leave me. I had done it before. In fact, I had used it as an excuse to end my romp with Catrina.

I don't remember the ride up, especially since the room at the top was like the one at the bottom, a lawn of green carpet and another jungle of plants, but no tiger skin anywhere. Instead, behind the empty receptionist's desk, was an original Peter Alexander textile collage, a good one from the '80s I think. It was over 10 feet high and about 8 feet wide, filled with floating biomorphic shapes in glowing florescent colors accented with sequins added for bling, all floating on deep blue black velvet. Peter always told everyone he got his best ideas while skin diving, but most people couldn't see the relationship. Its supple glow made me feel good and revived memories of him telling me he had sold it to Harriet Wagner which got me back on track. I wondered why Dr. Mazors' wife, Camille, didn't like contemporary artists and whether that included Brice and Peter.

"It does take you away, doesn't it?"

Ms. Struthers was about 55, dressed in a pleasant rose color, with pinkish-gray hair all fluffed around her gentle face and ornate glasses. She spoke in a soft, melodious voice that ended my reminiscing and pondering.

The Alexander collage was wonderful and a great joy to see again. I didn't even want to re-direct my eyes away from it, but I did promise Cisco I'd do my bit and the gods know I owe him. More importantly, I recalled Brice had once told me Harriet owned one of his paintings, and I was curious to know what Camille and Mazor thought about his murder.

"Mr. Terra? You can go right on in. Doctor is waiting for you."

Ms. Struthers had a flowing business-like manner as she gestured to a door near a large gangly looking fern that seemed starved for water and affection. As I headed toward it I recalled the last time I felt like an impending debacle was about to happen. It was when I realized I would have to change my lifestyle and explain myself to Catrina. As it turned out, instead of telling her the truth, I used the excuse that her family would never accept our relationship, she would never leave them for me and the whole situation would drive us both crazy. She didn't believe me and still doesn't. The thought brought back gut wrenching memories, but I walked past the fern and opened the door anyway.

I stepped in and let the heavy door slam behind me. The jolt made me feel silly, so I did a sort of half-assed goose step to the center of the room. It is a move I use when I want someone to believe I'm panicky. The room was not what I had expected. Its walls were covered with dark wood paneling divided into equally spaced sections. Centered in each section were framed prints of typical eighteenth century hunting scenes. The kind filled with golden retrievers, deer, pheasants, ducks and shotguns. I thought of old school country clubs where elderly men sit around in deep padded leather chairs and snore. Above the couch hung a real painting or so I thought. It was about 3' x 4' and had a sculptured, gold gilded frame. Attached to the wall beneath the frame was a brass plate. It read, "Dog Pointing Partridges in a Landscape, 1719, Alexandre-Francois Desportes." They only put narrative titles on paintings when they don't know what the original title was.

The dog, a black and white spotted hound, was eyeing two partridges hidden behind a curious looking tree. The strange tree's trunk and its two branches bore an uncanny resemblance to a human torso. It even had a knot hole for a belly-button. Growing all over it was a grape vine and positioned between the alert looking hound and the unsuspecting partridges, the tree seemed to be presenting the sparkling grapes as an offering to the hound. The glint of red in its eyes said he'd rather sink his teeth into flesh than tart grapes.

Hunting scenes have never ranked as high as historical, religious, or even Rococo froth for most lovers of eighteenth century art, so this one must have been created to meet the personal taste of a particular patron. My head tilted with the feeling I had seen the painting before, but surely not at Harriet Wagner's house.

The prints and the painting reminded me of the Psych 101 class Cisco and I took together. The prof talked about the many ways humans have used animals as a metaphorical means of representing and understanding ourselves. When he called upon me to give an example I referenced Picasso's drawings of the Minotaur copulating with two young women while Cisco cited Disney cartoons.

"Are you all right, Mr. Terra?"

The voice didn't sound like my father, but it did make me stand straight, pull my shoulders back and my stomach in. However, the light glinting off the dog's teeth reminded me I had to play the child in this scene so I bowed my head and let my shoulders slouch.

"Well, no ...I," I mumbled.

"From animals we learn strategies of survival and existence," Mazor noted as we stood looking at the painting and he continued speaking. "And we use them to express empathy too. Please be seated and let's see if we can locate the problem or are you here to sell me a painting?"

He had that all too familiar tone doctors hope for and psychiatrist deliberately cultivate. I didn't want to be put through a mental ringer, so I had to react fast. I decided to get right to the point.

I darted my eyes back and forth then spoke quickly. "I was at Brice Peregrine's when he was found dead."

Mazor didn't respond. The pale light coming through the room's only window made him look even drabber than I had remembered.

"I was jogging by and felt compelled to look in." I continued.

Silence.

"It was horrible, he..."

Silence again. I decided to go for gold.

"Have you ever seen a murdered person?"

More silence followed by a still hush. I felt empowered, but a little lost.

"Do you drive a mauve colored s560?"

That got him. He didn't move at all, but it was visible in his drooping eye lids and in the hardening of his chin. Then just as suddenly it was gone and he appeared relaxed. When he finally turned he spoke through a tight smile.

"Why no, ours is Blue, metallic Blue. Mercedes christened it Lunar Blue."

I felt cheated and shrugged impatiently. "Okay, it's immature. I know I shouldn't let it bother me, but those kind of sights always find a way of coming back when you are least prepared for them."

He looked puzzled and responded in a counterfeit manner "Mauve colored cars?"

"No, no, Brice."

"I see your point," he said slowly. "So you've seen murdered people before, I take it?"

I was in big trouble now. I really didn't want to re-digest my past with someone so buttoned. I regretted having followed my hunch by starting this silly game. "You know, I feel better all ready. It's funny how the mind works, uh?" I said as I stood up and moved toward the door. "I guess all I really needed was to hear my own confession.

Psychiatrists love that one. After a long minute Mazor stood and extended his right hand. His long bony fingers were cold and brittle, like the branches on the tree in the hunting painting.

"Correct," he said resolutely. "All we're offering is a chance to hear yourself."

"Well, send me your bill. I'm sure I will find it money well spent."

He looked down at some papers on his desk and pretended to read them. "Oh, there's no charge. I'll add it to Meyerhoff's account," he grinned. " Saturday isn't a regular office day for me."

I felt an overwhelming need to change the subject. "I see you used a different decorator than the rest of the offices."

I was thinking I could direct the conversation toward Peter's painting, Harriet's collection, and finally to Brice.

"Different, uhm, my wife likes to decorate. She did the outer offices and the main lobby downstairs," he said casually as he shoveled his papers.

"And this space is your man-cave I take it?" I don't know why I pursued the subject. I guess I was still trying to seem cured of my problem.

"Yes, yes, well good day Mr. Terra. Ah, Sketchy." He was no longer trying to disguise his dour manner. "Is that a term of endearment or a description of your character?"

Ouch, that was right to the point. As I stood in the doorway the contrast between the waiting room and Mazors' office seemed even stronger than when I came in. The sensation and his bluntness thrust me back on track. "I understand you inherited Harriet Wagner's collection?"

There it was again, a look of distress maybe even fear, in the deepest part of Mazors' pale eyes and in the entrenched creases of his forehead. He blinked, looked past me and it was gone. He had regained complete self-control and assurance.

"We're not going to keep it," he said with an insincere air of regret.

"Oh, why is that?"

"It's not our cup of tea, as they say."

"I see. Well, let me know if you need any help selling it. I know a lot of collectors and dealers or maybe we could even do a CALog about it."

"You are here to talk about art after all," he said after a long pause. "Much appreciated, but we've consigned it to Prescott & Roth."

"Well, they're the biggest auction gallery in town. I'm sure you'll get your price."

"Yes, well good day Mr. Terra."

He refocused his dark malachite eyes directly at me and spoke with a razor edge.

"Sketchy does suit you."

I hesitated for a long moment, but Mazor returned to looking at his disheveled papers, so I forced an insincere smile and stepped toward the lobby. He spoke while my foot was still air-borne causing me to make an awkward turn and knock my elbow on the door frame near the forlorn fern.

"By the way, what was that about an s560? Mauve colored you said."

"Oh, nothing really. According to the police one was seen in the area around the time Brice got decorated. I mean, murdered. I thought you might know someone, it's such an unusual color."

"No, no, ours is blue."

"Umm, so you said."

He seemed perplexed, but relieved as he picked up the now tidy papers and held them in front of his face this time. It was a signal for me to leave. I headed for the elevator feeling I had wasted my time. As I stood there looking at my own reflection in the polished brass elevator door, I kept rerunning those moments when he flashed a smidgen of anxiety. I don't remember the ride down to the lobby or even the drive back toward Ocean Park, only the look of dread and fear just barely visible on the very fringes of his ancient face.

"Sometimes a mere mortal exists behind the facade of a wise man," I said to myself.

Why would a young, sexy, unpretentious sweetie like Camille marry such an old irascible frog? Croaking spots, warts and all. Surely not for money. After all, if she is Harriet Wagner's heir, she certainly doesn't need money and I don't really know how I got the nickname of Sketchy. I've had it for as long as I can remember and I've always liked it.

Let's see now, one weird look from David and two streaks of anxiety from Mazor and one damn good Peter Alexander and why is it hanging in Mazor's foyer if he's not going to keep it?

My gut made a decision before my mind came to it. As it was almost lunch time and I wasn't ready to stop sleuthing for the day I decided to head over to Prescott & Roth. Plus I was real curious about Wagner's collection and Mazor hadn't been helpful filling in any blanks. Besides, a story about it would make a good segment for CALog and perhaps I could coax some info out of P&R's Director, Stephanie, if she would deign to take food and drink with me.

Prescott & Roth is on Broadway, near a cluster of galleries, east of Ocean Park. The building used to be the studio of Frank Samuels, but in the last recession even an artist as well established as he had been couldn't afford the rent. The last time I saw him, he was working on a massive painting and the canvas took up most of the studio floor. His agent in Europe had pre-sold it and when completed it was to be installed on the ceiling of some 19th century opera house or mansion in France or Belgium as I recall. Frank was going to complete the painting that very evening. He had made several small preliminary pieces about the size of a laptop and knew exactly what effect he wanted, nevertheless the scale of the huge canvas felt very intimidating to me. How he could envision the final image from so many small bits and pieces was beyond comprehension for his assorted gang of studio aides and me. And though I had tried to convince him to agree to letting my CALog crew shoot the painting session, he didn't go for it. I never did get even an interview or to see the finished painting. He has since died of some lingering illness.

I turned off Wilshire at 26th Street and made a right onto Broadway. Prescott & Roth is located in the courtyard behind a row of galleries. A narrow driveway, at the middle of the block, leads into the courtyard. It was still the lunch hour so there were plenty of empty parking spaces. I pulled my wheels into the one in front of the entrance to the Mountwien Gallery. They are always a little too snooty to artists like me or maybe it's because I've never made a CALog about any of the artists on their roster. Either way I like commandeering one of their parking spaces and not going in whenever I stop to visit Stephanie.

Small-leafed ivy covered the front walls of the building and its mint verde hue looked healthy against the burnt rust bricks. I could see the back of Stephanie through the window. She was leaning against the pulled out top drawer of a filing cabinet, with her long classy looking fingers dancing across several files. Her brunette hair glistened as it cascaded over her shoulders and led my eyes down her hale and hardy figure. She was dressed fashionable and smart as always and I was looking forward to seeing her smile again.

I went through the door quietly, thinking I could go past her to look at the exhibit first and casually come back to the office and surprise her.

"Well, it must be snowing in Malibu. Isn't that when you said I'd see you again?"

Christ, I had barely gotten three steps past the reception counter.

"Do you have eyes under your beautiful hair?"

I turned and gave her my best smile.

"No, but I can sense a rat at ten paces anytime," she snapped.

"You look great, really great," I said as I grinned even wider.

"Stop, don't say anymore, we've been down that path before and I'd love to take another trip," she said in a very seductive voice. "But not today."

"Yeah, we had a great ride didn't we?"

"James, it's wonderful to see you, but I've got clients in the VIP room now and I really can't afford to make them wait." She reared back and there was no sign of playfulness in her eyes. "I can give you only sixty seconds."

I took a deep breath.

"What do you know about the auctioning of Harriet Wagner's collection? I'm thinking of doing a CALog about it."

"Right. I knew there had to be an art reason you'd show up."

Her usual perkiness had changed to a disappointed tone and that was the second time in less than an hour that I had heard that dispiriting comment. The air started to feel a little like dry ice as we stared at one another.

"How about letting me treat you to lunch at your favorite café when you're done with the VIP's?" I was betting eight to five she'd go.

"Sorry, no can do," she said as she reached under the counter and pulled out a black and gold folder labeled The Wagner Collection.

"There are still some things I'm more than willing to do for you, but cancelling appointments with clients is not one of them." She handed me the folder. I thanked her and opened it to the first page.

"This says the auction was held two months ago."

"It was originally scheduled for then, but changed to the spring. You know, for the beginning of the new season. We haven't updated the catalog yet," she said in a business-like manner.

"So what is the real reason for the delay?"

With a gentle wink she offered "The family found a use for some of the works and is thinking about keeping some others."

The list of paintings and sculptures was several pages long.

"May I use your photo-copier?"

"No, since you do have some valuable contacts, you may have this copy."

Gallerists will do almost anything if they think there might be a commission in it, but I got the impression it was time to leave. She held the gallery door wide open and I went out.

"The offer for lunch was real," I said sheepishly.

"Another time, maybe."

"Oh, OK, by the way, do you know anyone who strongly disliked Brice?"

She crinkled her eye brows, but didn't answer. Stephanie and I dated for a while and still play a sort of love/hate game with each other, but the fire cooled after I met Nicole. Considering Stephanie is single and Nicole is married it's easy to understand why my closes friends think I'm batty, but they don't know about all the factors I had to take into account in making the choice. I still feel extremely lucky about even having had a choice or maybe I only think I had one. Maybe the choice was made by one of them.

When I got back to my car an officious looking young man was staring at me from the receptionist desk inside the Mountwien Gallery. I put my shades on and stared back. He wasn't impressed.

Once back in my studio it felt really good to be in my own space. Everything was where I had left it and wanted it to be. Duie was doing guard duty on the upper deck, or at least that's what I like to believe he does up there. Of course, all he probably does is sleep. He doesn't even chase the gulls away anymore. I suppose they're company for him when I'm not around or when I'm lost in the euphoria of painting or editing video.

I poured myself a glass of blueberry-pomegranate juice, took the catalog Stephanie gave me and sat down in my welcoming La-Z-Boy.

Prescott & Roth really know their business. The first page read like a sales pitch from Rolls Royce. They even implied since Harriet Wagner's collection spanned fifty-plus years any future owner would be crowned king of L.A. art collectors by both the Museum of Contemporary Art and the Los Angeles County Museum of Art. The thought brought forth a chuckle and a broad grin to my stubbly mug.

Swiftly Duie came running down the stairs and a minute later someone knocked on the front door. I'm always impressed with his hearing ability, but I decided not to react. I'd talked to enough people for one day, but the door swung open anyhow and in walked Cisco. I felt a little violated.

"I don't see you for almost three years and now you're here twice in less than 48 hours. Was it something I said?"

"Well it certainly wasn't your welcoming personality."

His voice was clear and hard as he quickly perused the studio and trained his ear toward the stairs. Satisfied no one was going to join us, he relaxed, but only a little.

"Why didn't you tell me about the brawl you started at the Verge Gallery?"

"I prefer to think of it as an accident," I said.

He moved along the wall like a kick boxer about to swing around and break something.

"Don't play cute with me."

His sneer revealed clinched polished teeth contrasted with a flushed russet face.

"Look, you asked me to help. I can't control every hot head I encounter," I said earnestly. "Besides, who told you about it?"

He looked me over, paused, took a deep breath, paused again, leaned back on the stool in front of the easel and shook his head wearily. I wasn't sure if his reaction was caused by what I said or by the yellow scalene painting his mystified stare was focused on.

"I guess I forgot how you and your art-nick friends treat one another."

He seemed exasperated. "Maybe it's not a good idea having you poke around in this. My Captain may come down hard if he found out. Perhaps we best let it go."

"Still think I can't handle it, uh? Think I'll mess up and you'll have to rescue me?"

I could tell my face was frowning as I squirmed deeper into the La-Z-Boy. In fact, I was sitting so low, I felt like I was back in junior high being scolded for asking too many questions. He looked at me, surprised I would open the door to the past. But, there it was, and about time too.

My stomach started churning and I found myself suggesting we have some lunch, in a public place. Maybe we could talk this out, like the friends we've been for over twenty years, instead of continuing to let it age both of us. But, it was no go. Cisco wasn't ready to re-focus the past so the only door open to me was to do something good in the here and now.

"Look why don't we do this together, like the old days?" I suggested.

I sat up and tried to balance on the edge of the tread bare seat cushion before speaking.

"We could use the graffiti art angle as a way to ask questions."

With both eyes fixed on me, he was chewing the side of his mouth with nervous determination. So I spoke quicker.

"With me doing the introductions, I can get you inside the studios and the gallery back rooms with no hassles and everyone will feel less stressed with me doing the introductions."

He bought it. I could tell because he ran his right forefinger across the bottom of his nose like a file. He always fidgets that way when he senses a good idea.

"No rough-housing. Only straight talk."

His finger was pointing directly at me. I nodded and said I would set something up for 10 in the morning. He took another long breath and headed toward the door.

CHAPTER 7

It was a short ride from my place over to Martine Jaquez's studio so neither Cisco or I had time to warm up to talking. Besides neither of us are morning guys. Martine's studio is in the back section of an old repurposed Four Square church. With a wall built across the middle of the nave two women artists share the front space where the pews used to be. The stain glass windows remain in place throughout the entire building and I've never understood how any artist can paint with the pious sunlight coming through and casting holy icons all over their canvases.

Cisco directed his car into a no parking zone and placed a Police placard on the dash. "Tell me again why we're visiting this particular artist" he said.

"He has strong contacts with the gangs in the area and the mess in Brice's studio reminds me of Martine's work somehow. Plus they once had a major clash about who actually owns the visual rights to the graffiti art here in the hood."

"Ok, let's do it," Cisco said as he studied how the front door of the church had been altered to look more arty.

Martine had told me via email he'd leave the wrought iron gate on the side of the building unlocked for us, but the pad lock looked secure as we approached it.

"Well, Mr. Insider, what do we do now?" Cisco snarled.

"It just requires an artist's touch." I was smiling broadly as I took hold of the hinge side of the gate and swung it open.

Martine had welded the latch side closed after a bunch of kids broke in and stole his Zune and all of his Nuevo Bandas music at this time last year. No doubt they wanted it for a holiday party.

For years Martine had paid his bills by working at a machine shop and his experience there had left him with some remarkable skills for the gate was a real work of art. It completely fooled anyone who only stood and looked at it. Cisco was not amused.

Like Cisco, Martine grew up locally and was well versed in Westside gang history. He had been a street artist for years and knows all of the current crop of graffiti taggers. If anyone knows about a possible rift between them and Brice, Martine would be the one.

The concrete walkway beyond the gate led down the south side of the church and was lined with every kind of cactus you could grow in the narrow strip of earth left between it and the nave wall. It was a challenge to get past them without being pricked. They led to the studio door which had a little roof added on that looked as though it had been pilfered from the San Fernando Mission.

"Typical peasant." Cisco shrugged.

I knocked only once and Martine yelled to come on in. Cisco insisted I enter first. As I stepped in the face of Moses glowed back at me from a stained glass window on the opposite wall. His right hand was pointing toward a lighting-bolt while his left held the fabled tablets. No matter which way I moved his stare seemed to be aimed right at me. Instinctively I turned to leave, but Cisco blocked my escape.

Martine introduced himself in his elegant manner while extending his hand to Cisco.

"Permitame que me presente Soy Martine Jaquez and it's always a pleasure to see you again Sketchy."

"Gracias senor." I said in the worst Spanish accent you can imagine.

"Nome gustan las pinturas oleos cuando son sagradas y religiosas," Cisco said with an almost comical look of distress on his face.

"It's obvious you two don't need me here, why don't I wait in the car?" I said.

"Ah, James, forgive me. I forget you're a New Yorker who can't speak L.A.'s native tongue."

Martine gestured like a toreador for us to sit on a deep purple crushed velveteen couch.

"Detective Rivas was saying he doesn't like religious paintings. I don't either, do I James?"

"Right! I suppose these are images of some new rock star?" Cisco blipped.

He was scanning the large grisaille paintings of the crucifixion and other biblical scenes stacked throughout the studio, all with life-sized figures. Grisaille is an old Renaissance technique whereby the entire painting is first completed in only shades of gray. Martine is especially good at it. His brush strokes are so beautifully blended you can't see a single one, and you'd swear the images were created by the 17th century master Diego Velazquez or some Flemish genius.

"Well let's say once I ordain them they won't seem so holy," Martine offered out of the side of his mouth as if Moses was listening.

Cisco turned to me with a look of total consternation.

"I thought you said we were going to talk to a Graffiti artist."

"I see your dilemma. Perhaps a little demonstration is in order here. After all it is Sunday," Martine said.

With a sparkle in his eyes he walked toward his paint canisters. My first thought was to stop him, but I could never pass up an opportunity to immerse Cisco's head in art. Besides, Martine had already began popping the lids off of six plastic quart size paint canisters. First the primary colors of red, yellow and blue followed by the secondary's orange, violet and green. He set them in a neat row on the floor at the point where the old altar used to stand, approximately twenty feet from the only blank wall in the studio. A large sheet of clear plastic covered the entire wall with two long nails protruding 2 inches out and parallel to one another at about eight feet up from the floor and five feet apart.

Moving swiftly now, the diminutive artist grabbed a painting from his storage racks without even stopping to look at which sacred image it depicted. With no effort at all he hung the painting by sliding the top stretcher bar along the top of the two nails. Standing now with his back to his guest and only the paint canisters between us, he paused, raised his arms as if he were about to conduct a symphony, went down on one knee, bowed his head as if to pray, reached back with his left hand and randomly selected a canister, swung it toward the canvas, and let its liquid fly. By chance, green fluid was now splattered across the left side of the grisaille image of Christ and oozing down toward the floor. Before it had reached Christ's knee a brilliant blue crowned his left ear, orange glanced his right shoulder and the bottom of his chin. The next canister was about to jettison a dazzling violet.

Cisco spoke, "Por que?"

"Porque me recuerdan la muerte inevitable y tengo miedo de la muerte!" Martine said in a calm, but breathless timbre.

The best I could make of that quick statement was something about the inevitability of death and not being afraid of it, but I may have got it wrong.

The distraction had caused Martine to turn to his right, sending violet off-target. It hit the corner of the room just below the roof beam and oozed down the nook like syrup on the side of a bottle. When it reached the floor it formed a flat balloon shape. The unexpected result created a giant, skinny exclamation point to the whole mass, I mean mess. Martine was especially captivated by it. All 5 feet of him was standing straight up now with his eyes fixed, in an unfocused stare, right at the center of the painting. Silence filled the studio to a nerve racking pitch while dehydrating fumes of acrylic paint smothered any thought of speech. The stench immediately reminded me of Brice's fume-filled studio.

Martine slowly turned toward us. His eyes were flooded now, but focused on Cisco.

"I had the blues yesterday, today I'm flying. Es un dia magnifico, gracias."

His voice sounded more like singing than speech. Cisco was still in a baffled stupor, but managed to whisper "El gusto es mio... my pleasure."

Our triad of hush was suddenly broken by an unnatural murmur, not unlike the white noise of an un-tuned radio.

"What a pity." said Martine.

Cisco made a gesture of apology, reached inside his coat and brought out a small cell phone sounding like the buzzing of a captured bumble-bee. He answered it, but something was preventing the call from clearly penetrating the sanctity of the studio so he headed out the door.

Martine refocused on me with that same look of continuance and camaraderie I had last seen in David's eyes the night he cut his hand. He smiled and turned toward the wall to study his newly graffiti-fied painting.

"It's a shame you didn't bring your CALog crew with you James," he said.

As I looked at the back of his head, his coal black hair seemed to reflect the light emanating from the face of Moses, with his eyes once again fixed on me. I closed my eyes and walked out the door. I was well past the cactus and all most to the gate before I could open them again. As I focused on the wrought iron gate its strong black bars reminded me of the holding cells down at the jail. I wondered if Los Angeles would always have this dual personality. One entity filled with creative, highly energized spirits and the other populated with morons and anarchists. As I swung the gate open its thin side view seemed a perfect metaphor for the group in the middle. Those hard working, peace loving people who only want a nice home, in a friendly neighborhood, people like Cisco, who was now signaling for me to hurry up. No one seems to have time to think of those folks anymore.

Cisco was looking intense when he spoke and gestured for me to hustle. "Get in, we've got a hot one."

"Well, let her roll." I said as I jumped in. "What's the call?"

"Fire and assault on the Northside."

"Oh, well why not let me out at Wilshire, I'll head over to Fromin's for lunch." I purposely sounded bored and I was famished.

"Don't give me that 'I don't care about the rich muck'. You're going to love this one," he said.

Cisco turned onto Lincoln and activated the siren. The shriek was deadly inside the car. I prefer moving though the community as quietly as possible, but Cisco was in his element and there was no way we could talk above the wail. Plus his race car driving mode always drove me panicky so I focused on the floorboard. When I finally raised my eyes, to confirm it still wasn't safe to look, I noticed his dashboard note pad. The scrawl read: Norten Peterson, Adelaide Drive. He glanced over at me with a delighted smirk and continued navigating through the heavy traffic. I decided to look undaunted and took out my cell and texted a brief note of thanks to Martine. Cisco leaned toward me, glanced at my cell and spoke loudly. "Hey, his mess looked a lot like the one at Peregrine's. Does he ever do his act with real bodies? And was that Hooker's Green he used?"

The look of complete vexation on my face brought a wide grin from Cisco.

Norten Peterson has had a full head of white hair since I first met him over 15 years ago and he must be in his late 60s by now. He's tall, trim, handsome, prosperous, and he'll probably always be. He collects art, exotic cars and women. He's also the person technophobes think of every time their anxious palms sweat having to learn how to operate some new computerized, digitalized nerdy wonder. Nine out of every ten new gadgets and programs on the market have innards copyrighted by him. His ultra-modern mansion is all white too, surrounded by a grove of tall thin eucalyptus trees whose pale mint green trunks are barely visible in front of the starkness of the house and its seven foot high security wall. On a sunny day as you're driving around this tawny neighborhood your first sight of the place is eye-popping. So much light bounces off it you feel a tan coming on by just being in its aura. To say nothing of the fact it signals big bucks ahead. We crossed Wilshire Boulevard and Cisco switched off the siren.

"Why did you pull the plug on the horn?" I queried.

"Boy, you have been out of it for a while," he said quickly while turning sharply on to San Vicente. "Noise abatement order. No unnecessary use of the horn in this neighborhood unless it's a matter of life or..."

He stopped his recital and the car.

"Look at that!"

Coming from over the top of the next ridge of houses was a huge cloud of dark gray smoke. Its ghost-like shape loomed as if a bomb had been detonated.

"It's going to be a bad-air day in Pacific Palisades." I said bemused.

Fingers of crimson red and orange were flaring up now. The allure of watching them play sky tag dissipated quickly with the thought that the entire canyon could go up, but just as swiftly their life force appeared to be extinguished.

Cisco drove on around the last curve and we were faced with an obstacle course of two gleaming yellow green fire trucks, three white and blue Police squad cars, a cherry red paramedics van, and a private metallic gold and cream ambulance. As Cisco deftly maneuvered the car through the gate and down the long driveway, passing busy men dressed in heavy fireproof gear, I expected to see the smoldering remains of material wealth and maybe a half dozen lifeless bodies. I was dead wrong. As we rolled past the last truck we were met by a half-acre of painted green lawn, flowering bushes, a full stand of trees and a completely intact grand palace. If there was an emergency here it must be in the basement I thought. Except for the heavy scent of fire in the air the place seemed pristine. Cisco leaned out and spoke to a uniformed sergeant.

"The place looks like a movie set. Where the hell was the fire? Or was there a real fire at all?"

"In the garage."

Cisco gestured with disbelief. "The what?"

With a similar look of incredulity the sergeant said, "The garage storeroom to be exact, sir."

Cisco took a long hard stare at the garage, which looked completely intact from our viewpoint. He jumped out from behind the steering wheel, walked straight up to the sergeant, toe to toe, looked him hard in the eyes and said, "I see, someone breaks into this, this mansion, conks the squire on the head, walks into the storeroom, the garage storeroom and starts a fire and you felt the need to call me. Is that correct Sergeant?"

"No sir. I thought you might like to look over the real situation, sir."

The Sergeant darted his eyes toward the back of the paramedic's van.

"The real what," Cisco snapped.

He turned in the direction of the Sergeant's stare and saw Norten Peterson seated on the back bumper of the van dressed in a colorful silk Hawaiian shirt, tailored white pants, white buck skin sandals and sporting a disheveled skull cap made of off-white bandages.

He was being consoled by two young ladies clad in string bikinis, Malibu Midnight brand, I believe. The honey blonde wore hot orange and had freckles leading down between her unnaturally round cleavage. The redhead was barely keeping herself covered by a fluorescent purple number trimmed with silver.

"Yep, it's a movie set all right, star and two bimbos," Cisco whispered as we approached the trio.

Nearby a small troop of firemen were fooling around with their equipment like jocks at a gym while maintaining their eagle eyes focused on Peterson's two playmates. Cisco sparked a glance at the sergeant, who got the message to put an end to their calisthenics. The men left the area.

"Detective Rivas, Mr. Peterson. Do you feel up to telling us what happened here?" Cisco said coolly as he flashed his shield.

Peterson glimpsed the badge and gestured to his two playmates to cease their attentions. "I don't know, really. I drove into the garage, got out of my car and wham, the lights went out. Next thing I know Honey and Cerise are helping me up and the garage is ablaze and full of smoke."

Immediately upon hearing their names, Honey and Cerise resumed their caressing and petting. Peterson gave them both a little kiss and patted their behinds, which was obviously his signal for them to leave. They politely smiled, turned, and bounced their way toward the pool. It was hard for Cisco and me to return our attention to Peterson, but when he coughed we managed to dither and vacillate enough to face him.

"You're a lucky man, and this place, this place could have been burned to the ground." Cisco paused. "Where were you coming from Mr. Peterson?"

"From my office in the Palisades. Why? And what are you doing here, Terra? There's nothing to video now," Peterson said with a measured degree of perplexity as he glared at me.

Cisco also stared at me, but with that old tag team look. "There's been a lot of this going on around here lately, and James has been helping us.

Peterson fidgeted with his bandages. "A lot of what?"

"Punks following people home and right on into their garage and jumping them.

What was taken?" I said.

Peterson became more annoyed with the unraveling head bandage. "Taken?"

"Your wallet perhaps, your ..."

Cisco grabbed Peterson's arm and held it up revealing a jewel encrusted Rolex. "No, robbery doesn't seem to be what's going on here. Does it Mr. Peterson?"

Peterson was now doubly irritated as he stood up and glared down at Cisco. "Yes, what is going on here, Detective, what is your name again?"

"Francisco Rivas. How did the firemen get here so quick?"

Peterson's chilled face now seemed haggard and about to explode as he drawled. "There's a direct alarm line to my security team."

"From the garage storeroom? What do you keep in there, spare parts for the Rolls?" Cisco said with a repulsive stare.

"Something a little more valuable, Lieutenant. My entire art collection was in there," he said. He looked at me and shook his head in a gesture of regret and sadness. Cisco rolled his eyes as he turned and looked at me too and then at the Sergeant.

"You see sir, that's why I called you," the sergeant said in a slow voice.

"No, I don't see." Cisco said over his shoulder as he turned back toward Peterson. "Why ... when you have a house like this do you put an art collection in the garage storeroom?"

Peterson sort of fell back and sat down on the van's bumper. "The entire inside of the house is to be re-painted and re-decorated starting tomorrow. And all of the professional art storage facilities in the city were full so I had a special one built in the garage. Damn it, bad decision." He moaned as he cradled his head in his hands.

"You were getting ready for your annual rehang right?" I said quietly.

"Yes, and I've been so busy with my new startup I forgot to reserve a storage space this year." He threw the head bandage on the ground.

The sergeant held up a manila folder marked 'Insurance' on the tab. "There were a number of Brice Peregrine paintings in the collection, Sir."

Cisco raised one eyebrow and looked at the Sergeant and me. We all turned toward Peterson, who was now staring cross-eyed at the ground. "I see, repainted tomorrow," Cisco said as he took the folder and angled his head for me to follow. "Neat, very neat. I can see quite clearly now. Well let's have a look," he grumbled as we headed for the garage. "Thank you sergeant for the phone call and your attention to detail."

The sergeant saluted and nodded in return.

As I looked back I could see the two medics from the private ambulance service hovering around Peterson and overheard the heavy-set one say. "You know sir, it might be prudent to let us take you to the clinic so there's a report on file. You know, in case there's any questions from the insurance companies and or any other authorities."

That last bit got Cisco's attention, but all he did was smile at the medic as Peterson shook his head in agreement.

From the outside, the garage looked large enough to hold six cars. But once inside it was obvious four of the spaces had been converted to a professionally designed art storage room built of metal and enclosed in heavy bars covered by a chain-like mesh.

Most of the smoke had faded to a light haze and had left a fine dust of black soot on a bright red Ferrari that was dappled in sunlight and coated by dirty water coming through holes in the burned out ceiling. Cisco noted the car had been parked as far away from the storage section as possible, plus the doors were closed and all its windows were up. "Neat, very neat," he said again as a couple of firemen continued to spray retardant on the smoldering roof beams.

The area looked like a giant oven had been left on too long, ruining the dinner and leaving only burnt, unrecognizable debris. There were large metal shelf-like structures, filled now with charred and burnt frames and sketcher bars plus fragmented pieces of curled up roasted canvas with blistered paint chips everywhere. All of which was bathed in water, fire extinguishing foam and piles of multi-hued ash.

Cisco stooped to pick up a few small pieces of blackened canvas inside the first storage shelf. "This guy was real efficient. He really knows how to outline a plot." He handed the remnants to me. "Hell, he could be a Hollywood director."

It was obvious the firemen weren't able to get any of the paintings out of the metal cage before the fire consumed them. No doubt the heat had been extremely intense, because the left side of the Ferrari was deformed and festered looking.

I cleaned soot off a small piece of burnt canvas, revealing the illegible signature of an artist. "It would be almost humorous if it weren't so extravagant."

Cisco glanced at the charred remnant and added the theoretical caveat, "It's often difficult in the crime game to look too far forward, but see what else you can find, Leonardo." He headed out the large, weighty metal security door at the back of the structure and I could see it opened onto a stone path leading to the pool and main house.

There didn't seem to be much else in the store room to look at, except numerous piles of ash and charred frames. Somehow, knowing those piles were once paintings left me feeling as though I was bearing witness to a mass crematorium ... one of those places where innocent victims are made to vanish. As I fingered through each heap of limpid black slag and embers, images of paintings flashed in front of my eyes, especially the ones Peterson often loaned out to exclusive exhibitions around town and those that I had seen throughout his house while schmoozing with guests at his numerous parties. I had even sold him one of my own paintings some years back. In fact, it was one of my best works. One I had held on to and had sold only because I was broke. The gritty wet dust coating my fingers suddenly seemed alive, as if all I had to do was smear it on a blank canvas and the painting would rise anew. But the sooty stain's grunge declared that the art was gone forever, it had evolved into a new reality. As I raised my eyes toward the huge burned-out sections of the ceiling I noticed melted security cameras mounted on opposite ends of the space.

I yelled at the fireman perched at the top of a nearby ladder. "Hey, were those things on when the fire started?"

"Don't know, but I believe the recorder is in the private security company's office," he replied. "Your sergeant knows about it."

Cisco and I scrutinized Honey and Cerise one last time and submitted our condolences to Peterson for his incinerated art collection. Then we drove away feeling somewhat puzzled.

Cisco turned the car toward the canyons, drove with uncharacteristic care, and seemed miles away. A sign near the entrance to the local Nature Center reminded all visitors to 'Leave only footprints. Take only photographs. Kill only time'. The car crawled to a stop near a small stand of yucca. Both of us emerged into the strong sunlight, eager to let nature rejuvenate our senses and fill our lungs with the fresh scent of sage. Nearby, a ground squirrel darted through the dry underbrush and froze at the sound of our footsteps. A few seconds later, a lizard slithered across the dusty trail, perched on a large boulder and posed cautiously. Each cocked its head and eyed us with suspicion. Cisco didn't seem to notice them as he gazed out over the rugged terrain. I had seen him like this many times before, especially when he was confronted by extreme wealth. Having come from harsh poverty, as he had, his reaction always seemed understandable to me.

There aren't a whole lot of connections one can make with the natural world when living in most large cities, but L.A. is surrounded by mountains and canyons that are fairly easy to get to providing you have a car. Many people like Cisco, who have experienced tragedy in their live, seek the solace those natural areas provide. He and I used to visit this very spot whenever we needed to get away from sirens, gangs and thugs.

Much of what goes on in a large city is completely out of one's control and even though nature is also beyond our control, somehow just being surrounded by it makes having complete control of life seem unnecessary.

After a few minutes of thoughtful silence and calm the sparrows and quails hidden in the brush had determined we weren't a threat and returned to their tweeting and whistles. The ground squirrel had vanished as had a hovering Harrier.

"Every CALog I shoot has a dozen possible story lines," I said thoughtfully. "Don't let this one subplot lead you away from the top story. The star at the helm of this current one-reeler is a non-pro."

Cisco picked up a small rock, threw it toward the bottom of the hill and stared out across the sun dried canyon. "You and I were a great team once. At the opening of each show I could always rely on you to come up with a detailed analysis, a description of the star, the set, even the plot." He turned back in the direction of Peterson's house then toward me and continued talking while struggling to see through the deflected sunlight glaring from the car's windshield ... which caused him to grimace as he spoke. "Some of your yak was laughable, but your instincts have always been true."

"It's a form of logistical regression," I said. "Like painting, it's holistic. The small parts, even if they're not all there, can tell you what the whole is going to look like. It's like articulating a pattern from someone else's mind."

"How do you stay passionate and yet clear about what you're dealing with when the external world is so erratic?" he said.

"It's your ability to deal with the fitful that made us a good team. All the maniacs you have to get close to on the street and on the force have always been too much for me. I work better in other spheres. More cerebral and intuitive, maybe even cellestial."

"Right," he said firmly after a short pause. "So you're still convinced the murder is an art thing?"

Perhaps it was the heat, but whatever it was, his reflective mood had vaporized like the ground squirrel and the Harrier hawk.

"Well so far, all the small parts are telling me it's at the very least a passion thing," I said with reluctant confidence.

"All the parts? I've got only two on my list," he replied surprisingly.

"Hey, by the way, how did Brice die? Surely he didn't let the murderer jam a brush down his throat," I queried.

With a shudder he said, "The coroner says he was most likely administered some sort of knockout drug, then drowned with paint. It will take a couple more days to get the lab results ... and who knows what we might find on Peterson's security disc if I can get a judge to sign off on the paper work." He turned his back to the sun and faced me. "So what other parts are on your list?"

"Look at the contrast between Brice's studio and Peterson's garage. One looks like a madman on a rampage destroyed it and the other looks like the house keeper burnt the brownies, but both vent passion and a noticeable level of obsession."

He headed back toward the car shaking his head "Yeah, that's true. They are both passionate, but maybe it's because they're both cunning enough to make it look that way."

"Well I doubt there is a real connection between the two events," I said. "And besides, introspection can often be inferior to the wisdom of gut instinct."

The lizard stuck out his long pale pink tongue and used it to remoisten his left eye. I wondered if it meant he could see us better or thought we'd look more tolerable all wet.

As Cisco drove the car back down the winding canyon road, the rhythm of the curves made my mind repeat silently "green paint ... green paint ... who hates, no... no ... graffiti art, graffiti art, who hates graffiti art ... David Bernkopf, that's who.

CHAPTER 8

An imposing solitary classic Greek column, Corinthian I believe, stood to the right of the entrance and an engraved bronze plaque at the center of the door read 'David Bernkopf, Artist'. It radiated an air of self-anointed stardom. There was no polite way to use the Cellini style cherub knocker, so I tapped the door with my shoe. To my surprise it swung open silently.

"Hey David, are you here, man? Its old salt of the earth James Terra."

Pausing only briefly, I stepped into the intimate foyer and was immediately drawn to a small painting on the floor. It was not much larger than a standard book and looked as though someone had simply dropped it there.

It depicted a group of nude males standing amongst some Greek ruins admiring a broken sculpture of a goddess. The image was flawlessly rendered with every reflected light and nuance of shadow done with perfection. Its clarity and cleanliness made the theme seem natural, wholesome even. I picked it up and laid it on an ornate doily atop a small French-styled table at the center of the hallway.

"Boy, you really keep things tight. I hope the cut on your hand hasn't caused you to loosen up too much."

I chuckled as I turned to leave the foyer and enter the studio, which had originally been the living room. Everything in the space was orderly, spotlessly clean, and as still as traffic on the I-5. There were only two things breaking the monotony. First, all of the large 300 ml tubes of expensive Holbein Vernet oil paint David always kept lined up on his work table were gone. As I stood there wondering about the missing paint, for the second time in less than a week, I ingested a whiff of mortality propelling its compliments my way. Suddenly I wished Cisco were with me. I headed down the short hall at the opposite end of the studio. As I entered, the fumes were wafting stronger as I approached the first door on the right, the bedroom.

The clear morning light streaming through two picture windows made the bed seem too big for the size of the room, and it was no secret David used it for more than sleeping. He also used it occasionally as a gallery when he held an open studio weekend so the walls were usually lined with several of his small, gold framed, paintings and the bed covered with portfolios of his exquisite figure drawings of male nudes. Today, however, it was obvious the foreplay had been for only one. All of the frames were completely empty and scattered about on the floor.

In the middle of the king size bed lay the master of the house, garnished with an untidy covering of shredded paintings from those empty gold frames. Bits and pieces of tiny images of nude body parts and ancient temples made a confetti-style blanket for his slim figure, while his face seemed hidden by an orgy of worm-like forms of Hooker's Green paint. You could smell the fumes of the oil as it simmered in the heat of the hot room and slid down his cheeks leaving long greasy stains. All of the other colors had been squeezed out all over his slight physique and the crumbled empty tubes were on the floor at the foot of the bed.

Once again there was a small gold object protruding from the victims paint filled open mouth ... a number 8 brush this time.

When the sergeant answered the phone I said, "Detective Rivas please."

After only a moment or two I heard a click and a voice, "Rivas speaking."

"This is James. I'm at Bernkopf's studio. There's some more brushwork here you need to investigate."

I started looking around for clues as to who was responsible for this wasteful destruction of life, talent and art, but my heart just wasn't in it. I walked outside to surround myself with flowers, vigorous shrubs, and the gentle embrace of manicured Mother Nature rather than be smothered by the constant proximity of death.

Bernkopf's house is one of those small, Mission Revival style boxes built in the 1920s or '30s. Its avocado stucco walls, terra cotta red tile roof, and rounded arched windows and doorways reflect a time before the marriage of nature and technology; before cell phones and flower vending machines; and before insanity became entertainment, but well within the confines of a Balkanized city of separate, unequal societies. If it had been located north of Wilshire Blvd., the house would be considered fit only as a tear-down even though the greenway running along the front was a plant lover's paradise and signaled pride of ownership. It even included Monarch Butterflies and Milkwood. Cisco was talking even before he stepped from his car. "Now correct me if I'm wrong, but this guy isn't a graffiti artist, is he?"

I felt eclipsed next to such blunt brilliance, so I shrugged my shoulders.

"Right," continued Cisco in a sustained gesture of gruffness. "Creative art BS has clouded your vision. You can't see the reality anymore and isn't this the guy you had the brawl with?"

The safety valve on Cisco's pressure cooker mood was dangerously close to broiling over.

"You're right, this game isn't for me. I think I'll stay out of it." I said as I started to leave. I barely got past the gladiolas when he vented, "Will you be at the studio or the club?"

"The club, I need a drink," was all I was able to say as I ambled to my car.

His disapproval was straight out of a behavioral science class, but fleeting. He had more important things to brood over, including the arriving throng of coroner's assistants, fingerprint experts, and assorted crime scene investigators. His ability to deal with those kind of minds has always amazed me.

The Indigo Blues Club is over on 4th Street near Colorado. It's one of those taverns where anyone looking for a full, satisfying, get-your-money's worth evening of blues and jazz can find it. The front door is always locked at that time of the day so I went down the alley to the kitchen entrance. If you speak unhurriedly to Leroy, the cook, he'll let you sample whatever he's fix'in on the grill for lunch.

Newly remodeled and ready to host another Tuesday night jam session, the lounge was empty except for owner harp man Spider Legs Washington. The sound from his metal mouth was melodic and matched the Chicago shuffle he was stepping to.

Spider never gained the fame he truly deserves and other than a small handful of recordings his work remains gravely overlooked. We grew up together on the lower east side of New York between Chinatown and Little Italy.

"I thought you said you weren't going to play the old school stuff anymore," I said as I reached for a beer from behind the bar. "That was Honky Tonk, wasn't it?"

"Wens somethin's gotsa holds of ya, yous gots-ta go wits it man. Don't fights its. You wits me?" He said as he smiled with his wonderful full grin.

"Well, I may be only an artist, but I think you forgot some of the notes."

"Wens yous goin' to learnts man. The notes yous leaves out is just as important as the extra ones yous puts in."

"Yea, you've been using that line ever since Miss Jackson said it to us during our eighth grade spelling bee remember? Oh and I thought you said you weren't going to use that tourist slang speak anymore," I said as I saluted him with the long neck.

"Uh ha, Ok, but she didn't get it then, just like you don't now." He paused and looked at me with as much concern as he cared to rally. "If life hands you lemons don't complain about the sour taste cause you could be pickin' cotton man. Either way the blues can make it sweeter."

As Spider leaned back on his stool the room filled with a smokin' swampy Mississippi sax sound from his harp. Molly, the cleaning lady, added to the mood by gracefully giving the piano a light once-over with her left hand while feather dusting it with her right. Whether it was the buzz from the harp, from the beer on an empty stomach, or from the humming I was trying to do in sync with Spider, slowly the big picture of the week's events was coming into focus. Some pieces were still missing and the composition didn't quiet balance yet, but the motif was taking shape.

The joint was starting to move with good vibes and life, when just as swiftly, Cisco walked in and everything came to a sudden halt. Even Leroy, who had danced out of the kitchen, looked worried and quickly retreated back to his grill.

Sensing the wave of anxiety he had generated, Cisco smiled and said, "Relax, I only came in for a cool one." He gestured for me to join him in the corner booth. "I just need to talk to Leonardo here."

I reached over the bar and grabbed a long neck for him. "You know good detecting is one of continuous synthesis," I said with renewed vigor as we slid into the booth. "An all but endless process of borrowing, absorption, dissemination, solidification and borrowing again with the process starting anew."

Cisco picked up the long neck and pressed it against my forehead. "Cool down, hot shot. Maybe you've absorbed too much sun."

I had to admit the cold glass felt good and did seem to make the ringing in my ears fade.

Cisco took a deep draw from the sweaty bottle, "What's got you going, man?"

"Look, why does anyone kill another human being?" I said with surprised clarity. "For love, hate or money, right?"

Cisco spread a small grin and took another draw on the long neck. "Yeah, but remember these are artists."

I chose to ignore his slight. "Look, I think we can rule out love. No body killed these two guys because of that. Right!" I said without breathing.

He began peeling the label off his beer bottle as his grin widened and he took another guzzle, "Are we starting to get some humility?"

I wanted to pursue that thought, but now wasn't the time. "Money seems like a sure bet, but passionate hate strikes me as the strongest possibility," I said as I finished my long neck. "Maybe hate generated by love."

Cisco was now frowning at his empty bottle, "Well, the sun raises in the east and sets in the west, but greed never seems to rest."

Leroy raised a fresh long neck from the cooler and gestured it toward Cisco, but he waved him off as he turned toward me with a weary glare.

"OK, so let's say you're right. First, how does anybody profit money-wise from killing Peregrine and Bernkoff?"

"They have to own paintings by them," said Cisco.

"Yes, lots of collectors own their paintings, but there's only one trying to sell them that I know of," I said, as I slid out of the booth and headed to point Percy to the porcelain.

As I stood there relieving myself I remembered it was Tuesday, which meant it was jam night at the club and the place is always abuzz with shared tastes and a feeling of being in the midst of a special time. Jazz and blues audiences are intelligent people, people who thrive on improvisation. When I returned to the booth I told Cisco about Mazor and Camille's plan to sell the collection they inherited from Harriet Wagner. I was a little surprised when he suggested I should look into it, but I sensed he had something else on his mind.

"Were there any clues or obvious pointers at David's for us to follow?"

"No, but there were a couple of oddities you might know something about."

He picked at the label on the empty long neck. "For starters, did you know Bernkoff wore a wig?"

"Uh, no I didn't, it is interesting though and explains why he grasped the back of his head when he tripped over my foot at the gallery instead of using his free hand to break his fall."

"Probably so."

"What else did you find?"

"There is a dog house in the back yard, dog food and a water bowls all labeled 'Ruff', but there was no dog anywhere. Did you see one while you were there?"

"No and I know there wasn't one there when we made his CALog last year. Do you think the killer may have taken it?"

"It's a possibility, I guess. OK, what about any relatives. Did he have any you know of?"

"I can't recall him ever mentioning any."

"What about a Hanna Bernkoffolla?"

"Hanna who, Bernkoffolla? Where did you find that name?"

"We need to notify the next-of-kin, so when we discovered his will in a small metal box of his personal papers hidden in the closet, we opened it and it stated he left everything to this Hanna woman. His house, car, bank account, insurance and what's left of his paintings. I'd like to talk to her."

"There was no contact info with the name uh?"

"Nothing and there is no phone, tax, or DMV listing of it anywhere in the state."

"It's possible my former assistant, Sally, might recall something. I'll call her."

Cisco stood and spoke in an offhand manner as he started to leave, "Ah yes, one of James Terra's famous resources. OK, I've got to get back to the station and fill out a ton of paperwork. Let me know if Sally knows anything. How do you like that beer?"

"The beer, it was cold and wet," I said as I glanced at the empty bottle and noticed its label had been peeled off too.

As I headed home around midnight, joyous moments of sheer musical delight remained with me all the way back to the studio and right on into my dreams of hiking along the Klickitat River last June and of one of my favorite northwest beers, Widmer Hef.

CHAPTER 9

It was dawning when Duie woke me and insisted on being let out so I decided to stay up and see if I could find my hard copy of Sally's old digital files. She had been a real trouper when I stipulated I wanted hard copies kept of all of her research and personal notes concerning each artists we shot for CALog. I can still hear how she laughed when I explained why I didn't trust the longevity of computers, CD's, flashdrives or the cloud.

When I opened the filing cabinet draw labeled 'James' Hard Stuff' I laughed out loud, but expected its contents to be completely organized and it was which made me miss Sally even more. She and her partner had moved to Albuquerque to be the Director of a new nonprofit art center in the heart of the downtown urban revitalization district and consistently tells me in her e-mails she is happy, is doing well, and loves the openness Albuquerque offers.

The folder marked Bernkoff had the usual stuff related to the artist's education, awards, and exhibition resume plus a few notes about major collectors who have acquired his work over the years. The only thing seemingly a little odd to me was his birthplace, Winamac, Monroe Township, Pulaski County, Indiana and it was not typed on the resume, but had been written, in Sally's hand, on the back. Few artists who are successful in L.A. ever come from small Midwest towns which can be insular and often even incestuous when presenting local arts programming. Perhaps David didn't want such a stigma applied to his formative years.

I put the folder back and went directly to my computer and googled 'Bernkoffolla Pulaski County Indiana.' Within two seconds a few listings appeared. Most were for individuals and businesses in Winamac while the others were for a region in east Poland, but none were for a Hanna Bernkoffolla. I surmised the name was of Polish/Russian or Polish/German origin and David had lopped off the 'olla' portion.

Everybody wants to be somebody else. David had obviously forgotten fame doesn't make you a new person. In fact, fame can be the worst part of being someone other than yourself.

I typed in 'Pulaski County white pages Hanna Bernkoffolla', hit search and got nothing. Either she didn't live in Pulaski County or didn't have a land line phone or got married or simply changed her name. I noticed a listing for 'Hanna' Garbozynski and decided to dial the number directly. After only two rings a woman answered so I asked her if she was Hanna Bernkoffolla and she quickly stated she hadn't used her maiden name since she married Mr. Garbozynski. I decided to e-mail the info directly to Cisco and let him deal with telling her about David and her inheritance.

Most galleries don't open until 11am, so Duie and I had lots of time to complete a good fast walk even though it was a little cool on the beach. By the time I finished lunch at Fromin's and got to the Heritage Gallery on La Cienega it was well past 1pm.

Ben Horowitz, owner and director of the gallery has been an art dealer in LA longer than any of the others. If anyone knew about the Harriet Wagner Collection, he would.

The drive down La Cienega from Sunset Boulevard had been slow going and the cracked pavement and aged buildings made me think about how some parts of LA always seem to be forgotten about. The worn carpet and drab walls of the gallery didn't seem inviting either. Ben was settled at his usual spot, a small desk over in the far corner of the second room. A lean man with grey hair and goatee, he is never without his pipe and a bag of pistachios.

"Good to see you, Ben," I said as I walked across to shake his hand. "It's always comforting to see that a real honest gallery can still survive in this town." I knew that comment would bring a smile to his venerable face and I meant every word of it.

"Well, I keep trying to stay on the straight and narrow, but it's getting harder all the time," he said as he reached his hand forward. "Have you brought some paintings for me to look at?"

I suddenly felt bad and a little embarrassed. Ben had been my dealer for many years and I had never really explained to him why I left his roster and didn't want to do another exhibit with him.

"No, I'm doing a little investigating for Cisco on the Peregrine/Bernkoff case," I said quickly in hopes he would forget about his query.

"Damn, James, I thought you gave that sort of thing up when you got the CALog gig," he scoffed. "Have you made any paintings at all this year?"

"I've been working on some new stuff, but it's going sort-of slow, so I needed to get out of the studio for a while. Beside you know I owe Cisco," I said softly.

Ben stared at me for a long moment and sat down wobbling his head. "OK, what do you need from me?" he said in an indifferent manner.

"What can you tell me about Harriet Wagner and her collection?"

A momentary look of bewilderment skipped across his eye lids, but didn't seem to slow his response.

"She had a great eye for all of the young ones coming up over the years," he said enthusiastically. "And didn't hesitate to go after what she wanted."

"The young ones," I said without really thinking.

"Come on James, surely at least once in your life one of those Beverly Hills socialites wanted more than a painting from you."

"Well yes, but not old lady Wagner. I mean, come on, she must have been over ninety when she died," I said sharply. "She couldn't have been trading sex for art during much of the past 15 years."

"Well she was a real looker in her day. There wasn't a young artist in this town who'd turn down any offer she'd make for a painting. In fact, I doubt she paid much, in money for her entire collection at least up until about 5 years ago. If she acquired more after that I didn't hear about it," Ben said thoughtfully.

"Mmm, yeah, I suppose you're right. There's a lot of art that changes hands in this town without a dime ever being spent," I said. "And yet, the Feds claim LA has more cash floating around than any other city in the country."

"What has any of this got to do with Peregrine and Bernkopf?" Ben said as he bit down on his gnawed pipe stem.

"Not sure yet, but it's part of the collage forming in my head, that's for sure," I said. "Let's see if we can paste some more bits of it together."

Ben's eyes twinkled as he tapped his pipe against his lower front teeth.

"For over 50 years, Wagner amasses a great collection, but doesn't seem to pay for it with much visible cash then 5 years ago she suddenly stops. Why? What happened?" I prompted.

"Well, remember by then she's in her 80s and there aren't too many artists around interested in that kind of ride," he said as he chuckled deeply. "The only thing I can remember is around that same time her husband died and her niece moved to Boston." Ben tapped his pipe against his desk top, "But I don't see how that could have anything to do with it."

"How do you know about her niece?"

"She'd often show up at openings on the arm of one or more of my artists and before leaving for back East she asked me to buy a couple of their works she owned personally," he said as he started looking through the filing cabinet behind him. "She needed money and her aunt refused to help her move."

"Did you buy the works?"

"Yes, but Wagner tried to convince me her niece had stolen them from her."

"Did she?"

"No, I checked with the artists and they both said they had given the works to the girl," he stated in a very convincing tone.

There was no reason to doubt Ben. During the many years I had dealt with him he had always been straightforward on every business deal. In fact, he was President of the L.A. Art Dealers Association and often served as an expert witness when the D.A. was prosecuting an art fraud case.

"Do you remember who the artists were?" I said as I stared at the filing cabinet.

"Yes, I do," he said with a sly grin. Jon Doh and Brice Peregrine."

My mouth must have been open a little too long because Ben threw a pistachio into it, which caused me to inhale and retch at the same time. While I stood up to get my throat clear, Ben pulled a file out and opened it.

"Yep, here it is. Jon Doh and Brice Peregrine. But I still don't see how that connects Harriet Wagner to murder."

"Mmm, no, but it seems to connect her niece," I said with surprise as I continued to gag. "Do you know where Jon moved his studio to? I haven't seen him since his old one was destroyed in the last quake."

Ben chomped his pipe again and reached for another manila folder. "Here it is, he moved to Ventura."

"You're kidding. Why would he want to live up there?"

He raised his thick eyebrows and said "If I recall correctly, he met a woman from there and bought some kind of business with her, but I don't have her name or address, only a phone number."

As he sorted through the papers in the folder a 5"x7" photograph fell out and the image immediately brought a smile to his face. "You know, when I questioned Jon about why he had given this piece to the niece, one of his best works by-the-way, he had an odd reply. He said, 'She deserves much more'."

He handed the photograph to me, "This is the piece you bought from Camille?"

"Yep and sold it right away, but alas, it was destroyed in that same quake."

Jon Doh is a ceramic Pop artist who specializes in whimsical teapots and has always refused to give his real name. After the quake destroyed his studio and most of his new work, he told everyone he wasn't going to make art anymore and was moving to the dessert. No one believed him. The photograph showed a contorted sculpture of what looked like two teapots copulating.

On the drive back to Ocean Park my mind kept jumping back and forth between determining how to find Jon Doh and the promise I had given Ben that I would definitely show him my new work. What new work, I hadn't finished anything in months good enough to exhibit. There was something very comforting about watching Ben find everything I asked for by opening an old filing cabinet and shuffling through a couple of manila folders. Obviously he has the same reservations about computers I have.

When I got home and googled "artist Jon Doh" only pre-quake stuff came up and the phone number Ben provided was no longer in service. When I tried "Jon Doh Ventura" nothing came up except a story about a drunken brawl at a bar in Oxnard near the Naval Air Station at Point Mugo and I couldn't imagine it was the same Jon Doh. The Jon I know would never switch from creating wonderfully imaginative sculptures to serving grog to sailors. My doubt was such that before making the drive up the coast, I decided to put the word out that I knew a collector who would pay anything for a new Doh piece. So I immediately posted a note on my CALog blog. If Jon was still in SoCal it would surely bring him out of the woodwork.

It was 7 am when I headed east on the I-10 to do a CALog shoot at Divya Diericks studio in the old downtown warehouse district. The shoot date had been set up over a month earlier and even though I'd rather have kept working the murder case, changing the shoot date would have caused too many people far too much trouble.

Downtown traffic was starting to dawdle as I exited the freeway, but I was sure I had time to stop at Zimmee Chan's Diner for a quick bite and some Sour Cherry tea. Chan's is between a ram-shackled meat packing plant and an open air Latino clothing mart. I once asked him why he had chosen the location and he answered, "A gem is not polished without rubbing, nor a man perfected without trials."

Zimmee is a bit cheeky and corny at times and he gets a real kick out of poking fun at old Hollywood actors his grandparents love. Zimmee had been a character actor in films himself for as long as I could remember.

The bouquet and tang of the tea plus Zimmee's pitter-patter jargon ricocheting in my sleepy noggin made me wonder who was trying to enhance what and how does eradicating artists help anyone.

Savoring the tea and musing was making me run late so I got my ass in gear and race-walked through the crowded streets to Divya's with hopes of arriving before my film crew.

The CALog project is a joint venture with PBS to catalogue and publish an online archive of interviews of art notables in the greater LA area. The searchable site is accessible to the public free of charge and features hours of interviews between myself and dozens of artists, art writers and a few musicians. I say interviews, but they're more like just talks. The project is complemented by 5 minute short versions running on public television stations throughout California. It's probably the most meaningful thing I'll ever do in my life aside from my early expressionistic figure paintings.

Divyas' studio is on the top floor of a large, mostly vacant, early 20th century concrete building on Olympic between San Pedro Street and Central. The exterior has been spruced up a bit with a few contemporary touches added to the loading dock area, but it looks like it would only take a 3.0 tremor to topple the whole place. The rent in the area is still reasonable, but the ever expanding Downtown Arts District is fast encroaching, bringing with it high end neighbors like SoHo House and a couple of headquarter buildings for social media giants which are definitely increasing the cost of living in the area.

When I exited the freight elevator, which opened directly into Divyas' studio, my crew of three were already there, set up and ready to go. Rather than proffering excuses about being late, I grabbed a mike, clipped it to my shirt collar and sat down in the chair opposite Divya.

"Good to see you, Divya. I trust the crew has been courteous and well-mannered while setting up."

"You know, James everyone told me you are always in a rush moving from place to place," she said with a coquettish smile. "But when I've watched your interviews you always seem completely present and calm. Why is that?"

The fact that I had immediately become the subject of the interview rather than the host brought a genuine smile to my face. "Interviews liberate time. It's my passion." I gestured for the camera to start rolling when I noticed they'd already done so.

"I see, so this project is really a new idea of what an archive can be," Divya enthused. "Are you aiming for a kind of slowed-down cerebral kind of audio file exposing the hearts and minds of artists or do you find the process exciting because of the new points of access it creates for the techno generation?"

Whew, I bowed my head and took a long, deep breath, but since I couldn't seem to recall any of Zimmee's mind bending proverbs the moment of dead silence was beginning to stretch the crew's nerves. I decided to take the straight and narrow path. "There are a lot of great thinkers out there who aren't already on the web, Instagram or YouTube or are just not in the public eye and we're hoping to locate those based here on the West Coast. So when one is mentioned during an interview as having had influence on an artist, as you were, we track that person down and here we are." I straighten up and moved a little forward on the chair.

Divya seemed slightly scared as she adjusted the sleeves on her shirt so I softened the tone of my voice and tried to look more relaxed. "With that thought in mind, tell us how you came to art through your interest in engineering."

She turned her head to the right away from me and said in a soft tone, "My dad grew up in poverty, slept on a dirt floor and read any old book he could find at the nearby dump. He was clever and wanted to go to school, but his father felt there was more money to be had if he worked fixing broken machinery for the local farmers rather than studying and dreaming of some utopian future. When he escaped the village and made his way to the nearest real city he was flabbergasted to discover people spent money on things like painting and sculpture ... so he redirected his natural abilities in engineering to creating geometric abstract sculpture ... captivating objects of beauty and grace which are also astounding feats of engineering," she said with a kind of crescendo. "I absorbed everything I could from him before he died of TB at 43."

My assistant Tilly gave me a 'now we're rolling' look and so I proceeded on as they say. "You're currently involved with two projects; one as curator, and the other as solo artist. Do you manage them differently from one another?"

"In both I'm selecting images and organizing them into some sort of narrative," she said with a warming smile. "I search for the correlative structure and points of similarity. Then it's only a matter of making each project as strong as possible."

Mmm, somehow she even managed to talk like an engineer. This seemed like the appropriate time to pause the formal part of the interview and direct our attention to her artwork, so I instructed the crew we would walk and talk our way through the works scattered around the studio.

After finishing up the walk-talk with a few more questions and making sure everyone was happy with what we'd done I decided to ample my wheels west on Wilshire toward the serenity of Palisades Park, where I could sit and overlook the beach. It's a perfect place to invigorate one's mind. Of course going down Wilshire meant I would drive past Dr. Mazor's office and that made my thoughts shift from Divya's fascinating work back to the nitty-gritty of two equally intriguing murders.

Divya's last words to me as I was leaving the studio were a compliment on having paid attention to the details of her work and her personal history. As I was sliding the safety bars of the elevator closed she looked directly into my eyes and bluntly said, "You really smell all the different things in the wind? Don't you? Not just the easy smells or the strong ones, but the harder scents too, the dainty ones, the essences. Yep, James Terra, you're no mongrel. You must know something about these horrible murders? Who's out to get us artists?"

I let that hang there and pushed the button for the elevator to descend. Did her first comment mean I'm a dog? Well one thing is for sure, I definitely need to take a closer sniff, ah, look at the details of each case. Especially the pieces that seem out of place and conspicuous ... no, no ... the ones that were surprising. What was the first surprise? Mmm, a Mauve colored s560 at 2am, next uhh, an out-of-place number 15 brush, Mac as King John, Cisco at my front door, offer to help, the anxiety spikes on Mazor's sour puss, the elation on Bernkopf's face, mmm, not only is that one a surprise it was really completely out of place. Why?

As traffic stalled, something in the far reaches of my mind was telling me the best place to start was at the Verge Gallery. "Maybe Christy noticed something during the ridiculous incident with Bernkopf you didn't," I murmured. "It could be worthwhile stopping by the gallery before zoning out in Palisades Park."

As I turned off Wilshire and headed toward Colorado, it occurred to me it was way too early in the day to usurp one of the private parking spaces behind the gallery or the heating and air conditioning offices next door. It therefore took a while to find street parking. When I finally did get into the gallery Christy was in the middle of reprimanding one of her exhibit installers for not buffing out some scuff marks that had accumulated on the polished gallery floor near the exasperating circle eight glass sculpture.

It seemed to me Christy was being way too hard on the young man. She went far beyond passive aggressive and was quickly drifting into sociopathic status so I felt compelled to intervene, but she was bent on having a real tantrum. When she stamped her feet near one of the scuff marks my eyes focused on the smear and glimpsed a startling and very unsettling sight.

"No wonder David had dollar signs in his eyes." I said in a sort of dumbfounded stupor as I continued staring at the floor. "Do you have a sign-in guest list for the opening the other night?" I blurted without looking up.

Both Christy and the installer stood stone cold glaring at me as I bent down to get a closer look at the abstract abrasion and to verify I wasn't imagining the smear of green, Hooker's Green to be precise.

Christy scowled, "What the hell are you going on about, James?"

The installer slipped quietly toward the back of the gallery and my mind was racing trying desperately to rerun every face I saw at the opening, but Christy was intent on being the center of attention. She walked beyond the reception desk, headed toward her office and screeched "James, James! Are you listening to me? No one around here ever listens to anything I say!"

I paused for a moment to evaluate the situation. Should I take the time to explain myself or let it be and depart? A voluntary sign-in list of names from the reception wouldn't prove anything and besides it had been several days since Brice's demise and those scuff marks could have been made at any time by anyone coming into the gallery. The only unquestionable thing was I felt assured the presence of that particular paint proved the killer is of the art community. I looked at Christy, smiled kindly and nodded my head as I turned and softly drifted out the door.

Heading toward my car, I envisioned Cisco asking me if I had taken a sample of the paint smear for the lab guys to analyze. Between that thought and still reeling from Christy's oppressiveness, sorrow began crawling up my back and would soon descend across my brow. The thought of a fellow artist as a killer was disheartening and downright depressing. The gloom and dismal prospect of confronting him or her left me feeling desolate and alone. It was definitely time to head to Palisades Park for some R&R and to watch the gray haired set amble among the flowered gardens, feel a gentle sea breeze sway the palms, and soak in some dappled sunlight, as winter approached.

As I drove west on Colorado toward the park my conjuring juices kicked in. Most likely while lying on the gallery floor David had noticed green paint splatters on the shoes of the killer. Had put two and two together and come up with a number he felt the individual would be willing to pay for his silence. So the main questions are, how did David contact the killer, what safeguards did he take, why didn't they work and why did he agree to allow the killer into his home?

Cisco was not impressed. In his judgment lots of artists use Hooker's Green and any one of them could have walked it into the gallery on the day of the murder or any other day since then. According to him, artists always have paint or any variety of odd substances on their clothing.

And even if Bernkopf had thought he could finger the killer, there was no way to know if he did.

I was at a stand-still and there didn't seem to be a direction to move in. Time and experience had long ago taught me when you're in that kind of situation sit still, preferably beneath a big tree, eat an apple and voila, a solution will present itself. Not having the luxury of that kind of time I decided to set about finishing up the editing of the Divya video. The process requires serious concentration, which was a good thing. It kept my mind from drifting back over the events of the past few days.

By late afternoon I was able to e-mail a finished copy of the video to my producer and take some time to peruse my calendar which showed there were two more shoot dates fast approaching. If I was going to be of any use to Cisco I'd have to pick my pace up a bit. OK, so back to my list ... who else have I encountered since the case started that had a peculiar look on their face. Mmm, the sour puss, Mazor.

While I was pondering Mazor's aberrant demeanor and facial expressions the distant sound of one of my favorite blues tunes resonated from my cell. Cisco was texting a missive ... "Artists were drugged with an overdose of a benzo dentist use to relax patients." Dentist, damn! There is no dentist on my radar screen.

Wait, wait, I do know an artist who is a dentist, or is it a dentist who is an artist. Either way, Bruno Brophy is a dentist to pay his bills and an iron mongering sculptor to feed his heart. Sophie, his girlfriend, tried everything and I do mean everything, she could a couple of years back to convince me to make a CALog about him, but that was the kind of thing that would get me the boot from public television. I need to talk to Bruno without the slightest suggestion I'm interested in his studio work and without Sophie present.

After only a few minutes of thought, it wasn't adding up in my mind. I never see Bruno at gallery openings or at any of the art charity dos plus no collectors I know own his work and he isn't on any gallery roster I'm aware of. The only thing he participates in is the Pacific Biannual Outdoor Sculpture Invitational which is really an open competition exhibit anyone can enter. I doubt he even knows who

Brice and David were. No, the best thing to do is to check with Stephanie at Prescott & Roth. If there is a dentist in this town who is a major collector, she will know him. Plus I need to go on line and look up the benzo's dentist's use so I'll sound a little more informed when I approach the guy, if I can find a way to approach whoever it may be.

According to a website I found the major problem with those sedation drugs is they can be a hit or miss affair. Apparently, it is impossible to know how well the drug will be absorbed and it may affect the nerve cells in the brain. Which means the response to these drugs is unpredictable and it's easy to give an overdose. Even body weight or gender are not good indicators of how high a dose should be. A standard dose might have virtually no effect on one person and totally zonk out the next. In fact, your brain may try to fight the effects or it may just make you go to sleep.

Mmm, maybe that explains why Brice was found in the middle of a major mess of destruction while David was just lying on his neat bed.

I remember, as I was being wheeled into my second surgery, I was given an anti-anxiety medication, a vial of liquid that tasted like peppermint and quickly made everything seem fuzzy like in a dream plus I felt very distant from the procedure and the results left me with some amnesia. They even told me afterwards the operation had taken over five hours, but it felt like only a few minutes to me. Which I was very happy about.

The website listed a host of trade names for the most commonly used Benzodiazepines or Benzos as Cisco called them ... Halcion, Xanax, Ativan. Sounds like a line-up of new exotic cars, but there primary purpose is the opposite, they are intended to tone down those parts of the brain responsible for excitement. In fact, in modest doses they induce a state of controlled fear. However, apparently their fluid boundaries can also easily led to overdoses resulting in coma or even death.

There's no getting around it, if Stephanie can't supply me with a name, I'll have to contact Sophie. Given that choice I'd much rather face Stephanie.

This situation reminds me of one of my favorite blues songs, Snake Eye Blues. Mmm, maybe Steph would respond to an e-mail.

Hi Steph,

Things are looking good for making the CALog about the Wagner Collection and it can feature you and Prescott & Roth, but for the moment I've been a little side tracked, it seems the network is working on an idea about cross-pollination and wants

*to know how many local, major art collectors and/or artists are doctors or dentists. Can
you give me any names?*

Keep smiling,
James

Stephanie's reply was swift and right to the point.

Dear Rat James,
*There are far too many collectors who are doctors for me to waste my time listing
them for you and the only dentist I ever heard of as being associated with a major
collection has been dead for many years. That was Harriet Wagner's late husband
Herman or Herschel or Hierman, whatever.*

*I'm not going to mention the CALog to anyone at Prescott & Roth yet because you
and I need to talk privately first!*

Cheers.

Wow, bull's-eye, a direct connection. What a rush, and what a deep plummet
into darkness it presents. I've often wondered why the centers of all shooting range
targets are black when they really should be gold.

Dr. Herman Wagner, or whatever his name was, was a dentist and is dead. His
mega art collector wife, Harriet, is dead and now two artists who were connected
to them are also dead. Maybe it's a coincidence, but the little malformed and
buckled spinal artery at the base of my throbbing brain was telling me it isn't. And
my grinding wisdom teeth are sensing sweet angel Camille is at the heart of it all.
How to pinpoint the crux, the very root of this misadventure that is the challenge.

Once again Cisco and I weren't on the same wavelength, to me the best lead
was the late Dr. Wagner, while for him it was dentist Bruno. When I told him I felt
he should speak with Bruno on his own, he suggested I was being an arrogant art
snob. That made me feel bad, but on the other hand I was glad to not have to speak
with Bruno and especially not to Sophie.

The one bit of intriguing info Cisco provided was that both Brice and David
had received the Benzo via a needle under the hair line at the back of the neck.
Which would cause the affects to be felt very quickly and implied they knew the
killer. Why else would they have allowed the killer to stand beside them?

As I sat there trying to visualize old Doc Mazor, young Camille, or iron monger
Bruno sneaking up behind Brice Peregrine, who was at least six foot tall and 250

pounds, Bruno seemed like the only possible candidate. Maybe Cisco is right, but what in the hell would have been Bruno's motive?

Before I could dive into that dark pit the funny little computer noise that tells you when a message has arrived in your In-box went off and at the same moment a T-bone Walker shuffle was emanating from my cell. I reached for the cell and noticed the call was from Elizabeth Weinstein, Executive Producer of CALog.

"Hi Liz," I voiced with deliberate cheer. "How are you on this fine day?"

"Hello James, I'm fine. I hope I'm not interrupting your painting or anything."

Mmm, she was also oozing deliberate charm. A knot was starting to form somewhere near my right temple as she started speaking quickly.

"There's a new artists in town and she would make for an interesting segment on CALog."

I took a deep breath and spoke as calmly as I could. "Well, you know the list of potential subjects is rather long at the moment, but I'll..."

"Yes, well I've already committed you to doing a segment on her. Be at her studio at 9 sharp tomorrow morning. Your crew has been informed," she affirmed breathlessly.

As she continued jabbering, I stammered "Can we talk about this?"

"No, look she will be unpacking crates of her new work and you can talk to her while she does so. It will make for a newer look to the show. I've e-mailed her name and address to you. Have fun." Her words trailed off as she hung up.

Damn. I was flummoxed and dismayed all at once. I quickly turned to the computer and clicked on the In-box. Yep, there it was, short and to the point ... a name and address. The name, Emerita Kooy, I did not know. However, the address seemed familiar. As I sat there trying to recall why I knew the address I couldn't stop wondering who would have suggested this escapade to Liz. Then it hit me the address was only a few doors from where artist Robert Graham's studio had been. Graham specialized in bronze nudes of young black women. He died a few years back and as far as I know the new owners of the studio wish to remain anonymous, aren't involved with the west side art community and had leased the building to a social media start-up created by a group of silicon/niobium beach nerds. Although it was hard for me to see how anyone could work in an ultra-modern space that beautiful and not be an artist or at least a collector.

Graham had been a very financially successful artist and thus was able to afford to have a custom studio built right on the beach, all the tools and assistants he needed, and lots of beautiful young models, which he had a predilection for, to pose for him any time he wanted.

Whoever this Kooy is, to live in that neighborhood she had to have money or a sugar daddy who does. To find out I went to my computer and clicked on the search button. The first listing was an article in New York's Gotham Daily Gazette:

"Artist Amerita Kooy has forged a wildly successful career out of being unclassifiable; constantly switching her creative processes and always counter to current art-market desires. Her early fame has risen from her embrace of a truly avant-garde sensibility. She is the sort of artist who employs conceptually loaded techniques. She has painted with mother's milk and menstrual discharge, created expressionistic images using only a dominatrix whip, and trained a live duck to rub its pigment-soaked ass feathers over raw canvases. What she does is punkish in its rejection of traditional techniques and established aesthetics. However, her rebellious counter-intuitive work attracts throngs of young admirers. Based on her most recent Tweets her new sculptures utilize chemical processes to create biomorphic abstract forms which are at once earthy and other worldly looking. For them she has mixed synthetic carbon fibers, metallic pigments, and diamond dust, which allows luminous afterimages to appear on the surface of each work. Kooy is of African-Asian descent, was raised in Thailand, and studied at Chiang-Mai University."

There seemed to be little need to read any of the other articles. I knew all I needed to know about Kooy and I believed I knew who convinced Liz I should interview her.

It was already dark outside, but at this time of year it starts getting dark rather early, so I rely on Duie to let me know when it's time for dinner and bed irrespective of what the clock says. That thought reminded me I hadn't eaten anything since breakfast, so I rose and started toward the frige, but once again the computer signaled another e-mail had arrived. Standing there trying to convince myself not to look at the screen I noticed my shadow was swaying a bit, so I sat back down and looked at the name on the e-mail. It read "Jon Doh". This was proving to be a very long day and may turn out to be an even longer night. The note consisted of only a phone number. A Ventura County number. I pick up my cell and dialed. Jon answered immediately.

"Hey Jon, how the hell are you man," I said happily.

"It's good to hear from you too Sketchy," he replied. "I'm doing well and happy to hear someone is still interested in my work."

That brought a grimace to my face and my empty gut, for there was no potential buyer seeking Jon's work. I just made the whole thing up and there was no way I was going to burst his balloon so I told him I was really happy to hear he is still creating new work, to send some photos and I was sure the imaginary buyer would select a piece. The thought crossed my mind I'd try to convince Nicole she needed one in her husband's collection or I'd buy a piece for myself. Either way I wanted to change the subject.

"Say Jon, that reminds me, uhm, I happened to see old Ben the other day and he mentioned the last time he spoke with you was when he bought one of your works from Camille Wagner."

"Yeah, I remember. How is Ben, he has to be in his 90s by now."

"Well his mind is still sharp, but the gallery is looking kinda shabby," I said. It was good to hear Jon's voice. I should get out more and see the old gang. "I was kind-a surprised to hear Camille Wagner had a collection of her own," I stated with hesitancy.

"Oh, she didn't buy the piece. I gave it to her as a present," he replied.

"A present? You mean like for her birthday or something?"

He chuckled and cleared his thought before responding. "Well let's just say it was my way of saying thanks for having been real nice to me, you know what I mean," he sniggered.

"I see. I didn't realize you had a thing going with her," I quipped. "You must have enjoyed that. I mean she's at least 15 years younger than us."

There was silence for what felt like a very uncomfortable stretch of time. "It was a short thing," he finally countered. "She's into that ecstasy stuff way too much for me. Drugs have never been my thing. I get high on life. You know, the real thing, not synthetic chemical junk. Hell, I don't even smoke pot, man, you know me."

"I hear you Jon and I'm right there with you," I concurred. "Did she offer you some X?"

"No Sketchy, she said her aunt gave it to her," he said with a tone of noticeable regret.

"I see are you sure it was X, maybe it was some kind of Benzo? You know, the kind dentists use. I mean after all her uncle was one and he probably had stuff laying around the house."

"Yep, you could be right. Well, I've got to get back to work man," he said.

"Yeah, I understand, I like to work in the studio late at night too."

"No, no man. I tend bar nights," he said in an even more somber tone.

"What? Are you kidding me Jon," I said with true astonishment. "What's going on?"

"I don't know man, I, I mean, between the last quake destroying the best work I'd made in years and the crazy LA art crowd with, with women like old lady Wagner I needed to make a big change. You know? I needed to feel freer."

I had to keep him talking. He was starting to open up and I didn't want to let him slip away. "Harriet Wagner? You had trouble with her," I said with as much bogus sympathy as I could.

"Well, James, I guess I have to admit it to someone sooner or later. God knows it took some doing to admit it to myself," he offered. "After all old lady Wagner is gone now."

The moment was way too silent on the line and I needed to say something before the only thing I'd hear would be a click. Yes, was the only word to come to mind and to my relief it worked. He continued.

"Wagner said she would arrange a date for me with her niece, with Camille if I'd donate one of my best works to her collection," he said with hesitation. "I was at a crossroads. The choice was clear, get one of my pieces into a nationally recognized collection and score some real fine nookie or insult a major collector and miss out on some pure sweetness."

"Yep, that is a hard spot to be in," I offered. "But I'm not sure I understand. I mean did Wagner actually guarantee Camille would be willing?

"Well, she said if I showed up at her place at a certain time, she'd make sure Camille was in a loving mood, so I did and she was and the deal was signed, sealed and delivered as they say."

Silence again, but before I could think of what to say next, he continued.

"Camille was real sweet, but I'm sure it had more to do with the X or the Benzo, whatever, than it did with my charm and, and you see Sketchy, that's why I gave one of my pieces to her too. I'm sorry to hear she sold it to Ben. She never mentioned that to me."

There was a short pause and he spoke one last time. "I've really got to get to the bar man, I'll e-mail some images of my new sculptures to you, take care of yourself." With that he hung up.

Well, there it was. Or at least to my mind it seemed clear cut, but it was hard to predict what Cisco might say about the whole thing.

It was good not to have to tell Jon the piece he gave to Camille and she sold to Ben and he sold had been destroyed in the same tremble he blamed so much on.

CHAPTER 10

Duie was extremely agitated when I left. He didn't get a chance to chase the gulls off the sand dunes before I put him up on the upper deck and headed for Emerita Kooy's studio. I was early, but I was hoping for an opportunity to observe where the crates had been shipped from, which art moving company had been hired, and most important of all whose name was on the shipping invoice.

The north bound lanes of Lincoln Blvd., which lead to the Santa Monica Freeway, were still bumper to bumper, but it was OK because I was in the south bound lanes and they were moving fine. The studio was right where I thought it would be, within sight of Robert Graham's former studio. Finding parking was challenging. However, since the art shipping truck was still blocking access to several spots I decided to park directly in front of it. As I walked past the truck I couldn't help but notice a clip board with what looked like a shipping invoice was lying on top of the dash. From the running board I could easily read the names on the form. The crates were shipped from the Sukhothai Company, Bangkok, Thailand and delivered to Brindle Scanlan, Scanlan Industries, Los Angeles.

Just as I was about to step down one of the art shipping company guys, dressed in teal colored shirt and pants, yelled, "Hey, what are you doing there?"

I jumped off the running board and said "Oh hi, I was wondering what time it is. I've got an appointment at 9 with the artist. Is she here? What time is it?"

He didn't seem to like my explanation or even my general appearance and his gesture directing me toward the back of the truck was not friendly. As I walked in that direction I thumb typed the info I had gleaned from the shipping invoice into the search engine of my cell.

The style of the studio building was bland and its battleship gray color hadn't improved it any. The sliding door that lead into its cavern-like interior was oversized, wide open, faced due east, and flooded the space with jarring morning sunlight. Inside was a maze of wood crates of varying sizes with two delivery men shifting them about in some sort of pattern which made no sense to me. In fact, their movements seemed annoying. As I weaved my way past them I could hear my film crew off to the left behind a wall shielding them from the glaring sun light. I rubbernecked my head past the corner of the wall and saw my crew had set everything up. My chair was in its usual position and I assumed the person seated to the right of it was Emerita Kooy.

She had streaks of fluorescent blue running diagonally across her opaque black hair, no discernable makeup, and was wearing a sort of platinum crop top with tight deep blue pants and cherry red high heels. From a visual point-of-view the image was somewhat appealing and did cause me to stop and stare.

"James, this is not an occasion for any tomfoolery," stated my right hand-man Tilly Tamzlin as she scrutinized my leer. "I have a meeting with management after this so we need to get this going now," she said with even more vigor.

Ms. Tamzlin wasn't my personal choice for an assistant. She was assigned to me by Liz Weinstein, over my strong objections. I've always felt her primary job is to report everything I do to Liz. I really miss my old assistant, Sally. She was a real girl-Friday and always made me feel relaxed.

It's not that Tilly doesn't know how to do the job. She's actually damn good at it, but she's a ruthless, ambitious New York bred control freak. She's constantly suggesting hair brain ideas to Liz and obviously this time it worked.

I leaned forward just enough to suggest aggression, glowered into her eyes, sneered and spoke through clinched teeth, "Well if you feel you need to leave Tilly you're welcome to do so. I'm sure the rest of the crew and I can handle everything here just fine."

That was all it took. She stepped back and moved closer to one of the crates. I hadn't realized how irritable I was feeling until I spoke so I took a couple of deep breaths and walked over to Ms. Thailand.

"Hello Ms. Kooy, I'm James Terra, host of CALog and I want to thank you for welcoming the crew and myself to your studio on such short notice."

My transformation was back in place so I gestured to the crew to start filming.

"I understand you are from Thailand and studied at Chiangmai University in Bangkok. Of course, the real name of Bangkok is the longest city name on earth, so I won't embarrass myself trying to pronounce it."

Kooy seemed immobile and kept looking to Tilly for guidance.

"Mmm, I'm told your work is impervious to the current tendencies influencing the LA art scene," I said sternly, but with a smile. "What are you planning for your first exhibition here?"

After a couple of nondescript gestures from Tilly, Kooy finally refocused and spoke. "I'm going to include contemporary dance and maybe some poetry," she said with a charming Asian influenced dialect.

"I see, so you are open to other disciplines and I assume these cumbersome crates surrounding us hold sculptures rather than your usual abstract paintings."

It was obvious from her facial expression that she was going to speak very politely and she did, "Yes, they do."

"You designed the sculptures, but they were actually fabricated for you at the Sukhothai factory in Bangkok, were they not," I said with a wide grin.

Her left hand rose almost as if it was ready to deliver a sharp slap to my face, but she decided it would be better used to twirl one of the blue streaks in her hair.

She assumed a faux nonchalant attitude and replied, "Yes, they were. How kind of you to mention it."

"A number of artists these days have their work fabricated by shops in Asia and they complete a little bit of the finish work themselves. No doubt it's a way to still feel connected to the work, is it not?"

There was now a decided flush to her cheeks and her hands were clasped tightly together. Tilly looked downright incensed.

Kooy threw her head back and ran her fingers through the hair along both sides, then spoke very softly, "Many artists throughout history have had studio assistants including Rubens and Da Vinci. It's not a new idea."

"OK, let's have one of your assistants open a crate and we'll have a look at this new work from the Sukhothai factory," I said.

Kooy swallowed hard and gestured toward a small crate stacked on top of a big one. Her assistants converged on it and quickly had it completely dismantled leaving an object about the size of an overstuffed pillow which appeared to be seal wrapped. The camera man swung around and positioned himself accordingly while Kooy and I moved to opposite ends of the larger crate and the sound guy adjusted his equipment appropriately.

"Why don't you tell us about this piece before you unwrap it," I suggested.

"What do you want to know," was her somewhat lame reply.

"Is it from a series or is it a one off," I offered.

While gesturing to the other crates she said, "It's from a series. In fact, all of these pieces are from the same series."

"And the series is titled what?"

"Dawn of Happiness," was what it sounded like she said.

"Well let's see it."

She slowly began removing the plastic seal wrap revealing a sort of deep brownish lumpy form that resembled a large potato with violet colored bruises and welts. As the crew readjusted our portable lights the form's translucent aspects became apparent.

"So do you have a poem or dance to go with this piece?" I asked. "Or perhaps a song?"

"Not yet, but soon I will. See how it sparkles in the light. That's the diamond dust. Isn't it pretty," she said in a captivated manner.

"So what part of this one did you finish yourself?"

Except for Tilly's groan, there was only silence from everyone else.

I waited for her reply for about 60 seconds before speaking in a booming voice. "Mmm, OK folks that's a wrap. Let's pack it up so Tilly can get to her big meeting."

Everyone paused to see if Kooy or Tilly were going to respond, but neither did.

"Thank you again Emerita and good luck with everything," I offered as I took off my mic and headed toward the door feeling I only half ploughed the unknown terrain of a mine field.

In the short seconds it took to get to my car Tilly was right behind me, but I was ready for her. "What the hell do you think you're playing at," I said heatedly. "Liz has enough on her plate, she doesn't need you scamming her with this kind of crap. This is the kind of thing which will make the top execs cancel us."

She looked indignant and sounded so too. "Kooy's a hot artist. Some universities and a couple of museums already have her works in their collections."

"Oh yeah, did you take the time to see if they purchased them or someone donated the stuff to them?"

She was still fuming, "What do you mean?"

"I mean most likely her sugar daddy gave the works to them along with a sizable donation in cash," I said as I got into my car and closed the door. "He probably even paid for the fabrication of the pieces and shells out for the rent on this beach house too!"

"What, who are you talking about?"

"Brindle Scanlan, President of Scanlan Industries, that's who. Look it up, hot shot," I said with complete conviction as I rolled up the window and drove away.

Over the years I've met several artists, both men and women, but perhaps more young attractive women than men, who have managed to get themselves a sugar daddy who will buy their work, turn around and donate it to a nonprofit and take a big tax write off. It's another aspect of the art game. Scanlan was a new name to me, but I was betting he fits the description perfectly and no doubt he also gets some enjoyable benefits from Kooy in the deal as well or perhaps he's a relative.

Which reminded me, I needed to find a way to talk with Camille and driving directly to her house wasn't it. I was now heading north on Lincoln and the traffic was still moving sluggishly. As it inched forward past the Girls and Boys Club, which uses an old converted schoolhouse for their activities, I recalled Camille had said she was in Nell Myerhoff's art appreciation group.

It occurred to me perhaps I could get Nell to bring the group to my studio to see my new work. Of course I don't know what new work I was thinking of. I hadn't finished anything worth showing to anyone in a long time. My second absurd idea was to organize a painting demonstration for her group and that dumb thought was so completely laughable it made me bring my car to a full stop. As traffic started moving again a kick ball flew out of the Girls and Boys Club playground and slammed against the side of my car. The jolt rattled my brain and lit a spark, "more action" is what Liz said the CALog needed so how about expanding the idea of doing a segment on Dr. Mazor and Camille selling old lady Wagner's hot collection of contemporary LA art. It could include a group interview with several of the living artists from the collection. The more the traffic stalled the more I was liking the idea and betting I could get Nell to convince the Mazors to do it.

I don't recall the rest of the drive back to my place and apparently I didn't hear my cell buzzer either for when I picked it up it showed I had missed several calls, most of which were from Liz. I decided to answer the one from Cisco instead.

After letting Duie outside to do his business I hit the speed dial for Cisco and he answered immediately and more importantly he liked the whole Mazor-artists group idea. The only thing we weren't able to resolve was how he could be involved. I told him we should think about it for a day or two and I needed time to sell the idea to Liz anyway.

Speaking of which, as soon as I hung up a blues riff started and I recognized the phone number. It was Liz. I hit the talk button and said "Hi". I fully expected her to really be furious, but she was incredibly calm, which made me feel concerned about my immediate income potential and for all the artists I had promised I would make a CALog about.

"Look Liz, could we do this face to face, I mean its only right, lets meet at Fromin's on Wilshire. I'll even pay for lunch," I said with my fingers crossed.

"OK see you there at 1," she said quickly and hung up.

Duie was happy to see me as he danced impatiently about and scratched the sliding glass door while I fiddled with the latch to let him out. I was obviously preoccupied with having dodged another bullet for I couldn't seem to tell whether Liz had been angry or calm, was I going to be fired or was Tilly or worst of all, was the show going to get cancelled. My head was spinning and throbbing. I needed to sit down and relax. The last thing I needed was to have another brain aneurism with my damn twisted artery. The darn thing can't be operated on anymore and the only item that seems to relax it and keep it from collapsing completely is one of those notorious blue pills and taking one of those can lead to all sorts of other issues to deal with, the least of which is an obvious impediment to walking comfortably.

I had about an hour before I would have to leave for Fromin's so I took only half of a pill, sat down in the La-Z-Boy and tilted it all the way back. It was important to keep Duie nearby because he's one of those dogs with a sixth sense about impending physical doom and if he were to curl up near my feet I would need to get to the hospital a.s.a.p.﹒

It was 12:35 when I awoke and left for Fromin's. The blue pill had done its job at both ends of my torso. My head felt better and I solved my need to walk with care by carrying my coat over my arm in front of me. After all it was winter time.

It took only 15 minutes to get to the restaurant and I felt lucky to find a space in their parking lot. Once inside I noted Liz hadn't arrived yet so I headed to my usual spot in the far corner booth. From there you can see anyone coming in the front door and pretty much most of the other tables in the main room. I liked that.

While I was waiting it seemed like it would be worth having a quick word with Nell about the CALog idea. I hit the speed dial on my cell. Nell didn't answer, but her maid did. While I was on hold I remembered Nell's son, Jeffery, had died in a printing accident a few months back.

"Hello Nell, I hope I haven't called at an inconvenient time."

"Hello Sketchy. It's nice to hear from you. Are you keeping well?"

She sounded very much as she always has so I decided to move forward. "We haven't had an opportunity to speak very often since..."

She interrupted me.

"Its fine, I understand. I appreciate your concern, but I'd much rather not discuss it any further."

"Yes, well sure, of course," I said with as much decorum as I could. "Are you aware that Dr. Mazor and his wife Camille are planning to auction off Harriet Wagner's collection?"

"Why yes, in fact, I've had several talks with Camille concerning it. She's in my group this season you know," she said in an unexpected demure manner.

"Mmm yes, she did mention it to me and I understand from others in the group she isn't comfortable with contemporary art. Do you think the feeling extends to the artists as well?" I said without much thought given to being tactful.

"Well you know, I've known her since her parents died in a terrible car accident when she was 16. That's when she moved in with Harriet in her big mansion and it wasn't long after that her uncle Herschel passed," she said in a rather solemn manner. "Which left Harriet completely on her own in dealing with blossoming Camille and her raging hormones."

Liz was now coming through the door and looking around for me. I sat up and waved my free arm so she would find her way. I was still listening to Nell as Liz approached.

"I know she dated some of the artists Harriet bought works from, or perhaps I should say acquired works from, but I've never heard Camille express dislike for any of them," she concluded.

"I see, well I'm here with Elizabeth Weinstein, Executive Producer of CALog and we were discussing how nice it would be if you could help us with convincing Dr. Mazor and Camille to let us shoot a segment about the art collection along with several of the artists," I said in my best CALog host manner.

I could hear excitement in her breathing. "Oh, what a wonderful idea, yes, yes, I would love to help."

Her spirits had definitely been lifted. It was a good feeling. "Great Nell, let Elizabeth and me discuss how to proceed and I'll call you back a little later." We hung up and Liz, who was now sitting at the opposite side of the booth and staring wide-eyed at me while leaning forward with her chin firmly supported by her clinched hands.

"Would you like something to drink or is this going to be strictly a business meeting," I said calmly.

Liz took a deep breath and smiled civilly, while I however was feeling queasy and beginning to slouch.

"How did you know about Brindle Scanlan," she snipped.

I hadn't seen that one coming. I thought for sure she was going to talk about Tilly or maybe even Kooy, but not Scanlan. "I have my sources," I said as I sat back up again.

"OK James, I concede, you and your sources are why you got the job of host in the first place," she said in a matter of fact way. "And, no doubt, my bullying you about doing the Kooy shoot made you come down hard on Tilly, but now we have a bigger problem."

Hard, grap, Tilly obviously bamboozled Liz. "What problem? Do you mean the shoot, I can fix that in the editing," I said sternly.

"No I don't mean the shoot, in fact, we're dumping the video. No, the problem we have now is a lawsuit," she said as she waved for the waitress.

"Kooy is filing a lawsuit? Hell, I can convince her that would not be in her best interest," I stated confidently.

"No, Scanlan is filing one," she said as the waitress approached. "I'll have a glass of red wine. A large one."

Two surprises in a row, Liz conceded to making a mistake and Scanlan is filing a suit. I was speechless. According to Liz, Scanlan is a mover and shaker in the Los Angeles Central Business District Association and a number of their members make large annual donations to the station. The lawsuit is about me having caused damage to one of Kooy's sculptures by bullying her into instructing her assistants to open one of the crates. Which seemed totally absurd and ludicrous to me and down-right bizarre.

"How the hell can that be proved and why isn't the suit being filed by Kooy?" I insisted.

"Scanlan owns the sculptures, not Kooy," Liz replied as she took a big gulp of wine.

"All of them?"

Her eyebrows arched as she replied, "So it appears. He's a real sugar daddy, that's for sure."

Liz and I discussed what the station may or may not be willing to do once their lawyers actually review the suit; how to proceed with organizing the CALog shoot of the Wagner collection; and what to do about Tilly. I suggested we do nothing about Tilly. She's basically a good kid and knows how to do the job well. She only needs some serious guidance and maybe a good spanking but, there was no way I could suggest one, especially since we didn't need to provide cause for a second lawsuit. Perhaps the aftereffects of the blue pill were causing my mind to stray.

We talked outside on the sunny sidewalk for a few minutes before heading in separate directions. Liz had assured me she would stay on top of the lawsuit and I could move on with pursuing the Wagner gig. We said our good byes and I decided to walk down Wilshire to Palisades Park and sit beneath a big tree to soak up some rays quietly while I pondered the day's events. The clean crisp November air had a hint of the Pacific. A gentle breeze was rustling the palms and the sun felt good on my back and everyone I passed as I ambled along seemed as contented as I. There are times when California seems like the best place in the world to live and no problem is too big to overcome.

When I skipped off the curb at Ocean Ave. and took a sprightly step toward the park a metallic dash in the form of a jet-like motorcycle rocketed around a stopped car to my left, through the crosswalk, and headed straight at me. I stepped back quickly and the cycle came close enough to sideswipe the coat I was still carrying in front of me. Its roar created a rush of air that spun me around as a mid-sized flatbed truck with an oversized bumper guard charged straight at me from the opposite side of the intersection. I instinctively jumped back onto the sidewalk and the truck clattered up over the curb. Panic set in instantly as I lunged into a large concrete planter box a few feet away.

By the time I emerged from the jungle of evergreens both the truck and the cycle had vanished. Everyone standing nearby paused and gawked for a moment, but none seemed overly concerned about my well-being. No doubt they too were wrapped up in their own individual shrouds of California bliss or maybe they simply mistook the whole thing as just another movie shoot stunt, which are a routine occurrence in Santa Monica.

I was shaken, scratched and a little bruised, but I was able to climb out of the planter box and stand on my own two feet. As I dusted myself off I became thoroughly convinced I had certainly rankled someone on this fine day and they were out to get my attention. Instead of heading to the park, I walked back to my car and drove home.

It didn't seem possible Mazor or Camille would have discovered that they were in my sights or that they would have used death by vehicle as their weapon of choice. However, Scanlan and his girl-toy Kooy may have.

I ruminated that if it was Scanlan, he must be in love with Kooy. Why else would he send goons to visit harm upon me? Plus in order to know how to find me, he would have to have been told by Liz or someone in her office which seemed very unlikely or by someone who had been following me since I left Kooy's studio. That seemed very likely.

Such a thought was enough for today. To Duie's surprise when I arrived home I went upstairs and laid down on the bed to take a nap and to give my artery time to calm down. As I dozed off I was happy in the realization that the effectiveness of a portion of a little blue pill had eased the pressure on my touchy artery and enabled me to traverse the turmoil of the day.

CHAPTER 11

The next morning I felt rested and my bruises weren't looking too bad, so Duie and I headed out for our usual bit of exertion. As we got to the end of our loop, near the cul-de-sac where the mauve 560 had been when this inexplicable adventure started, there stood Cisco.

As I inventoried yesterday's events for him he registered a high level of interest and I'm happy to say, some real concern. However, he didn't feel compelled to invest time in Scanlan or Kooy and since his talk with Bruno the dentist was a dead end he wanted to concentrate all our efforts on Dr. Mazor and Camille instead. Plus he wanted to make sure we weren't overlooking some other possible suspect. I agreed.

As we started to walk toward my place another 560, a soft cashmere cream one I knew well, pulled into the cul-de-sac. Nicole emerged wearing a wonderfully small hot pink bikini. With that tantalizing image coming towards us, Cisco gave me a salute and headed for his car. He managed to look back only three times before driving away with a face full of beaming smile.

As Nicole approached I couldn't help but notice that when she spoke she was staring at the front of my trousers. "You must be happy to see me."

The potency of even a half of one of those blue pills is really great for my brain artery problem, but can also be extremely untimely when it comes to its lingering after effects. The only thing I could do was smile back.

Nicole and I spent hours in bed and I enjoyed every second. As the noon hour approached I also felt some hunger pangs, but was reluctant to mention so. To my utter surprise she darted out of bed, threw on my shirt, and headed down stairs with Duie in close pursuit. By the time I pulled my trousers on and descended the stairs I was astonished to find her in the kitchen nook fixing lunch.

Something was obviously up so I felt compelled to sit, pay attention and enjoy the great view: each time she reached up to a shelf or bent over to pull out one of the bottom draws every angle and nuance looked lip smacking yummy and she knew it too.

When she finally placed a scrumptious looking plate of food before me I knew something big had to be coming because Nicole had never ever made a meal for me before.

With a feeling of impending doom I swallowed hard and said, "Do I have to ask or are you going to spill the beans? Uhm, no pun intended."

"Well darling, here it is. Patterson wants a divorce," she said as she stared into my eyes. "And my dear, he is willing to give me whatever I want."

"A divorce, why? What happened?" I said as I pushed my chair back from the table intending to stand. "Did he find out about us?"

"No, he says I'm too young for him and he needs someone more connected to his lifestyle. Someone who shares his drives and is willing to work with him. What he really means is he wants a 'business' partner, someone who gets excited about stocks, acquisitions, mergers and all that boring stuff that drives me crazy." She straddled my lap and sat down right on target.

We spent most of the remainder of the day discussing our new relationship from every perspective imaginable and by late afternoon we had concluded since she had not signed a pre-nup the most important decision for her to reach quickly was to come to a financial and property settlement they both could live with and get it in writing, which would require the expertise of a attorney. At which point, Nicole felt she wanted the advice of some of her closest girlfriends so she dressed and left.

I was smiling widely as she kissed me goodbye, but the moment her car was out of sight I could feel my entire being starting to slump. Nicole's declaration of love for me should have made me very happy and a large part of me certainly was. However, an equally large part was deeply panicked. I had never told her about my precarious health condition as I had never told Catrina or even Cisco. In fact, no one other than the great team of doctors and nurses I had at St. Johns Hospital has any inkling or suspicion. I never liked the idea of being treated as though I was infirm or incapacitated in some way so I never mentioned it to anyone.

I ran away from facing up to that decision when my relationship with Catrina reached its apogee and I've always regretted having made the choice. Now I was faced with it again. It felt like I'd taken a fork in the road only to find it lead me right back to where I had started.

"Surely you're man enough to admit it isn't worth taking the same route again. Besides, all good trips are completed by a rigorous experience," I said out loud to convince myself.

Maybe a walk along the beach would clear my mental fog or at least help clarify the current state of affairs. What a morning it had been. When I slid the glass door open, Duie charged out startling the gulls and their earsplitting screech instantaneously brought back the memory of the raucous squeal of those motorcycle tires that had almost left their impression across my forehead. That shudder spurred me to turn around and head to my computer where I sent the following message to Liz, "Please e-mail me a copy of the Kooy shoot, I want to check on something." In the state of huff I was in when I left the shoot I had forgotten to take my customary flash-drive copy from the camera man. I was happy when it arrived in my In Box from Liz within thirty minutes.

I was thinking maybe the shoot would show mug shots of Kooy's assistants, but even after viewing it a couple of times there didn't seem to be much point. None of them looked like they could harm a fly. Yet, as I was about to close the file, an old sixth sense feeling at the back of my neck was telling me to look at it again. So I did, again and again, until it hit me. At the beginning of the shoot there are three delivery guys moving the crates around, but at the end there are only two. With the aid of a photo program I was able to make mug shot enlargements of all three and one of them looked very questionable, the one who had vanished before the end of the shoot. I wasn't sure what to make of that, but it seemed worthy of remembering. I wondered what Cisco would make of it. Mmm, most likely he would tell me to stop wasting my time with Scanlan and focus on Dr. Mazor and Camille. And doubtless he was correct, solving a murder is more important than worrying about a lawsuit or the near miss from a motorcycle or even an errant flatbed dually. Before I gave a second thought to running the choice by Cisco, an Albert King blues ditty started resonating from my cell. It felt so good to my ear drums and my soul I wanted to let it play until I looked at who was on the line.

"Hey man, you must be psychic, I was about to phone you."

"Yeah, sure, that's why I knew another one of your arty friends was going to get himself decorated," he said in a distressed manner. "I'm almost at your front door so lock up Duie and get yourself outside."

I hung up lickety-split, ran Duie upstairs, sprinted back down and straight out the front door.

Cisco was there with his car turned around and ready to go. "We've got to get on top of this thing, Leonardo. Heat is coming at me from all sides. My captain is boiling over, the mayor is threatening to dissolve the department and start with an amalgamation of greenhorns from other departments. I mean, shit, I've even got the Chamber of Commerce's Director of Tourism and your pals at the Arts Council breathing down my neck," he said in complete desperation as he drove like a madman toward the industrial section near the Santa Monica Airport.

As coolly and calmly as I could I said, "Who's dead?"

"What, oh, ah, some dude that makes abstract photography. Whatever the hell that is."

Still calm, I said, "So there's no green paint this time?"

With a snicker he replied, "Hell I don't know. Ahm, maybe, maybe he's covered in green film."

After encountering very little traffic as we headed east on Ocean Park Boulevard I could tell Cisco was starting to cool down. No doubt he only needed to blow off some steam. I knew the feeling and hoped that was all it was.

We stopped in front of one of the multi-purpose buildings which looked as though it was originally build for storing and repairing airplanes. The usual assortment of police and emergency vehicles crowded the main entrance door with its fairly new looking marque above that read 'Airport Art Studios - South.'

Once inside, it was easy to see the cavernous interior had been divided into separate live-in studios: twenty of them, as it turned out. We headed down the central hallway toward the far end passing a mixture of a half dozen or so young want-a-bees, some paramedics and a unit of Blue-bulls. The side walls of the hall were covered with an array of amateurish, inept looking paintings and drawings created by the resident artists. Each one had a large hand written label showing the artist name and the price of the piece ... real class.

On the wall next to the murder victim's studio were large color prints of nude females. They looked like they had been photographed with a camera lens covered by benday screens, which resulted in moray patterns camouflaging each exquisite figure. They didn't look like a greenhorn had made them, but they weren't really unique or creative either. There were no labels on the prints, but there was a nameplate on the door, Collier Robischon, that ignited a spark of recognition.

"I know this guy," I whispered to Cisco as we passed by the Sargent. "He's older than us."

The space was set up as a photography studio with light stands, tripods, background screens, and several types of cameras situated about. In the far corner was a curtain drawn back revealing an untidy, empty bed with an assortment of clothes hanging on a nearby portable drying rack and a small end table with a plain looking lamp on it. I had seen that exact scene in one of the photos displayed at the front door except it had a nude female lying on the bed.

Toward the back was a wall with a doorway on the right side covered by a blackout curtain. Another officer was standing near it and as Cisco approached he pulled the curtain back which allowed a green glow to escape from the dark interior. Cisco and I looked at each other. I shrugged and gestured we should go in.

Inside was a typical photography darkroom with trays of chemicals, several negatives hanging about, and some fresh prints floating in a small sink. The small green ceiling lights, while not a Hookers Green, still managed to make everything look bizarre.

Seated on a stool was the figure of a man leaning back against an enlarger. His arms were hanging limp at his side and his head was at an extreme angle. Even in the glare of the odd lights I could tell it was Robischon. His hair was grayer and there was less on the top and more at the back than when I had seen him last. His eyes were wide open and there, even in the dim light, you could see the end of a brush protruding from his open mouth.

Cisco took out his ink pen and gently lifted Robischon's hair just a few inches past his right ear. There it was, the puncture wound from a needle. "Crap, that makes it number three and all hell is going to break out down at the station and City Hall," he said. With a facial expression of complete exasperation he motioned for me to follow him out of the darkroom. "You better high tail it out of here. It won't look good if you're here when the brass arrives and they're going to show up for this one for sure. You know what I mean."

I must have looked disconcerted because his last word to me was "leave". So I did.

CHAPTER 12

The events of the past couple of days had been exhausting and very worrying for everyone. Cisco had his hands full of brass, businessmen, and busybody media types. Nicole was liaising with lawyers and multitudinous lady friends. I, on the other hand, spent my time in the quiet solitude of my studio painting and at the club absorbing blues and brews.

Good art and engaging music are both consistently impelled by humanity, often impossible to capture in words, yet instantly and entirely immersed with one's inner being and I needed a lot of it. Either one can also grab you like a whirlwind and put high demands on your concentration or leave you dumbfounded and trying to knit the pieces together into a cohesive whole. Plus like a mystery, they both can be at once comprehensible and evasive, even hard to pin down ... "Like the mystery of the brushwork," I said out loud to Duie, who sat up and lifted his ears. Then, after seeing me do nothing, rolled over and ignored me.

The weather at the beach was still beautiful for November, but the 'brushwork' mystery, the 'ever changing relationship to Nicole' mystery, and the 'what to do for the fast approaching holidays' mystery were giving me pause and I needed to be creative to solve each of them so I began singing to Duie who not only got up, he soared onto the La-Z-Boy and began shaking his entire rear end.

"I've got those palm tree swaying, lemon drop sun setting paradise b l u e s," I crooned as Duie's tail was thumping to a four-chord beat. "Sand dunes of rosy hue, drones flying high looking for someone just like you, I've got those palm tree swaying, pink bikini clad paradise b l u e s." Duie was up on his feet dancin' now. "Got those Mauve colored 560 cruising, green paint splattering paradise b l u e s."

My mood was just starting to pick up when a Scatman Crothers track began on my cell and I knew I could never compete with his resonant voice. It was one of the favorites I hadn't heard in a long time, but considering the incoming call was from Cisco, I had to cut Scatman off.

"Hey Cis, I sure hope you're not going to tell me about another nightmare swathed in lurid green."

"Nope, not this time, thank goodness. I just thought maybe you'd like to hear about some of the details that the lab guys came up with," he said in an unhurried manner.

"OK, fire away."

"It seems all three of the murder brushes came from Peregrine's studio."

"Mmm, so our killer has obviously been planning ahead," I said cautiously. "Ah, how did the lab determine that?"

"Well, all three are the same brand and all are new and all came from the same manufactures lot. Which matches with the statement we got from Peregrines' girlfriend. She says she purchased a new set for him last month because she broke several old ones during a quarrel they had. The new brushes were a sort of a make-up gift."

"Is that it?" I said. "Nothing more?"

"What, you're in a hurry? I suppose you've got a date with that hot pink number." He quipped.

"No, no, I was just hoping for more."

"Well, there are a couple of things, but one seems like a long shot to me."

"Give me the good one first," I said hoping for a zinger.

"Well, two of the brushes have DNA on them and it isn't just from the victims, but it is from the same individual and wait for it, it's female and wait for it again it isn't from Peregrine's girlfriend."

"Wow, DNA from brushes that were jammed down a throat. Makes sense I guess. Which two victims?"

"Ah, Bernkoff and Robischon."

"So the killer is a woman," I said with a level of revelation that even surprised me.

"And both samples are from the same woman?"

"Yep and it was really ground into the bristles of each brush. That's how it managed to survive being dunked into the throat of each victim."

"What does that mean?"

"Well, my artist friend, it means that each brush was rubbed real hard and repeatedly against one particular woman."

"But we don't know if the killer rubbed them against herself or if a male killer rubbed them against his girlfriend or who knows who rubbed against whom or something like that. Right?"

"Uh, right. Interesting, that's for sure."

"Yes it is and puzzling too," I said with complete honesty. "It could mean there are two killers, a man and a woman."

"Yep, it could mean just that."

"OK, what is the other thing the lab found?"

"There were some strands of hair found on the first two vics, but not at the photo studio. And they don't match either of the vics', but they are from the same individual, maybe they're from the killer."

"With all of the wiz-bang high-tech gizmos available today, can't the lab get more info out of them than that?" I said with a low level of rancor.

"Only that they are a brownish color and probably male. The crime scenes were just too contaminated to process them fully," he said, disheartened. "You know, all that paint thrown around and too many people going in-out not to mention a dog."

I couldn't help but look over at Duie who was still smiling and wagging his tail.

"I see, I wonder why there weren't any strands found at Robischon's?"

"Most likely because the killer no longer has a need to demean his victims, he just wants them dead, so he didn't mess around moving the body and thereby leaving his or her hair on the guy." Cisco said matter-of-factly.

"Or maybe he didn't have time."

"What do you mean?" asked Cisco.

"The walls between the studios in that old hangar looked very insubstantial to me and there are a lot of people living there. The killer probably was worried that someone would hear something. So he um or her took the quick and quiet way and split immediately after the deed was done." I was on a roll. "Maybe someone heard something, but they didn't recognize it as a fight. How about if I drift over there and see if I can ferret out something?"

I wasn't sure if I was feeling optimistic or just wanted to divert myself away from everything else on my plate.

"Ferret as in quiet, discreet, and unobtrusive?" Advised Cisco.

"Absolutely, totally, unequivocally," I vowed.

"Seguro, yo te creo que cuando lo vea." Cisco mumbled.

"What?" It sounded like something about 'sure you will' although I wasn't 100 percent certain.

"Nothing, just do it right." He hung up.

As I sat there thinking about when to go to A.A.S.S. I found myself staring out at the heat waves wafting up from the hot beach sand and wondered why you can see them, but you can't smell them. In a flash from light bouncing off a wave my mind skipped, hopped and jumped to the fumes I had smelled while in Robischon's darkroom. I recalled there was a tray of developer, one of fixer, and another of stop bath. All of which you need to make black-and-white prints, but the lights were a blue-green color, not the red or amber lights you need when making black and white prints. Plus, blue-green light would destroy color film and prints for they are sensitive to all parts of the visual spectrum and must be kept in complete darkness until properly fixed.

The prints on display at the entrance to his studio and hanging about inside were all in color and I could tell they weren't analog developed prints, they were all natural pigment prints made from digital files. The only prints in black and white were the few floating in the sink and hanging on a string in the darkroom. The looks of the whole place just didn't add up correctly. Most likely, the darkroom, the black and white prints, and the few 35 mm negs scattered about were just props, just there to create the atmosphere of a professional photographer's studio where film is developed and prints are hand-made.

More importantly, something major was missing, where was his professional level digital printer? I couldn't recall seeing it in the studio. Surely the killer didn't walk off with it. Printers capable of making the large digital prints most contemporary photographer artists prefer weigh over 100 lbs. and are over four foot high and wide and at least a foot deep. Not an easy thing to move around. Robischon either hid his or the killer took it or someone stole it.

It was going on 11a.m. and seemed like a good time to head on over to do some snooping around. I wondered if there was an Airport Art Studios North, or East, or West. I hoped not because if there were it would mean I was losing touch with what was happening in this town.

I was surprised when I arrived at the building for there were plenty of vacant parking spaces including the one labeled Robischon, so I parked in it. Just inside the main entrance a list was posted on the wall providing the names of all the artists and their respective studio spaces. I had missed it when I came in with Cisco. I was further surprised to note there were a half dozen or so empty studios available to rent.

In past years these kind of live-in studios were in great demand, but I have paid less attention to the housing market ever since one of the TV executives at the station agreed to let me have his rental beach condo for a very reasonable rate. I think he realized even though I was an artist, given I really wanted to keep my job as host of CALog, I wouldn't trash his pristine, unsullied condo and I'd be there year around so he wouldn't have to deal with the constant turnover of tenants.

How to select an artist from the roster to speak with seemed somewhat daunting especially when remembering the empty parking lot. My choice was obviously limited to who was home. No doubt the high cost of living in LA was causing even more artists to get a day job to support their art addiction. As I walked past each door listening intently for sounds of life within I came upon a very engaging ink drawing. It was of modest size and simply rendered in black ink on plain white paper, but its skill was immediately noticeable. The name on the label read Jenni Fields. I knocked on the door and there was a moment of silence then numerous shuffling sounds as if the occupant was quickly straighten things up. Then the little peep hole in the middle of the door flickered, latches snapped and the door opened.

Jenni Fields looked to be about 23 or 24. She was as tall as I, with dark hair and clear blue eyes. The outfit she was wearing, though it suited her and looked attractive, I would never be able to accurately describe to anyone. Which made me feel even older than usual. She was holding her cell up to her right ear and said quickly "I'll have to phone you back Jake I've got company." She slid the cell into an unseen pocket somewhere.

"Oh it is you, jeepers, gee, you're. You are James Terra. Heavens, right here at my door. Golly, please come in."

Wow was right. Her look was great, but her personality was especially captivating and for some odd reason made me feel like I wished I'd become a father. I happily walked in. "I hope I'm not disturbing you, Ms. Fields. I was hoping I could talk with you about this wonderful drawing."

She was glowing now, which made her seem even more enchanting.

She took the drawing from the wall and handed it to me. "Oh, you like this old thing, here it's yours, please take it, it was meant for you."

"I couldn't I, uhm, I'm not allowed to accept gifts from artists," I said in my best CALog host voice. "Especially if I invite them to be on the show."

I was a little surprised at myself for having blurted that out, but deep inside I knew I had felt it the moment I had seen the drawing.

"Oh, yes of course, I understand, professionalism and all, wait you're considering inviting me to be on CALog?" she said with a look of sheer terror on her face. "I just graduated, you know, I don't have a resume of exhibits or awards or anything," she gasped.

"Don't worry about that. We're going to start featuring emerging artists on the show and I'd like to consider you for one of the spots."

The fear on her face was still there, but she managed to smile through it. "I see, uh that sounds great. So I assume you want to see more of my work, right?"

Yes and no. I really would have liked to seen more of her work, but if that's all I did while there Cisco would be furious. "Not just now," I said as gently as I could. "I'm a little concerned about what's been happening here at A.A.S.S. with the murder and all."

She blushed a little and graciously gestured toward the seating area which caused me to turn and look at the inside of the studio for the first time. The furniture and decorative items in the living room area had a decided feminine look as did the kitchen nook, which was mostly in shades of pastel yellow. Opposite the nook was the studio area with a drawing table, adjustable lamp, and sketches pinned to the wall.

I sat on the mini sofa and Jenni pulled the stool from in front of her drawing table over and sat just to the right of me. I could tell the arrangement was being used just as she had hoped it would be because from my vantage point I could easily view all of the framed drawings on the facing wall and her.

"Tell me Mr. Terra, how did you come to select me? I mean who told you about my work? Did you see it somewhere or something, on my Facebook page or website or Instagram maybe," she said in what I'm sure she felt was a very formal and professional manner. It was sweet, but made her seem even younger than I had initially thought she was.

"Let's just say I have my sources," I said smiling broadly.

"Oh, well I wouldn't want to have to be beholden to anyone if you catch my meaning," she said as she tilted her head down a bit and then stared straight back through the top of her eyes.

"Don't worry about it. I can assure you no one is going to come knocking on your door and ask you to repay them," I said as I looked over at the door and noticed for the first time the profusion of locks and chains.

She noticed my obvious interest. "That's not a result of the murder. I'm just naturally cautious," she said as she clasped her hands together.

I couldn't help but think if she were my daughter I wouldn't let her live on her own even if she were 25. There are just too many eccentrics around.

"Mmm are there any weirdos living in this complex?" I said as I pondered why I was having so many paternal feelings.

"Do you mean art wise or creepy like?"

"Creepy like I guess. I mean the police don't seem to know if the killer was a visitor here or a resident."

"There's only one guy I'm a leery of. He's in the unit a couple doors past old man Robischon's space," she said. "His name is Finsel Larkey and he's a mixed media artist. He makes photographs and then draws on top of them with everything like pencils, chalk, and ink and probably a whole lot of other stuff."

"What kind of photographs?"

"Mostly landscapes, why?"

"No, I mean are they old school or digitals," I said.

"Oh, they're definitely digitals. He's always complaining about how expensive it is to get them printed, especially since he has his prints made on high quality Rivas printmaking paper," she said while adjusting her posture. "I'd like to use it too for my drawings, but it's beyond my budget."

"I'm aware of the process. Most digital printing paper comes only in rolls, but the Rivas is only available in sheets so it has to be hand fed into the printer and that makes the process much more expensive," I noted as if I was teaching a class.

"Oh I see."

"Making landscapes doesn't make a guy creepy," I suggested.

"Oh no, he just acts in an unsettling way. He keeps asking me out, but I don't want to have anything to do with him. Besides, I've got a boyfriend," she said with a noticeable level of pride and an even stiffer posture.

"Jake," I said with a smile as she blushed.

Before I could think of my next question, a classic Jimmy Reed beat rang out from my cell. I checked the screen and it was Nicole on the line so I gestured to Jenni I would have to answer. Jenni got up and walked into what I believe was her bedroom area. There was a pink glow that emanated from the space when she pushed the curtain aside to enter it.

"Hi babe, have you signed any papers yet?"

After I apologized for thinking only about business and money, Nicole and I agreed to meet for dinner and to walk Duie along the beach. Jenni returned the moment she heard me say goodbye.

"Was that Jimmy Reed I heard," she said to my astonishment. "My dad listens to a lot of those kind of blues stuff. The one I like is Joe Bonamassa or something or other."

"Yep, the blues are my muse," I said as I stood up.

Jenni giggled and looked a little worried. "Is that it, you don't want to talk about my work or anything, I mean, what happens next?"

"Oh this was just a preliminary interview to make sure you would be able to handle being on camera. It's standard procedure." I said with a bit of a grimace. "My assistant Tilly will contact you to let you know when we'll be able to fit you into our shooting schedule. Just be patient it could take a while. The important thing is to keep drawing."

She was smiling while she unlocked the main latch and opened the door, I said good-bye and headed down the hall toward the exit. No doubt she would rerun every detail of our conversation in her mind over and over again every day while waiting to hear from Tilly. I on the other hand was focused only on one small part of it, 'Finsel Larkey'. I wondered what the origin was for such a name and the name Bonamassa.

As I got into my car and stared at the name Robischon stenciled on the wall in front of me an old derelict looking van pulled in a few spaces from me. A short, stocky young fellow with disheveled hair and wearing a worn denim shirt and jeans got out and hurried to the back of the van. The name stenciled at that space was Larkey. From my vantage point it was difficult to see what he was doing, so I got out and walked toward him quietly. Just as I got close I could see he had retrieved a large cardboard box from the van. He froze when he saw me approaching and he was obviously frightened.

"Larkey," I said sternly. "I want to have a word with you, lad."

He looked at where my car was parked, began to shake and said "Yes officer, sure whatever you guys want, I'm happy to help you guys anyway I can."

His nervousness only increased when I reached inside my coat and pulled out my small note pad. "It says here you usually have your prints made at a professional printers."

He looked even more alarmed. "Ah, well yes usually. Why do you want to know?"

"Because I want you to explain why you are holding a box of pigment cartridges. The kind only used in large digital printers like professional shops have," I said with a forced sneer.

His head drooped as he sat down on the bumper still hugging the box.

"You stole Robischon's printer, didn't you, lad?"

A fallacious half-smile crossed his face, "He loaned it to me."

"Do you really want to add lying to the authorities to the list of charges against you?" I was almost growling now.

"No, you're right I stole it but, it's ok I didn't damage it or anything I just used up the pigment making my prints." He was looking totally forlorn. "I can put these new cartridges in and put the printer right back."

He was surprised when I said, "Come on, bring the box with you. Let's go look at it."

We headed inside the building and I was hoping Jenni Fields wouldn't emerge from her studio before we reached Larkeys' and I was also hoping he wouldn't recognize me. I mean I thought every artist in LA was familiar with my mug. Jenni was right, this kid really is a weirdo.

As we walked passed Jenni's door I could hear her talking on the phone and immediately assumed it was to Jake.

When we got to Larkeys' studio, he put the box down to retrieve his keys and I was still worried Jenni would pop out and spot us, but he managed quickly enough and we stepped in as I made sure the door was closed. When I turned around, right in the middle of the studio was the printer still mounted on an old piano mover.

"Ok kid, tell it from the beginning." I said returning to my imitation of Cisco. "Start with telling me how you knew Robischon was dead."

He sat on the only chair in the place still tightly holding the box of pigment tubes. "Well you know these are not real walls in this place. They're made with just one-by-two's with no installation and only quarter inch drywall."

A quick scan of the sparse looking studio revealed only a chair, a small table with a hot plate and a small assortment of art supplies on it, an old army style cot, a cardboard box full of dirty clothes, a few messy dishes in the sink and a metal box filled with what looked like old carpenter tools.

"Are you really an artist or a construction worker?" I inquired.

"Both," he said, looking completely dejected.

"All right, go on you were going to tell me what you heard."

"Well, ever since I moved in here I've heard just about everything that went on in there. All the chicks he banged. All the phone calls with clients."

"What kind of clients?" I interrupted.

"Oh the usual stuff, wedding planners, baristas, aspiring models and actresses. You know he was a photographer."

"Right. So what happened?"

"Well one of the chicks showed up a few nights ago and she was real miffed because he refused to give her the original photos of a party or something," he was smiling now. "The walls really shook when she slammed out of there."

"Did you hear a name or see her when she left?"

"Nope not then anyway, but the next night a man shows up and he's not happy either. He talked a lot quieter than the chick, but I got the general feeling he was talking about the same photos the chick wanted. The man said something about camels and I heard a kind of thump and some scuffling. Then someone left and it was completely quiet."

"Camels? As in desert nomads or cigarettes?"

"Well Robischon said something about them being hot so I assumed he meant the kind you smoke. The one thing I heard the visitor guy say was 'I want those photographs' that's why I thought he was probably a client or something."

"So how did you know Robischon was dead?"

"It was the next morning, when I was leaving for work. You know I have to be on the job by 6 so I leave early and I noticed a light coming out of his door and found it ajar, so I looked in, didn't see anyone, you know, so I thought I'd just have a look around, you know, to make sure that everything was alright."

"Uh ha, more likely to see what you could steal," I said as I turned my attention to the printer and noticed that there was a small computer screen near the control panel. "Does this thing have a hard drive or file for storing images?"

"No!" Larkey said quickly.

"Look lad, either you cooperate or I'll make sure the book gets thrown at you." He was quivering again.

"Ok, ok well, yes there is a file that was uploaded recently, but it just looked like porn so I, I just ignored it."

"Sure you did, show it to me."

"Uh, its kind-a graphic you sure you want to ..."

"Open it!"

The screen was not much bigger than those on a Kindle and as I strained to see what was going on in each photo Larkey handed me a magnifying glass like the ones you see in old Sherlock films. When I scowled at him he just shrugged and gave a sheepish grin.

With the glass I could see the first image was of three nude males surrounding a bed with a young woman lying in its center. In the next image the woman was on her hands and knees with one guy mounting her doggy style and another in front of her with his knob in her mouth. The third guy was standing on the opposite side of the bed and the woman appeared to have his knob in her hand. Making each guy happy seemed to be her goal.

The next image was shot from the end of the bed and showed her straddling the top of a guy while she was facing his feet and the camera. It was obvious she was riding his knob while the other two guys were standing to each side of the bed. It was an ungainly looking image because the woman's arms were extended out and her right hand was holding a knob and her left a set of nuts. The most surprising part of the image was her facing directly into the camera and smiling.

It was definitely Camille, a much younger Camille, but there was no denying it was her.

And though she was smiling her eyes looked vexed and the general demeanor of her face seemed fretful.

At first glimpse all the images looked erotic, but the more I studied them I could tell the staging and lighting were so ingeniously nuanced it revealed a level of affection for Camille. The gentle curves of her flowing hair; the simplicity of the shadow along her neck and slope of her breasts showed her youthful softness. Even the detail and delicacy of her elegant fingers was celebrated all while exposing her vulnerability. This was the work of an artist, not a pornographer and since Robischon wasn't in any of the photos, but had them in his printer he mostly likely was the artist who took them. However, the room the party took place in wasn't his studio. The bed and the other assorted pieces of furniture partially visible in each shot looked dated and had a tropical flair.

"Zonked," said Larkey.

"What," I said while still fixated on Camille's smile.

"The girl, she looks zonked, you know high on drugs or something."

"Yep, she does at that. Can you make an 8 by 10 hard copy of her face from this last image," I said while still fixated on it. "And a print of each of the photos?"

"Sure can, officer, just let me put in these new pigment tubes and get to the control panel," he said as I stepped out of his way. "Say, what is your name anyway?"

I moved away from the printer and turned my attention to Lackey's mixed-media drawings hoping he would concentrate on making the prints rather than on what my name might be. His art was tacked to the wall and appeared naive looking, but on closer study I could see it had a very strong neo-expressionistic touch. I was surprised, but wondered why he makes each image on top of a landscape photograph. It didn't seem necessary, but as my mind and eyes were still filled with images of Camille's sex-a-pade I really couldn't seem to concentrate on why Lackey would do anything.

Before I had awakened from my revelry he finished adjusting the printer and pushed the print button. The thing came to life and you could hear the ink jets as they whizzed back and forth across the paper. The photos slowly rolled out of the top. Larkey grabbed each one and handed it to me.

"That's it officer. Pretty hot looking chick uh?"

"Ok lad you've been real helpful and I want you to do two more things for me."

"Yes sir, whatever I can do. I'll help all I can."

"Right. First, don't touch this printer again and don't talk to anyone until Detective Rivas arrives. Second, if you're lucky enough to get out of this mess, give me a call."

I gave him one of my business cards. His response was a real eye-opener for me for he didn't recognize my name and the title of the show didn't seem to mean anything to him either. It was then I noticed there was no television or computer in sight.

"Does this mean you're not a cop that you work for television?" he said, mystified.

"I work undercover. Remember, don't talk to anyone, don't touch the printer or leave here before Rivas arrives," I said sternly.

"Undercover, I got it and wait for Rivas, will do."

On the drive back to my place I phoned Cisco and filled him in. He was thrilled I got some real helpful info for a change and managed to do it without messing up. The only thing we didn't agree on was what all of it meant especially since we still didn't have any proof the man who wanted the photos was Dr. Mazor or the earlier visitor had been Camille. Plus we didn't have any real evidence or a strong motive for any of the murders plus neither Larkey nor anyone else ever saw Mazor or Camille at any of the crime scenes. The only thing we knew for sure was Camille seemed to enjoy being gang banged or was drugged into doing so or enjoyed being drugged while doing so. By the time I clicked off the blue tooth with Cisco I didn't know if we had moved forward or we were sinking further into a quagmire.

When I got home I was happy to see Nicole was already there and was in the kitchen preparing food. Duie seemed happy too. Of course when food is anywhere nearby his tail gives him away. Nicole greeted me at the door dressed casually, but ever so sexy and my small dining table had been transformed by the addition of a new lace-like table cloth, two scented candles, and a bouquet of flowers. After a wonderful meal and a couple of glasses of wine she proceeded to tell me about how negotiations were going with Patterson and his legion of lawyers and hers. We were both convinced the lawyers would end up with most of the money. As we took Duie out for a walk along the moonlit beach there were lots of opportunities for me to tell her about my spinal-cerebral artery problem, but I just didn't feel up to it and didn't want to ruin our peaceful time together. Since we've known each other we've always had to limit the amount of time we could spend relaxed in each other's company and I wanted to savor this one.

After a night of wonderful physical hijinks with Nicole, in the morning I didn't have the energy to walk Duie on our usual track or to complete the unfinished painting on my easel. My mind was still flip flopping around yesterday's events. So I found my cell and phoned Nell Myerhoff. By the time her maid managed to get her to the phone, I was ready for another round of revelations.

"Good morning Nell. Isn't it great we are still having all this wonderful weather while the rest of the country is knee deep in snow and icy chaos," I said in a surprisingly upbeat way.

"Good morning to you too James," she said in a surprisingly non-snooty manner. "I feel for all those good folks back east and hope they come through this round of storms with their families and homes intact."

There wasn't much I could say except maybe, "Yes, I hope so too." At which point there was silence so I decided to move forward. "Have you had an opportunity to speak with Mazor and Camille about the CALog idea?"

Silence was still there so I moved forward again. "I spoke with Stephanie at Prescott & Roth and she's all for the idea. Would you rather I ask her to contact them?"

"No, no. James, there's no need. I'll invite both of them for dinner tonight and speak with them then. It will be a more friendly and congenial approach than Stephanie's business manner," she said earnestly. "You don't need to speak to her."

I wasn't surprised that Nell responded that way. The one thing you can count on with her is her desire to be in charge.

"OK, see if you can find out why Camille seems to dislike contemporary artists."

"You said this before. Why do you need to know," she said briskly. "And I'm not sure it's true anyway."

"Well, I wouldn't want her to come across as angry or anything on camera. You know, CALog is an upbeat program not a rage journal."

"I see. You're right. Leave it to me James, I've known Camille for a good long while."

We agreed to talk again the next day and anyway I had an itchy need to make a synopsis of the case to date. Inventorying has always helped me find my way when no direction seemed obvious. So I found pencil and paper and started a list, more or less in chronological order, of all the incidents to occur thus far and felt significant. Pencil on paper still feels more natural to me than typing, perhaps it's because I'm an artist.

- *Metallic mauve s560 after midnight- Hooker Green paint on dead Brice Peregrine*

- *David Bernkopf's look of jubilation- Dr. Mazor's look of anxiety, metallic blue s560*

- *Fire at Norten Peterson's mansion- Hooker Green paint on dead David Bernkopf*

- *Hooker Green paint @ Verge Gallery- Dentist's Benzo from Dr. Herschel Wagner*

- *Jon Doh had sex with Camille- Motorcycle/flat-bed truck attack*

- *No green paint on Collier Robischon- Sexy art photos of Camille & 3 boyfriends*

-*Artist paint brushes stuck down each artist's throat*

After much mental re-running and cogitating of all 13 items only two seemed to have no potential connection to the case: the fire at Peterson's mansion and the motorcycle/truck attack on me.

Peterson most likely set the fire himself, probably for the usual insurance scam purposes. Although it was hard to believe he needs money bad enough to commit such a stupid crime; then again he did mention he was in the process of launching a new start-up so maybe he does need money. Either way it would be very disappointing to find he is cold hearted enough to destroy such a wonderful collection of top rated art. In fact, I'd swear he loved the collection more than he did his own fame and fortune. Plus, he may have started the fire, but he certainly didn't whack himself on the head and I couldn't imagine Honey or Cerise would do anything hurtful to anyone.

As for the rather crude attempt to run me down via vehicle mishap that was most likely the result of my sabotage of the Kooy shoot. Obviously her sugar daddy, Scanlan, keeps a close watch on her and is very emotional about protecting her from any unpleasantness, especially the kind which comes from men like me. So he probably sent a couple of his goons to intimidate me.

Still the biggest link missing from the list or in sight anywhere was the reason or purpose someone was killing contemporary artists? How does the killer benefit? Or more to the immediate point, what do we know about the killer or killers?

Well, he or she has access to Benzo; has access to artists, even the ones he or she doesn't like; likes or dislikes Hookers Green; may drive a metallic mauve 560; doesn't want anyone to know Camille has had or has sex with multiple partners.

Since Cisco discovered, via the DMV and the local Mercedes dealers, no s560 comes from the factory with a metallic mauve paint job, he has had his team checking with the independent paint shops and the custom car guys. But so far that clue has been a dead end. So it could be there is no mauve 560 connection to the case at all especially since the witness who saw a 560 parked in front of Brice's studio the night of the murder, wasn't sure what color it was. Plus I was very fatigued when I saw it so I could be wrong about the color. After all, I had been staring at a yellow scalene for hours, so maybe my eyes eased that tension by creating the complementary color of violet and the street lamp simply softened it to mauve.

Cisco's lab crew determined the Benzo used in each killing is a generic brand which is used by hundreds of dentists nationwide. So where does all this leave Cisco and I? Is there anyway further I can help him move forward? Before I could resolve that conundrum, Buddy Guy's raspy voice resonated from my cell.

"Como esta Cis?" I sang.

"That's it? That's the best you can do after living here for over twenty years? When are you going to take that conversational Spanish class you promised Catrina you would take? No doubt, when you dumped her you dumped that commitment too."

"Let's not go there OK? I mean after all, no one can go through life without breaking a few promises."

"Right, well sooner or later you're going to address those issues and a host of others you've been side stepping for years."

"Damn it Cis, give me a break man," I said with complete vexation. "Do you have anything new on the case?"

"Si Senor," he said mockingly. "I had that Finsel Larkey character make blow-ups of the three dudes in the party pix's with Camille and I want you to ID them."

"Yeah, well I gave that some thought when I looked at their mugs under the Sherlock glass, but I'm not sure who they are. I mean, think about it for minute Camille looks at least five years younger than she is now and the guys look a little older so that would make them maybe in their late 20's or early 30's when the pix's were taken."

"So what, I want you to take a look at the enlargements maybe something will click in that visual brain of yours."

"Right, I need to get out of here anyway so why don't we meet at the club around noon."

"Si Senor," Cisco said with even more mimicry as he clicked off.

Well there it was, my way to move forward, but I was disappointed I didn't have the courage to tell him I had completed a conversational Spanish class and was saving letting everyone know until I found an opportunity to use it on CALog.

The day had become clear and warm which made me feel the need to get outside and walk so I called Duie down from the upper deck and we headed toward Neilson way. We then continued on to Ocean Avenue and when we reached Colorado Avenue Duie headed toward Palisades Park while I wanted to turn right. Duie won, so we headed for a bench under our favorite tree. The city doesn't allow dogs in Palisades Park, but lots of people ignore the signs and bring them anyway. We had been there often so Duie knew the drill, I sat in the middle of the bench and he sat right next to me with his front paws on my lap, that way, should a blue-bull come by, it wouldn't immediately be obvious I had a dog with me. As we sat there looking out over the bluff toward the beach and the open sea I did some deep breathing exercises and then took out my list of significant events in hopes concentrating on it would bring whatever I had missed to the surface, but there was just too much activity going on around me. Kids on inline skates, young mothers jogging with a baby strapped either to their chest or back, elderly couples ambling along or feeding the birds, and of course the occasional vagabond seeking a handout. It sure didn't seem like winter was fast approaching.

As I rose to leave I noticed a particularly sullied, earthy looking vagrant bending over to pick up a smidgen of cigarette. I sat back down to watch what seemed like a classic Red Skelton skit from the 50s ... like the ones that are so popular on YouTube.

He fussed and groused around with the cigarette and finally put it up to his lips. It was then my mind did a hop, skip and jump first from the vagrant to Red Skelton's dimpled smile, then to Dr. Mazor sitting at his office desk looking bored to death by my lackluster performance while resting his chin on his right hand with his two tobacco stained forefingers extended along his cheek and finally to a cigarette being ejected from the driver's window of the metallic mauve s560.

"Mazor is a smoker and may be a killer," I muttered. It was a long shot, but I found myself craving for a connection. Larkey had mentioned he heard someone talk about Camels, but then again perhaps the person actually said Camille, not Camels.

"What," garbled the vagrant as the trifling between his cracked lips disintegrated and he brushed it from his tattered shirt. "Hey, you got a smoke buddy?"

I handed him a 10 spot and told him he'd be better off getting some food then gestured to Duie and we headed up Colorado toward 4th Street. The itinerant moseyed in the opposite way.

The walk to the club was a blur as I pondered the next two things on my list. The only thing I could think of for #2 was the name 'Hooker's' could have some kind of double meaning to the killer. Perhaps he or she associates it with the kind of Irma da Duce services offered by the chickie-doodles down at Rose & Main in Venice, but probably not, because most people don't know one shade of green paint from another.

Not too long ago there was a Hooker's Green pop/electronic/indie music group that had a No.1 download. The first time I heard their name I remember thinking it was odd for a group making that kind of sound. But most likely none of that relates to the case at all either.

One of my favorite old art professors used to tell his greenhorn students that Hooker's Green was named after some British illustrator dude from the 1800s who became famous for making still-life paintings of fruit and vegetables with green leaves. Sir William Jackson Hooker would probably be amazed to know that in this century his name has been appropriated for something much more vivacious than paintings of fruit in a bowl.

As for #3, David's look of jubilation probably did come from seeing Hooker's Green on someone's shoes or clothes during his pratfall at the Verge Gallery and he probably did put two and two together and concluded he could make some easy money if he contacted the person. Right, so how would he have contacted Mazor or Camille? Most likely by phone. He would have phoned their house or Mazor's office, and there should be a record of it somewhere.

When I reached the club I was momentarily taken aback when I went to open the door, the green door. As I stood there in a visual trance the old song 'What's Behind the Green Door' began playing in my head.

Green door, what's that secret you're keepin'?
There's an old piano and they play it hot behind the green door
Don't know what they're doin' but they laugh a lot behind the green door
Wish they'd let me in so I could find out what's behind the green door

When I finally emerged from my flashback, Duie had cocked his head to one side and was looking at me as though he wasn't sure who I was. I felt the same.

"Let's find out what's behind this green door, hey boy, come-on." We entered the club and headed straight for my usual booth in the far corner only to find Cisco already there.

"Did you come by way of Wilmington or something?"

"No, no, Duie needed an outing so we walked up Neilson Way that's all. What time is it?"

"After 1."

"Mmm ... have you had lunch already?"

"Yes, I didn't want to listen to your gringo elocution on an empty stomach," Cisco said, smiling broadly.

It was good to see him relaxed. We ordered beers and tried to sum up the bits and pieces of our separate thought patterns, but there just wasn't a coherent blueprint for murder emerging especially in the motive department. Why kill these particular three artists? That was the biggest missing slice of the pie. Cisco agreed that it was worth checking David's phone records, but he had already done so with the land line and there was no record of a call to Mazor's office or his home. Plus no cell had been found at David's house, but Cisco was having his team check with cell companies anyway to see if he owned one. Given the current legal restrictions that process would probably take some time and he may have just used one of those prepaid cheapie throwaway burners and tossed it or the killer took it.

I was impressed with how professional my old friend had become.

The last thing we needed to cover was to look at the blow-up photos Cisco had Larkey print of Camille and her gang of boyfriends or partners or whatever they are. Considering how sexy Camille looked, focusing on the faces of the three dudes was a challenge. One thing was for sure, neither David nor Collier was in the trio and there wasn't a really good face shot of the third guy to make a sure identification. The third guy did look a little bit like Brice in general body build, but his face was turned down and away from the camera so all you could really see clearly about him was his Elvis style sideburns. Of the other two, the shorter one looked like a joe-college jock, while the only marked thing about the other was his deep tan which isn't really unique around here.

The real challenge for me was to select who to show the photos to and I was thinking that perhaps Nicole might have some thoughts on the subject.

"Look, show these things around discreetly to see if anyone recognizes any of these guys. In fact, perhaps your lady friend in the hot pink bikini might recognize one or all of them," Cisco said in a soft whisper as the waitress came by and sneaked a peek at the up-side-down photos while clumsily picking up our empty beer bottles.

"Are you trying to insinuate something about Nicole," I said between my teeth.

"Oh boy, he's coming to her defense. It's serious uh?"

I could feel the heat rising in my ears and across my forehead, but before I could detonate Cisco took his sweaty beer glass and pressed it against my forehead.

"OK, cool down. I didn't mean anything. What do you think of this beer anyway? Do you like it?"

I took a second or two to calm myself before speaking. "You mean it wasn't our regular brew? What is it?"

"A new local called Repriso Premium. It's made from reconstituted waste water," he said with a chuckle. "Which means the draught has pushed us to drinking our own piss."

Cisco walked over to Spider and spoke to him in a low murmur, then the two of them laughed and Cisco walked out the red exit door which was actually the back side of the green entrance door.

I put my glass down and just sat there. That's when the thought of drinking reconstituted anything made me belch and my mind do another ricochet.

Most beers look pretty much alike and people who don't like beer think all beers taste bad. People who don't know artists think all artists are the same so while Cisco and I keep thinking David was murdered because he tried to blackmail the killer, more likely, it was for the same reason Brice and Collier were murdered. It's just a fluke David saw something which could have identified the killer. The truth is, he was on the hit list to begin with. So since all beers have things in common, what besides being artists, did Brice, David, and Collier have in common? Brice and David both had their works in Harriet Wagner's collection, but not Collier or did he?

I hit the speed dial on my cell. "Hi Steph, hope all is going well for you and the gallery."

"Not you again, what do you want now?"

"Gee, Steph I know you're trying to sound hard, but I can hear you smiling."

"You've got three seconds."

"OK, did Harriet Wagner have an official photographer of her collection?"

"She had each piece photographed for security and insurance purposes shortly after purchasing them and the photographer of most of the collection was Collier Robischon. Why?"

"Robischon, yes indeedee. Thank you. Bye."

Wow, there it was again. Everything leads back to Harriet Wagner, which leads to Mazor and Camille. Which leads to murder? Maybe, I'm still not sure. Somethings seems to be missing.

Before I could complete the thought a Stevie Ray twanged from my cell and while staring at the number I found myself hoping Mazor hadn't turned down Nell's dinner invitation.

"Hi Nell."

"James, why don't you join us tonight," she said with mandated authority.

"It's good to know the Mazors accepted your invitation and so shall I," I said with sureness and a smile to myself.

"Good, I'll expect you at 8 and bring along Nicole," she said with complete confidence.

"Ah, ah, how did you, I mean, what?" I said in a muddle.

"To be natural is a very difficult facade to maintain, is it not James," she said.

With that there was a long stretch of voiceless air before I stiffened my chin with resolve. "City life nourishes our more civilized qualities so yes, I will ask Nicole if she would like to accompany me," I said as precisely as I could. "But before I do, please tell me how you knew."

"A woman who moralizes is invariably plain and that is not a goal I aspire to," said Nell in a very ladylike manner. "Besides, I was at St. John's dealing with some family matters on the day you had your surgery last year."

"Mmm, ok, so you know about the surgery, but how do you know about my relationship with Nicole?"

"Well, silly, she was there too."

"Oh, yes, of course and no doubt you've heard about her impending divorce from Patterson."

"That is the one thing every woman on the west side has heard about darling, but don't worry about your surgery secret, Nicole and I agreed we would never mentioned it to anyone unless you did first. As for your relationship with Nicole, after the divorce notice ran in the Times yesterday no one will ever be surprised to see the two of you together."

I don't remember how the call ended or how long I sat there dumb founded, but when Duie started jumping against my leg I finally got up, left the club and walked to the pier and down onto the beach, then removed my shoes while Duie frolicked in the surf.

I've never felt a sense of belonging to a specific time or physical age, but standing at the very edge of the open ocean is an experience unlike any other. The rhythmic sound of the endless waves, the sparkle of the water, the smell of the salt scented air, and the feel of the wet sand between your toes, all resonate with my core. I've always felt if all people world-wide embraced this primordial experience, humanity's ills could be surmounted.

"Accepting oneself does not preclude striving to become a better person," I said into the wind.

As I stood there mesmerized, the realization my life was about to change sleepwalked out of my soul and into my conscious being making me feel liberated and happier than I'd been in a long while. And it was solely due to having Nicole enter my life.

That surge also unshackled my view of the future as well. There was no longer a reason to fret about explaining my health issue to Nicole but, I'm sure she'll demand an explanation as to why I hadn't told her myself or anyone else either.

However, at this moment, the best course was to stay focused on the next challenge; how to invite Nicole to Nell's dinner with Mazor and Camille; and how to prepare myself for questioning Mazor without tipping him off Cisco and I suspect he's a killer.

When I was first invited to be host of CALog the station gave me some basic pointers on how to prepare for interviewing guests without sounding like a journalist or detective and part of that training included rehearsing my questions. So it's been my custom to write down a basic overview of my thoughts and then drill them into my head. That way I don't look like an amateur by reading them off of a piece of paper or 3x5 cards.

I whistled for Duie to follow me as I took one more look at the ocean, inhaled deeply, and walked back to the studio then straight to the pile of Times newspapers lying just inside the front door. I grabbed yesterday's edition, turned quickly to the society page, and spotted the article immediately. It provided all of the basic info about the couple and their general backgrounds then finished with: "Volkov is a millionaire hedge fund owner and is already on the hook for nearly 5 mil per year in support of his first wife whom he divorced only 3 years ago. He spends staggering sums on a private jet, vacation homes and his ever expanding art collection. This divorce case threatens to be one of the biggest settlements in the country. He is citing irreconcilable differences from his estranged wife Nicole Volkov. According to California law, she is entitled to continue the lifestyle they enjoyed during the marriage. The marriage included five homes, household staff and 24/7 security services. There was no prenuptial agreement."

Better him than me is all I could think of, plus the fact I would never be able to provide Nicole with a lifestyle at such a level. If I kept thinking about it I'd surely go wacky. I needed to get my mind back on track so I found pencil and paper and began writing.

Favoring the kinds of questions rarely, if ever, addressed by historians and critics who write art books, the following list of questions for Mazor and Camille came flowing out of me

- Without being too psychological about it, what were Harriet's motivations for collecting; what were the origins of her passion; what gave her the first inspiration to be a collector?

- Often artists play a big role in steering collectors in one direction or another. Which artists had a strong influence on Harriet? Which ones did she have a close personal relationship with?

- Which artists did Harriet feel were the most important in her collection and why?

- How did your aunt's taste develop over time and how did she perceive influences from her peers?

- Looking at works of art from the point of view of the owner speaks to culture more than to art because it's about personal perceptions and sensitivities, do you agree with that?

Having an opportunity to address those ideas in a CALog appealed to me greatly and could provide some insights into whether the Mazors are capable of murder.

Since I needed a shave and shower before facing Nicole I stripped down, tossed my clothes toward the washer under the stairs, and took the steps two at a time all the way to the top. Duie did the same and given he's older than I, in canine years that is, his drive was impressive.

The shave went well and the shower felt good, especially when I let the warm water massage the back of my neck where my old surgery scar is. As I was beginning to zone out I felt a soft form snuggle up behind me, gentle fingers kneading my groin, and a soft yet firm hand grip my stiff manhood with quickening strokes.

I turned around to kiss Nicole, but she had squatted down and was taking my knob into her mouth. I was in heaven and began humming "There's A Moon Out Tonight," one of my favorite doo wop songs. By the time we had finished playing my mind felt like I could conquer the world, but my body needed sleep first and I certainly didn't want to go to Nell's or face Mazor's sour puss.

At 7pm, Nicole woke me and said we needed to get dressed. I was thinking casual, but she had already laid out one of my dress shirts, slacks and a sport coat. Her dress was semi-formal and perfect for her wonderful figure. I could feel my entire body smiling just by looking at her.

When I turned around to slide the wardrobe door closed I noticed my clothes had all been pushed to one side and the other side was now filled with hers plus both the top shelf and the floor were covered with her shoes. I couldn't help but wonder if we would ever make a go of it as a couple. I cautiously asked, "Have you moved in for keeps?"

She turned and sashayed over to me. Her hips looked so good I had a hard time concentrating on her words as she began fussing with my shirt collar, but I think she said something about not completely leaving the house in Beverly Hills until Volkov signed the divorce papers and gave her everything she wanted. What I got from the statement was she had a lot more clothes still to come.

At 7:30pm, having made sure Duie had plenty of water and a chewy, Nicole and I headed to the door. Once outside she handed me the keys to her 560, which brought a broad smile to my contented mug.

"You've told me a thousand times how much you've always wanted one of these, now you've got one, of course, you have to take me in the bargain as well," she said as she stood there with one hand on her hip and the other extended toward me.

I took her hand and felt like I was the luckiest man on the planet. "This is a special occasion," I said as we stood looking into each other's eyes.

"Well it's a nice car, but there are other things in life a little more special," she said as we headed toward it.

"I was referring to the fact this will be our first official public appearance as a couple."

"Oh James, you're going to make me cry," she said, then kissed my cheek. The 560 drove like no other car I had ever driven and caused me to almost forget to explain the purpose of going to Nell's. In the process I quickly realized it would be best to stick to the CALog line and not mention anything about Cisco or that the Mazors might be connected to the murders. It seemed better to save that part of the story until we got back home, especially since I was going to have to show her the sex photos of Camille.

When we arrived and walked up the steps toward the front door of Nell's stately mansion, I glanced back at the 560.

"It will still be there when we come out," Nicole cooed.

"Oh, no I was just wondering how you managed to get all of your clothes and shoes into it."

"All, darling, you haven't seen anything yet. Besides I'm good at putting big things into tight spaces," she said as her eye lashes flashed.

I was beaming and probably still blushing when Nell greeted us and explained her husband Paul had to make a quick trip to New York on a business matter.

CHAPTER 13

Nell was gracious at welcoming everyone and a perfect hostess throughout the dinner. It was obvious she hosted these kind of events often and loved every minute of it. After the meal she led the group on a tour of her home to show off some of her favorite art. It presented the perfect setting for discussing the CALog project.

"I was last here on a cold morning in February, amid your annual rehang and there wasn't an artwork in sight. You were surrounded by house painters carefully patching the drywall to prepare for the influx of all your new acquisitions," I said.

"Yes, I was getting ready for the Spring Art Fling home tour," said Nell proudly.

"Well the space has definitely been drastically transformed."

Speaking with pride and looking at Dr. Mazor, Nell said, "I open the house frequently for charitable organizations and collector groups. By the way, did you hear about the fire at Norten Peterson's house?" Her eyes grew wide as she continued, "Apparently he was getting ready to do his rehang and had stored his collection in the garage and the place caught on fire and destroyed his entire collection."

"Yeah that's a real loss to L.A. art history," I said as I looked at Nicole. "I hope your collection is safeguarded."

"You should have 3-D scans made of all of the paintings and sculptures in your collection. That way if any of them are destroyed a very accurate duplicate can be made that will be precise right down to the smallest brushstroke or texture," said Mazor to everyone's astonishment. "The Van Gogh Museum in Amsterdam has successfully completed doing just so with some of his masterpieces."

Wow, that was totally unexpected and left us all speechless, but I could tell Nell didn't like being upstaged. So while fine-tuning the automatic UV shields used to protect the room from harmful sun rays coming through the south facing windows during the day, she continued her museum docent style tour much like a stage actor giving her 1000th performance. She even gave a nice concise footnote about how ultraviolet rays can destroy works of art very quickly then waited to see if Mazor had anything to add. When it was obvious he didn't I decided to ask him a question.

"So you are interested in how high-tech can be used to preserve valuable works of art?

"Not really, I just find it interesting how some things have been considered good can so easily be seen as bad, evil even."

"What things are you referring to?" said Nicole.

"Why, the scorching sun, of course. It is being seen as less benevolent and more sinister with every record breaking temperature. The whole epoch of global warming has induced increasingly flagrant strategies to reckon with it. Everything from UV screens to digital misters. The biggest irony is solar powered air-conditioning." Mazor said as he gave Nell an unkind sort of gawp.

It was obvious Nell wasn't going to take that kind of statement lightly. "Well, Paul and I feel strongly original art is meant to be shared and seen, not duplicated," she said of their annual habit of changing over the works on display. "As a collector, you either have to be confined by the boundaries of your walls, or commit to store and rotate everything. It's a shame Peterson didn't think to install a digital fire sprinkler system in the garage storage unit he had built for his collection and I'll bet he didn't have 3-d scans made of the works either," she said as she stared at Mazor. "He didn't use enough of his knowledge of high-tech gizmos to protect his own wonderful collection."

I felt the conversation needed a new direction.

"Nell and Paul caught the collecting bug in the '80s when Nell's childhood friend Larry Giles had a solo exhibit in New York," I said as Nell gave me a node. "Is that not correct, Nell?"

"Yes it is. We went to the opening early and we found a painting we both liked, and Paul felt we should acquire it so Larry would have something sold before anyone else arrived and so we did," she said nonchalantly, but with lingering tenseness. "From there, we began to look at work by emerging and mid-career artists and to build personal and lasting relationships with many of them. Your aunt, my dear friend Harriet, did the same, didn't she, Camille?"

Camille smiled, but did not reply.

"Your commitment to fostering art has blossomed beautifully and you're both on the boards of several art museums. It's amazing how you and Paul have enough time for hosting so many social events." I said with admiration. "You travel the world to attend openings of the artists whose work you collect and to scout for new artists at international art fairs and this beautiful home really reflects your passion." I was hoping such statements would encourage the Mazors to agree to the CALog project just in case they didn't turn out to be the killers.

"We've developed lasting friendships with the vast majority of the artists we collect, but what's most enjoyable is the camaraderie of the artists within our collection. Harriet was especially good at bringing that feeling out during her varied social events. She had a great passion about collecting, but also about fostering a community around it."

"It all comes down to a shared sensibility," Nicole injected.

"Yes, it does. And so far, we've managed to really like all of the artists we've acquired works from," said Nell. "That's really why we are committed to collecting several works from each of them and to protecting those works."

As we approached a painting by young local artist Thadeus Longfellow, I recalled a wonderful story I'd heard about him and Nell. "I seem to remember you got into a bit of a skirmish with the County Museum over one of Thadeus' early works. Correct?"

"No, well yes and no. I saw a painting of his at the LA Art Fair and put a hold on it, then someone at County saw it and wanted it for the permanent collection. That's when Paul said it would be better for Thadeus if it went to the Museum instead of to us. Which meant we ended up having to buy his later works."

"How much later is this one?" asked Mazor.

"A year or so," Nellie said with a sigh. "That doesn't sound like much, but I like to be in at the beginning."

"Huh ah, the old virgin syndrome," Mazor groused.

Nell wasn't amused by the comment. Nicole rolled her eyes and Camille turned and walked into the next room with this parting shot: "Not everything in life comes down to sex, Dr. Mazor. There are more important things in the world."

Her emphasis on the word 'Doctor' made Mazor groan and look ticked off or at least very annoyed, it was hard to tell from his scowl. To me it seemed the perfect opportunity to provide him with a chance to redeem himself and to proffer the CALog project.

"The story behind a great collection is usually as important as the artworks in it," I said while looking at Mazor, but he didn't respond. "If the collector is regarded as a great arbiter of taste, then others, including critics, curators, and even artists, will follow their lead. Do you think Harriet was such a leader?"

The room was feeling a little anxious when Mazor turned and spoke. "I didn't really know Mrs. Wagner well. You knew her better than I," he said in a somber manner through a thin smile. "You seem to have made a complete recovery from your, shall we say momentary despair Terra."

It wasn't much and I could have done without the personal comment, but it was at least a start and seemed to have abated the tension between everyone, for which I was grateful. Nicole gave me a what's-up look and I gestured we will talk about it later, which Nell mistook as her cue to keep the conversation going.

"Harriet's ideas about everything else from interior design to politics was somewhat dated, but when it came to cutting edge art she certainly was a leader," Nell offered with a more generous smile. "And didn't hesitate to go after what-ever she wanted for her collection."

Camille looked a little too self-conscious at the remark so I spoke up. "Thank you for that, Nell. I've been thinking of doing a special edition of CALog just about Harriet and her collection. It would be wonderful if you two would appear in the segment as well. We could even include Stephanie from Prescott & Roth. What do you think? Does the idea appeal to you?" I said to Mazor and Camille.

Nicole, sensing Camille needed more encouragement, took her arm and walked her toward one of Brice's pseudo graffiti paintings.

"Camille, if you don't like the idea of being on camera and talking about your aunt, I'm sure James understands and could just feature the art works. Right darling?"

I was liking Nicole more and more.

"No," said Camille as she whipped around to face Mazor. "It should feature the artists, especially the ones who are still alive."

I couldn't help but notice Camille positively glows when she's adamant, a quality I've seen in only a couple of people before in my life, and both were well known tinsel town celebs.

"Yes, yes of course you are right. Perhaps, since you know them, you could co-host the segment and assist me with interviewing them?" I was keeping my fingers crossed as I waited nervously for her answer.

Mazor was strangely silent as he scowled again at Camille and stepped toward her. Camille broke off her returning glare, moved away from him and shifted toward me while extending her right hand. I returned the gesture by grasping and shaking it with both of mine. Everyone, except Mazor, gave a sigh of relief and Nicole winked at me.

Bending down to look at the signature and date on Brice's large colorful painting Camille said, "This must be one of the last paintings he made."

"Why yes, it is," replied Nell. "I acquired it about a week before he was murdered. I will miss him. His work was just starting to come into its own."

"I miss him too," said Camille. "He was a nice guy."

Mazor grimaced and pouted through an insincere grin so I decided to broach the unspoken topic of the evening. "These murders must put you in a difficult position. I mean on the one hand they were all friends of your Aunt and you and on the other, their deaths increase the value of your inherited collection."

Mazor just glared at me and stiffened his fingers. Camille looked deeply moved and spoke with genuine sadness. "I don't care about the money, it was their friendship that meant the most to me and my Aunt."

With the statement still hanging in the air Mazor put his right arm around Camille's waist and gripped her left arm with his other hand, then forced walked her away from the painting toward a large bouquet of yellow flowers spouting from the open mouth of a life sized ceramic pelican.

After pausing to dab a handkerchief to her eyes, Camille stooped to sample the fragrant aroma wafting up from the arrangement. A full smile overtook her youthful face. "Oh, isn't this an early Jon Doh?" she asked as she wiped full tears from her cheeks.

"Yes it is," replied Nell. "How clever of you to know."

"When I was a kid I always looked forward to visiting my aunt just because I would get to see Jon's work. In fact, I think she acquired many of them just because I responded to it. He's a real special man, too."

Again, Mazor grimaced and pouted like a scorned fourteen year old as his hands curled into lumps. "Does he still live in L.A.?" Everyone shrugged and moved on.

We spent another hour or so strolling through the house stopping here and there at each painting and sculpture created by an artist Camille knew or had at least met before moving to Boston. When we approached the front door and began thanking Nell for a wonderful evening, Nicole decided to put some final questions to the couple.

"How did you two happen to meet? Was it here or in Boston?"

"Boston. Why do you ask?" Mazor said in a disingenuous manner.

"Oh just wondering. I mean you seem so different from one another. That's all. What made you pick Boston?" she said to Camille.

"My girlfriend from high school was going to college there and I wanted to experience something different from L.A. and I needed to get away from the crowd I was hanging with. You know what I mean?"

"Yes, I do although I did it the other way around. I left Philadelphia and came here."

Everyone laughed, except Mazor.

"Ok, so you both were in Boston, but how did you meet?"

"Well you know my folks had died in a horrible car accident and old uncle Hershel passed away. Plus I was feeling a bit stressed about everything and what to do with my life. I wasn't sure about going to college or finding a career so I got some counseling, that's all," Camille said as she fussed with her coat sleeve.

"I was her therapist," said Mazor resolutely. "Now we have to be going, good night."

"Thank you for a lovely evening Nellie," said Camille. "It was special."

"I will call you in a couple of days about the CALog shoot," I said as they walked down the steps toward their car. "Perhaps we could invite the artists to your house and do the interviews in front of their works insitu as it were." Neither of them turned around or acknowledged my parting words as they got into their car and drove away.

Nell suggested that we have something warm before calling it a night so we all walked back into the living room and she instructed the maid to make three flat white coffees.

"Well that was a success even if it was a little like pulling teeth," Nell said as we arranged our selves around a small marble table in the form of a life-sized genuflecting nude female figure. "It's a little hard to believe Camille is in love with him, but I'm convinced he is fanatical about controlling her."

"Yes, he is a highly intelligent, educated man, but he's obviously overly intense," suggested Nicole. "I mean, every time she mentioned she knew an artist or liked his work, he seemed down right saturnine."

The coffee arrived and after a few sips we all felt relaxed so the maid placed a small plate of seductive looking pastries on the glass tabletop. They looked so suggestive I had to ask what they were called. Nell replied, "Venus' Nipples."

I wasn't sure whether to bite or lick the one in my hand, which brought a big smile to Nicole's face and a slight blush to mine.

"So is it official, I mean can I tell everyone that you two are an item," asked Nell.

"No, not just yet," Nicole said flatly before I had even considered the question or finished my pastry treat. "The settlement papers haven't been signed yet and if I can't get Patterson to agree to my demands then the whole thing will have to be settled by a judge and I don't need any unnecessary complications screwing anything up."

"Yes, of course, you are right. We'll keep it on the QT for now," relented Nell as she glanced at me. "You're looking a little muddled, James. What's on your mind?"

"Oh, I was just thinking about Mazor's state of mind. Most likely he suffers from a bad case of possessiveness and jealousy", I said.

"Which is a recipe for a relationship headed toward total annihilation," said Nicole.

"I was wondering if I should strike while the iron is hot and phone Camille tomorrow morning."

"You know dear, Camille seems perfectly capable of doing the CALog shoot with just you and the artists. I don't think you need to include Mazor or Stephanie. What do you think, Nellie?" Nicole said as she touched my knee, but looked at Nell.

"Yes, that's right James. Besides, it's more appropriate since she is Harriet's niece and only heir. Having Stephanie there would only make the whole program seem crass and commercial, below your high standards. You don't want that do you," said Nell.

"No, of course not," I said as Nicole and Nell smiled at me and then at each other.

I was being ganged up on and I instantly knew it wouldn't be the last time. "It will be fine, I can make it work with just Camille."

CHAPTER 14

It was another mellow November night so when Nicole and I arrived back at the studio we went out onto the upper deck to bask in the mood of a golden moon backed by a deep blue sky with sparkling silver stars and each other. All of which compelled me to speak. "We need to talk about where and how we're going to live together."

"OK, but what do you mean exactly?"

"I mean you're used to living in a mansion surrounded by luxury and pampering. I'm an artist. I live in a small, messy studio. Granted, living as I do is sort of a 19th century concept, but it still holds true for most artists, especially in this age of selfies."

"Selfies? Ahh yes selfies, yes I understand, the establishment of an image of oneself, self-fashioning, with all its assorted strategies, is more important than ever for an artist in this time and place."

I was stunned by her instant comprehension of what I perceived as a potential deal breaker to our blossoming union and my pause only spurred her further response.

"Artists like you not only look for an answer to who they are through the creation of their art, but through how they are perceived. Right?" She said with sincerity. "For me, it's your voice that defines you, James."

My head tilted back toward the Big Dipper and I swallowed a mouthful of her engaging perfume, "What?"

"Do you know how I came to be aware of you?"

My head tilted back down as my eyebrows crinkled and my mind slipped into gear at the sight of her enchanting face. Unable to speak, I shook my head from left to right.

"Well my dear, it was at one of Nellie's classes. I had arrived a little late on the day she was introducing the group to your CALog program and from where I was sitting I couldn't see the screen, but I could hear your voice," she said with a heartfelt smile.

I cleared my gravely throat. "Mmm, so what is it about my voice?"

"It's warm, calm, commanding, projects sincere gravitas, and is never off-putting. It's almost a paternal presence that invites everyone into the story and makes them feel their attention is essential and vital."

"Wha ah, but does it make you want to look at the art?" I said with genuine honesty.

"Yes, it's just a comforting presence making learning and discovering enjoyable. Do you understand now why I asked Nellie to introduce us?"

"That's right, it was her that introduced us," I recalled.

"I want you in my life as a continual presence whether it is in a mansion or a messy studio. I am emotionally bonded to you, James. You are my North Star."

"Stop, I can't live up to that level of commitment."

Her eyes sharpened their focus on me as her shapely thighs stiffened.

"What do you mean?" she said as her eyes began to fill with tears and her hands went to the top of her hips.

"The sense of an individual one gets from their public persona can often bear little resemblance to who they actually are," I said with as much conviction as I could.

Her face took on a tender smile, "That's true, but in your case, your private persona is even better."

I felt my chest heave as I exhaled deeply. "This moment has arrived much sooner than I had anticipated, but it's here now and must be faced."

"James, what are you talking about?"

"Tell me how you knew I was going to be at St. John's Hospital for an operation," I said in what I believed to be my paternal voice.

"Your former assistant, Sally, although she wouldn't tell me what the operation was for."

"I forgot she knew about it and about you. She couldn't tell why, because she didn't know."

"But you're going to tell me now, aren't you James."

I took another deep breath and her hand while staring at the North Star. "I have a birth defect in a major spinal artery at the base of my brain and it cannot be operated on any further and could collapse at any time. So my love, I won't ever be able to give you a mansion and I may not be able to give you much of a future either."

The tears welling up in her eyes made their color turn even darker. "Do you know how much time?"

"No, it could collapse tomorrow, next week, next year, or even never it's not a sure thing one way or the other."

She moved into my arms and we stood embraced in silence for what seemed like a very long time. When she finally looked up at me, I had prepared myself for hearing her give me a sweet goodbye.

"Is there anyway to stall the inevit ... the ..." She just let it hang there.

"Only one thing, no overexertion that might cause my blood pressure to spike."

"I see, that's why I never see you run with Duie or jog on the beach, why you won't play volleyball or tennis, or why you never seem to lose your temper. Isn't it?"

"Yes and no."

"And what does that mean?

"I do lose my temper, but I've learned to do so without raising my blood pressure too high."

"Wait a minute, what about all of our lovemaking?" she said as she released her arms from around me and stood firmly with her shoulders squared and her hands on her hips again. "Doesn't your blood pressure rise then? Uh?"

"Well, obviously it does, but I've learned to control that too." I was smiling again and it felt good.

Still standing firm she said, "OK Mr. Control Man, we have no problem then, do we, with care we can make this work right?"

"Right," was all I could think of to say, so I said it in my best commanding voice and then picked her up and carried her to the bed.

Throughout the next day, something kept telling me to hold off on pushing Mazor or Camille about moving forward with the CALog shoot, and I had learned long ago to listen to my inner voice. However, Cisco and Elizabeth were being insistent, plus I had yet to ask Nicole for her help in identifying the mystery men in the gang-bang party photos. I decided to start with Nicole who had left in her new metallic blue bikini for a walk on the beach with plans to return before dark.

Around dusk, Duie and I went out onto the deck to wait for her. I turned a chair towards the pier fully expecting her to come from there since that's where she likes to go to watch sunsets. Duie, however, faced himself toward the cul-del-sac. After only a few minutes Duie sat up and began wagging his tail. I turned my chair around and sure enough, as the street lamp lit up Nicole came into view at the far end of the block. It had only been a little over an hour since I had seen her leave and I could have sworn she had been wearing her blue bikini, but now she was in a metallic mauve one. My manhood felt concerned.

"Where have you been, baby?"

"What do you mean? I walked to the pier."

"Make any stops?"

"No."

"None at all?"

"No, none. Now what the hell is this interrogation about?"

"Let's go inside where we can talk in private," I said as I gripped her arm above the elbow and felt my blood pressure rising.

She pulled away from my grip and said sharply, "Yes, let's do so."

I opened the door and gestured for her to enter first. She took only a couple of steps inside and quickly turned around to face me head-on. I was fully prepared for our first fight, but the wind went out of my sails instantly and my knees almost buckled.

Nicole's face turned pale as she rushed to my side and put her arm around me with her shoulder tucked-under my armpit to steady me.

All I could do was to mumble, "What color is that bikini?"

"You better sit down if that's what's affecting you."

With her aid I ambled over to the La-Z-Boy and sat staring at the canvas that had been on the easel for the past three weeks. I was very happy to see that the scalene was still yellow. Before I could refocus, Nicole stepped in front of me in a manner that demanded an explanation.

"Take that thing off," I blurted before I could get my brain in gear.

"Should I phone for the paramedics?"

"Please just do as I say and I'll explain everything. Take it off!"

"Damn it James this better be real good," Nicole demanded as she took the two pieces of shiny clothing off, handed them to me and stood there completely naked with her arms tightly folded in front of her. I took the bikini and walked out the front door with her close to my heels until we reached the deck. Then I headed toward the street lamp in the cul-de-sac and she grabbed the deck chair to cover herself. At the lamp it only took a moment to observe the effect, so I whipped around and held the bikini up and waved it at her.

As she strove to keep herself covered she gave out with a frustrated yell. "I don't get it!"

Duie ran excitedly back and forth between us as I stood there holding the bikini in my hands, fascinated by how the glare from that new hi-tech bulb in the street lamp made the fabric's color appear mauve instead of blue. As I turned my back to the lamp and held the pieces close to me they appeared blue again. The effect had to be caused by the metallic nature of the fabric. No wonder Mazor had looked so perplexed when I had mentioned a mauve colored 560. The bulb had changed the perceived color of his car too, but from inside the car he hadn't noticed the effect. I wandered if the tinted windows had prevented him from seeing it.

Nicole ran to me wearing one of my dirty shirts from the laundry basket. "Please tell me there is a real good reason for your behavior. I just can't deal with another crazy man in my life right now."

I picked her up and twirled us both around and around in the wonderful night air. "You are a precious, precious revelation," I said as I carried her back inside the condo.

It didn't take long to explain everything Cisco and I had done searching for the killer of Brice, David and Collier but, Nicole wasn't completely convinced. To her, killing three artists simply because Camille liked them years ago just wasn't a strong enough motive for a highly educated man like Mazor. Sure he has an obsessive personality, but he's not crazy. Not even the added prospect the deaths increased the value of Harriet Wagner's collection moved her to agree.

Her hesitation was based mostly on her woman's intuition, which had told her there had to be something more going on, something which struck at the heart of Mazor's manhood beyond his obvious need to be authoritative and control everything Camille said, did or thought.

Listening to her explain her reasoning process was a great eye-opener for me. Up to this point our relationship had been nourished primarily by our mutual interest in art and of course, sex. It was becoming more and more clear to me she was also very committed to becoming a community art leader as Harriet Wagner had been and Nell Meyerhof was close approaching. No doubt the perceived liberty of her impending divorce had bolstered her self-confident drive to achieve the goal.

Back in the last century, before collector and uber art investor lists were omnipresent on the web and in every major art magazine, such individuals were not just rich, their importance was based more on their abilities to be movers and shakers in their respective social spheres. In today's world, the selection process for those lists is cloaked in secrecy and the process has been distilled down to names appearing only on business documents, such as auction house sales reports, major donor award bulletins, and especially in publicity and marketing campaigns for international art fairs. All of which has more to do with money and power politics than cultural leadership. As a result, the likes of Harriet Wagner and Nell Meyerhof are never included, but on a local level they weld a great deal of weight. Nicole was after that level of recognition. The scenario also suggested my presence in her life would most likely bog down her quest.

For the first time, I realized Nicole's talent rests in her awareness of her own natural charisma and her complete understanding of her movement through real time and space, an uncommon gift in the age of the selfie. That said, the one thing I felt very concerned about was her assured sense of unapologetic entitlement. I concluded perhaps it was simply because she was a beautiful woman inside and out.

It was at that moment I realized I had been standing there staring at her for well over a realistic length of time given the circumstances of what had just occurred. She brought me back to earth when she took the bikini from my hands and led me back inside.

"I must confess I'm somewhat surprised to learn you are some kind of unofficial sleuth who works with a bona fide homicide detective," Nicole said as we slipped into bed. "How many other major things do I not know about you?"

"Nada," I said as I rolled over and pretended to snore.

In the morning, after speaking with Cisco I had to admit the street lamp bulb phenomenon didn't provide any real proof Mazor was the killer. He suggested again I show Nicole the gang-bang photos to see if she could shed some real light on the identity of the three mystery men.

My reluctance to do so was two-fold, I wasn't sure what my reaction would be should she know any of the men and should it turn out she knew them as Camille did I would feel some-what intimidated for all three were well-endowed, handsome, athletic looking guys.

"Baby, there is some evidence found which may be related to the case and Cisco has asked me to share it with you in hopes you may be able to help us determine its value," I said dispassionately as we finished our breakfast.

"OK, what is it? I would love to help."

I spread the photos out on my drawing table and stepped back so she could review them, but quickly realized in doing so I wouldn't be able to see her reactions. So I moved them to the coffee table and sat on the opposite side. Now I could observe not only her facial expressions, but also her body language.

She studied each photo carefully and only paused once for a closer look then bit her lower lip twice and spoke matter-of-factly, "OK, I've looked, so what is it you think I can tell you?"

"We don't know who these guys are. Do you recognize any of them?"

"This is Jeffery. Didn't you know him?"

"Jeffery as in Nell's dead son?"

"Yes. Where were these found?"

"In Collier's printer," I replied. "You know, I didn't really know Jeffery at all. I recall seeing him briefly a couple of times at Nell's maybe two or three years ago, but only in passing during her many art socials, not really to speak to. How well did you know him?"

"Mmm not as well as Camille obviously did, but well enough to know why she would be his close friend and huh, sex partner."

"What was special about him?"

"You mean beyond the obvious, well, perhaps under the current circumstances, it could be because he may have been the killer's first victim."

We both were surprised at the statement and took another look at the photo before facing each other.

"I thought he died in a printing accident," I questioned.

"As far as I know, he did."

"What kind of printing was he involved in?"

"He made high end offset reproductions of old 18th century paintings from his grandmother's collection, I think. She lived in Pasadena and he inherited them from her."

My mind instantly flashed back to the painting 'Dog Pointing Partridges in a Landscape, 1719' and the related prints I had seen hanging in Mazor's office. As I described them to Nicole her eyes enlarged and her head kept bobbing up and down.

"Do you think we should speak to Camille about this?" she suggested.

"It's always best to respect people's private lives, especially if you want them to be candid about what went on in their thinking."

"No, no I didn't mean about her sex activities, I meant about Jeffery maybe being the very first murder victim."

"Well, you have to admit it's got to be more than a coincidence these photos were in the possession of the third victim and he was most likely the photographer who took them in the first place. I mean look how artistic they are. They weren't shot by an amateur."

"Do you want me to show the mug shots of the other two guys to Nellie and maybe some of the women in the class?" she ventured. "I mean after all, they should be located before they become the next victims."

"I'm not sure. Cisco and I were working under the belief someone was targeting artists, but if you assume Jeffery was murdered by the same killer our reasoning doesn't hold up and it may also mean these other two guys are not artists, either."

"Do you know if any of Camille's other sex partners have died recently?" Nicole queried.

"Well, we only know of one other guy who has had sex with her and as of a few days ago he was still breathing."

"Who is he?" she demanded.

"Jon Doh," I said without thinking.

"Really, the artist who made that dreadful pelican sculpture?"

"Yep."

"Did she have sex with Brice and David too?"

"We don't know."

"So the only connection is Camille knew them all because her aunt Harriet acquired art from each of them. Correct?"

"Yep."

"Well, having seen the photos of these three guys and speaking as a woman I can tell you I can see why Camille would want to have sex with them, but having known Brice and David I doubt she would have selected them," she said as she looked at the photos again. "But then again, she did have sex with Mazor and Jon Doh which I find hard to understand too."

"Well Jon was five or six years ago."

"You mean when she was a teenager?'

"Yes."

"Wow, you and Cisco have been busy haven't you and during all this time I thought you'd just been sitting here staring at this silly scalene in a state of euphoria.

Oh, I'm sorry, you did take a day or so to film and edit a couple of CALog segments, didn't you."

It hurt a little to hear Nicole call my painting silly, but it probably was time to finish it so she could develop a better appreciation of what I'm trying to convey. I had actually been considering going back to enhancing its cosmic sense of movement more.

That night, sleeping didn't go well. Nicole's words about the case, the two unknown studs and our potential future together reverberated with every toss and turn I made. By morning I felt exhausted and drained of energy, but Nicole and Duie were up early doing stretching exercises. It was all I could do to straighten up and walk to the toilet. As I approached the bathroom door I could see Nicole's reflection in the full length mirror she had purchased at the local hardware store and which was still leaning against the wall because I'd been too lazy to install it as she had requested. When she bent over to touch her toes my mind lit up.

"Hey, aren't you a member of the local gym?" I said with renewed vigor.

"Yes I am and you should be too. In fact I know a great trainer who could get you in shape real quick," she said as she stood up and turned to face me.

"That's it," I said as I darted down the stairs.

"What? Geez, not again."

By the time I reached the coffee table both Nicole and Duie were right behind me. I quickly sorted through the photos and picked up the one showing Camille lying in the center of the bed with the three guys standing around it and all facing the camera.

"Look at the way our two mystery guys are standing. Does that stance look familiar to you?"

Nicole took the photo from my hand and studied it closely. "Yes it does. You are absolutely correct. These two guys are weight lifters."

After a brief discussion we agreed that she would take the mug shot photos to the gym to see if any staff could identify the men.

I was sitting at the kitchen table eating my usually breakfast pick-me-up of yogurt with blueberries and walnuts when she came down from the bedroom and headed for the front door.

"Hold on. What are you wearing?" I said as I jumped to my feet.

"Just my gym outfit, why?"

"It looks more like what my old mom used call a 'ninon over none on' than an outfit for exercising in."

"Well my dear, that just goes to show you how little you know about going to the gym. Besides, what if I see those two guys you want me to be able to talk to them don't you?" she said as the door closed behind her.

I knocked over the yogurt as I rushed toward the door and yelled, "NO I DON'T."

I was too slow. By the time I threw a towel over the yogurt and got the door open she was in her car and driving away. My first thought was to put some clothes on quickly and chase after her, but on reflection it seemed best to let her follow her own instincts even if I didn't agree with them. I decided to phone Cisco and fill him in on what was happening.

Cisco wasn't in his office and neither he nor Nicole were answering their cells. It seemed like forever waiting to hear from them. I was feeling worried and useless when Elvis' Steam Roller Blues seared out of my cell.

I didn't recognize the return number, but knew I had to answer it anyway.

"Hello, this is James Terra, how may I help you," I said in my best CALog voice.

"Hi Sketchy. It's Camille. Is Nicole there?"

To say I was stunned would have been a gross understatement. I coughed and cleared my throat before attempting to reply.

"Huh, no she isn't. Is there something I can do?"

"Oh, she left a text message inviting me to join her at the gym earlier this morning, that's all and I just wanted her to know my cell service just delivered it," she said in her wonderfully feminine way. "Silly thing, it never works right."

"Oh, I see, well if you hear from her please tell her to call me ASAP, OK."

"Will do, take care Sketchy. Bye."

This whole thing was getting out of hand. Nicole was way too far out in front which could be dangerous. I was resolved to have a serious talk with her the moment she came through the door. There was nothing I could do though, so I picked up my sketchbook and started making another portrait of Duie. Drawing has always been my preferred way of quelling my anger and calming my nerves to say nothing about lowering my blood pressure. I had just about completed the drawing when Nicole waltzed in around noon.

"I'm very happy to see you back. Please sit down so we can talk," I said in her favorite voice.

"Oh come on James, don't tell me you're going to scold me. We're not married yet, you know, and after all I'm a grown woman not your daughter."

I took a deep breath and her hand then sat in the La-Z-Boy and guided her onto my lap. "Under normal circumstances I would be happy about just about anything you would do, but three, possible four, people have been murdered so yes, I worry when you run out the door wearing practically nothing and fail to contact me when you arrange to meet one of the suspects," I said in a voice gradually rising in volume.

She paused and chewed her lip a little then spoke softly, "That's sweet but, what do you mean arranged to meet a suspect?"

"Camille called and told me you invited her to join you."

"Oh that, I just thought if we could have some girl time alone to talk I might find out something useful, that's all. She's not really a suspect is she?"

"We don't know yet. Mazor probably is and if he is, then Camille may also be involved."

"Well, based on what she told me I don't think so," she said with a big smile. "Are you going to spank me now?"

"Ah no, but it sure would make me feel better if I did. Just tell me what happened."

"Well, after she spoke to you, she texted me and we arranged to meet."

"And what did you talk about?"

"Mostly men including the two mystery guys," she said beaming.

"I see, did you show her the mug shots?"

"Don't be daft, I wouldn't do that. We just talked about if she knew any guys around the gym who might be interesting to date, you know, considering my divorce and all and she walked to the trophy case and pointed out one of the guys from the photos. He won third place in a weight lifting competition a few years ago. His name is Rollie Copius and he is not an artist," she said with a flash of her eyes.

"Were there any others she suggested you should date?" I was hoping there weren't.

"No, he was the only one she knows at the gym and she's seen him only once since coming back to LA, but doesn't know where he lives. After she left I asked about him at the front desk and was told he is a movie extra and often works out-of-town."

"Yeah, movie extra probably for the adult film industry," I suggested with a smirk.

"I think you are correct," she said with an unsettling smile.

"What do you mean?"

"I got the impression back when Camille was planning to leave for Boston she needed money and Jeffery told her he knew a guy who could help her, you know by making a sex tape or something. That's probably where those photos you found came from. Don't you think?"

"Yep, probably so and I think this is something that Cisco and his team should look into."

"You mean you don't have any contacts in that business," she said coyly.

"No I don't."

"Too bad, it might be fun for us to make a sex tape," she said as she pulled her skimpy top off her shoulder to reveal her left breast.

The next hour or so was the most fun I'd ever had on that old La-Z-Boy. Nicole chose the moment when I put my pants back on and was about to zip up to say, "You know, I also asked Camille about her relationship to Jon Doh and you'll never guess what she told me about him."

"Just tell me, what?" I said as I paused to face her.

"She knows who he really is."

"What do you mean? I've known Jon for years. He's a ceramic artist."

"Yes, but what do you know about his background?

"He graduated from California Arts & Crafts in San Francisco."

"And before that, where did he come from?" she said with a somewhat girly smugness.

"All right, I don't know. Just tell me." I was having trouble with my zipper probably because I was thinking Jon would turn out to also be a porn star.

"His real name is Jon Doheny. As in Doheny Drive, Beverly Hills."

I almost snagged my manhood in the zipper and Nicole laughed out loud.

"He's a member of the Doheny family?"

"A nephew and Camille really likes him a lot."

"Wow this is a surprise. He always seems so anti everything their name stands for."

"Yes, but apparently old lady Wagner knew his father well and thought Jon and Camille would make a perfect couple. From what I could gather from Camille, I think Harriet even tried to get the two of them together or something, but Jon felt he was too old for Camille."

"Geez Nicole, you are truly unbelievable. All of this in one morning. What a day this has been," I said with complete astonishment. "I've got to get a hold of Cisco. He is going to be amazed by all this news."

"Well there is one more thing you should know before contacting him, but I think you should sit back down first, you know, let your blood pressure ease up a bit. We don't want your brain stem thingy acting up or anything."

"Nicole, don't treat me that way. It drives me crazy. If I think I'm going to have a problem, I'll tell you, don't you try to second guess anything. OK? Do you understand?" I said in a manner probably harder than necessary.

She rushed to my side and leaned against me, "Yes James I get it and, and I'm sorry, you did tell me before and I won't let it happen again. I promise."

"I'm sorry too, I shouldn't have sounded so mean."

"Isn't it nice we can talk to each other in a congenial way without shouting," she said with a warm smile.

"Yes it is. Now tell me what else happened today."

"Oh, Camille said she doesn't really want to sell Harriet's art collection. It's Mazor's idea, not hers. He believes if they keep it, it will remind her of too many bad memories from her youth like it did when she saw Brice's painting at Nellie's dinner."

"Right, well that definitely kills the CALog project and means I've got to phone Liz, she's not going to like this turn of events at all."

"You know, believe it or not, Camille spent more time asking about my divorce than she did answering my offhand questions about men. I think she would like to leave Mazor and she may even be afraid of him. I have to say I actually sensed that feeling in her at Nellie's."

"Yes, but I've known many couples over the years who seem to thrive on a love/hate relationship and still manage to stay together. It's as though their love for one another blossoms on friction and antagonism to fuel it," I said as I hit Liz's number on my cell's speed dial. It took only a couple of rings before her assistant answered and less than a minute later for Liz to say hello.

"James I'm so glad you called. I've got some news for you," she said with enthusiasm. "Scanlan made a settlement offer and we've accepted it, so we can all relax. Now we can move on with developing a really good CALog to finish off the season."

The lift in her voice was so noticeable it generated a smile on my face, but something was telling me there had to be a catch somewhere.

"That is news. What did we have to acquiesce to," I asked hesitantly.

"Scanlan Enterprises agreed to be a three year CALog sponsor and you will re-shoot the Kooy segment sometime next year. Isn't this great?"

"Well it certainly is unexpected. He either loves the girl or has made a sizable investment in her art, or maybe both, but I still don't see why we had to agree to anything."

"James, you're missing the most important part, Scanlan signed a pledge contract which means the show is good to go for three more years."

"Yes, you're right, it is good news. Unfortunately, I have some bad news."

"Oh and what is that?"

"We will not be doing the Harriet Wagner Collection shoot. The family is delaying or maybe even cancelling the auction," I said as carefully as I could.

"What a shame, but I think we can get past it. I'm sure you'll use your famous resources to come up with something just as good or even better. Just don't take too long. OK?"

After convincing Liz I would definitely come up with something new and exciting I phoned Cisco again and was fortunate to find him still at his office.

"What's up, Leonardo," Cisco said in a somber way. "Nothin's happening here, but at least there hasn't been another murder, I know of anyway."

"I've got lots of news which will kick-start you out of your dull mood," I said on an upbeat note. Cisco was genuinely amazed at all the blank spots Nicole had filled in for us in just one morning of sleuthing. Twice I had to assure him, yes the info was gathered by 'the chicky-doodle in the hot pink number and I was real glad we had the conversation on the phone rather than in front of Nicole. She would have exploded at being referred to in such a manner.

"La vision de ella inspira amor," Cisco commented.

"Come again," I said even though I agreed with him, Nicole is a lovely vision.

"Oh never mind, I've got one bit of other info for you. You remember the security tape from Peterson's garage?" Cisco said.

"Yep."

"Well we got a judge to sign off on it and it shows the miscreant."

"Great. Who is he?"

"He is a she, a Latina. In fact, she's one of Peterson's former playmates."

"Really, well it's not a bombshell, but it is a surprise."

"It seems she is miffed he dumped her for Honey and Cerise so she conked him on the head, but claims she didn't mean to set the garage on fire."

"Mmm how do you accidently start that kind of fire?" I replied.

"Exactly."

"What did Norten have to say about it?" I asked.

"He doesn't want us to press charges and prefers the whole matter to be written up as an accident. He will probably have to let the insurance claim go too plus pay for all Fire Department and Paramedic expenses."

I was real happy to know the attack didn't have anything to do with the murders and especially happy that Peterson wasn't responsible for the destruction of his wonderful art collection.

After a little more discussion Cisco felt the best way to move forward with the search for the murderer was to make sure Camille wasn't involved and to see if there was a way she could help us find enough evidence or motive to arrest Mazor. We both felt that required a feminine touch and he suggested I ask Nicole. He also felt it was time to start a 24/7 watch on Mazor and a search for Rollie Copious which neither he nor I believed was the guy's real name.

By the time I got off the phone Nicole and Duie were not in sight. I walked out onto the deck and couldn't spot them so I went up to the upper deck and took a look around with the binoculars. I spotted them running along the water's edge just as they turned toward the studio. Nicole looked great in her metallic blue bikini. It was a joy to watch every part of her figure in continuous motion and to think about how the rest of our evening together would go. When she returned I suggested we drive up the coast to Paradise Cove for dinner.

She said yes and added, "Are you sure we're doing this so we can have a nice evening together or so you can drive the 560 again?"

There was no way to answer, so I just smiled.

As we drove north on Pacific Coast Highway through Malibu I was still reeling from Nicole's skillful handling of the day's events and felt compelled to know how she accomplished it.

"How did you entice Camille to come to the gym?"

"Well, while we were in the powder room at Nellie's dinner party we exchanged phone numbers and email addresses so I just texted her an invite. I also gave her your cell number. Is that OK?"

"Mmm, it was simple ugh?"

"It was a natural. I had already asked her what she did with her time while Mazor was at his office and she told me she was always looking for things to do.

You know, women talk this way to each other all the time. Don't worry, it wasn't a forced conversation at all."

Paradise Cove was beautiful as always and the restaurant wasn't too crowded probably because it was November. The drive back was somewhat of a blur due to my excessive desire to put the 560 through its paces. I slowed down only when Nicole reminded me that stretch of the PCH has the highest number of accidents per mile of any road in the county.

In the morning, Nicole left for the gym early to meet with Camille and I resisted my strong desire to suggest she add some more pieces to her workout attire. So Duie and I just went for our usual fast walk, which was even faster than normal while I vented some. When we got near Brice's studio the events of the last three weeks flashed in front of me like the roller coaster at the pier and made me anxious about Nicole being at the gym again. She had promised to phone me by 10, but when Duie and I returned home it was only 8:01 so I decided to look through Sally's old hard copy files to see if I could come up with an idea for a new CALog. The landline phone rang at 9:28.

"Hello, this is James Terra, how may I help you?"

"Sketchy, it's Jon Doh. Have you got a few minutes to talk?"

"Absolutely Jon. Good to hear from you. What's up?"

"Well I've been working on a special project for some time now and thought maybe you'd be interested in doing a Log about it. I realize you don't usually do more than one program on an artist, but this is a very special situation," he said with a noticeable level of desperation in his voice.

"I am interested Jon, but I can't drive all the way up there right now. Can you send me some photos of the work?"

"Oh, no, no it's not that kind of work and it's not in Ventura. It's in a canyon just up PCH a short drive."

"I thought you moved to Ventura County's inner sanctum?"

"No I just work up in Oxnard on weekends, that's all."

"At a bar?"

"Right, the Mud Pit. The rest of the time I spend at a little place I have off the grid in the canyon near Leo Carrillo State Beach."

"Off the grid? I didn't know those kind of places still existed along the coast," I said as I felt my eyebrows rise.

"Well this is one of the reasons why I'd like you to see it before they make me destroy it."

"What are you talking about Jon? Someone wants you to destroy your artwork? What law did you break," I said.

"This is a site specific project, James, and I didn't get a permit to build it and now the local Council says I have to tear it down. If it was filmed by someone with your credibility and integrity there would at least be an official record of it and if you come I'll make sure there's plenty of cold beer in the frig."

"I thought you said it's off the grid?"

"It is, but I've got solar and wind."

"Right. OK, email me driving directions and I'll try to arrive by noon."

"Great. Thank you, James. I can't tell you how much this means to me, man. I'll see you around noon."

By the time I got off the phone I noticed Duie sitting at the front door wagging his tail and heard voices approaching. So I grabbed one of my finished paintings from the storage rack, set it in front of the scalene painting on the easel and headed for the door. Opening the door revealed a sight I wasn't prepared for but Duie was excited about. It was Nicole and Camille in bikinis sunning themselves in the deck chairs.

"What a lovely, wonderful vision you both are."

"Ah isn't he a sweetheart," Nicole said with a wink.

It took only a moment to tell them both about Jon's invitation and to ask them to come with me, but Camille was reticent. She was concerned Jon would not want to see her and she didn't have the right kind of clothes with her. To me the two thoughts didn't really relate, but I could see from the look Nicole flashed me she knew what to do.

"I'll tell you what, why don't you keep me company while I change and maybe we can find something for you too," Nicole advanced.

It didn't take long before all three of us were in the 560 and heading toward the far end of Malibu.

"When was the last time you and Jon were together," Nicole asked Camille.

"Oh it's been over five years, but we used to email each other when I first went to Boston. Brian made me stop when we got married."

I handed my cell to Nicole and asked her to read out the driving direction Jon had texted, but Camille interrupted.

"We won't need those. I know how to get there," she said with complete confidence.

"You do?" Nicole and I said in surprised unison.

"Jon took me there a few times when he first started building things up there. I think its part of an old land grant his family had from a long time ago. He always wanted to keep the area natural rather than develop it. He's really a sensitive guy."

Nicole reached over, squeezed my leg and smiled at me. We were passing Trancas Beach and traffic on PCH was very light so we were definitely going to arrive at Jon's on time.

"James, let's pull in here and pick up some food and drinks just in case Jon doesn't have anything."

"Yes, we could have a picnic," Camille suggested with a perky smile. "He likes to picnic in a little grove of coastal oaks up there. I know just what he would like."

Nicole smiled and winked at me so I pulled into the parking lot at Trancas Deli/Mart. "You two go ahead, I've got some calls to make so I'll wait here," I said as they hurried into the store.

My cell wasn't picking up a very strong signal so I got out of the car and walked up a little hill at the back of the store and the signal gained enough strength to enable me to dial Cisco. Several rings passed before the front desk answered, but it was only one click to reach Cisco.

"Hey Cis, you'll never guess were I'm headed."

"It better not be to the Club, it's not noon yet," he answered in a deadpan manner.

"No, no man, I'm working on a Log and on the case. I've got Nicole and Camille with me and we'll be at Jon Doh's in a few minutes. How's that for a start?"

"You're in Ventura?"

Cisco was just as surprised as I had been when I told him about Jon having a place near Leo Carrillo Beach and he was very happy to know Nicole and Camille were bonding.

"Anything new on the murders?" I asked.

"Yeah, a couple of things. First Rollie Copius' real name is Raimond Hortense Puissant."

"Geez, are you sure he's an individual? It sounds more like a law firm."

"He's a Creole from Louisiana. And as you suspected he is an extra in the porns, but doesn't get any leading roles because he speaks in a high pitched voice with a heavy accent."

"Do they really care about how he speaks? I would have thought he was hired for his more obvious physical attributes," I said with a chuckle. "Does he live on the Westside?

"This we haven't been able to determine yet. We even checked with the gym and they said he's not a member. He just buys a day pass once or twice a week. His agent says the only way to reach him is through his cell and we don't want to yet, it might spook him into absconding."

"Makes sense. So what's next?"

"The Vice Squad says most of the x-extras hang out at a karaoke bar in West Hollywood so we're keeping an eye out for him there. If he shows up we're going to tail him for a while before bringing him in for questioning. The best thing would be if we spot him with Mazor or something along those lines."

"Mmm well, if Mazor is our man, it's hard to see how he and Hortense have any kind of relationship other than their personal involvement with Camille."

"Yea and Mazor doesn't sound like the kind of man who'd share. Just make sure Nicole goes easy with Camille. We don't want to spook her either. She may be our only hope of snaring Mazor. See if you can discover why anyone may have killed her friends."

"Right, I've got it," I said as I saw Nicole and Camille loading their purchases into the car. "Gotta go man, I'll check in with you when we get back."

As we got near Leo Carrillo Beach I noticed in the rear view mirror Camille wiping tears from her eyes, so I reached over and nudged Nicole who immediately realized I wanted her to speak to Camille.

"Did you and Jon spend time at this beach?" Nicole said softly.

"It's one of his favorite places. During the summer you can really see the stars at night here. It's magical."

"So you met him when you were 19," Nicole inquired.

"Oh no, I've known Jon since I was a kid. He knew my folks and I'd often see him when we visited Aunt Harriet. He probably still thinks of me as his little sister."

"Really, how old were you the last time you actually saw each other?"

"Mmm, well I was about 19 then, but I was stupid."

Nicole turned and faced Camille to speak softly, "How so?"

"I tried to prove to him I was no longer a kid and he should see me as a woman, you know what I mean," she said as she tilted her head down and then raised her eyes up in a kind of girly vamp way.

"I see, so what happened?"

I could tell Camille was feeling a little uncomfortable by the question so I pretended to be more interested in driving and the scenery.

"Boy, this car handles real good on the curves. It's going to be fun when we head up the canyon," I said as I glanced at Nicole and smiled.

"I'm glad you're enjoying yourself dear. So what happened with Jon," Nicole said as she redirected her attention back to Camille.

"Oh, we had a real good time, but I may have shocked him, you know trying to convince him I was willing to do anything he wanted."

"Anything?" Nicole let it hang there.

"Well yes I liked him and I wanted to get away from my Aunt," Camille said, looking embarrassed. "I was hoping we'd have so much fun together he'd want me to move in with him."

"That's nothing to feel repentant about. Besides you're all grown up now and I'm sure he'll notice especially in the outfit you selected."

Camille was smiling again, but looked like a deer caught in headlights. "Turn right here," she said while taking a small mirror from her purse. "Go about two miles up and look for a small, plain looking wood gate on the left." She adjusted her makeup and put on some unusual looking ear rings as the 560 effortlessly glided around each curve.

"Those ear rings look like the bristle end of fan paint brushes," I said as Nicole whipped around to get a close look at what Camille was doing.

"Yes, you're right they are. Jon gave them to me on my 16th birthday. I always carry them with me. It makes me feel good to look at them and I'd like him to see that I still have them."

"Is that paint I see on the very tips of the bristles" noted Nicole.

"Yes, it is. It's a special shade of green Jon created. He says he got the idea from looking into my eyes. He calls it Chartreuse Emerald."

A rush of erratic thoughts raced through my mind as we passed the two mile mark and I began to wonder if Camille really knew where she was leading us. Thinking we would probably have to turn around and wanting to get a more studied look at those brushwork ear rings, I stopped at an overlook on the right side of the road.

"We've gone more than two miles. Does anything look familiar to you," I asked.

"Oh, I'm sorry I just guessed at the mileage. I don't really know how to measure distances, but I do recognize this view. The gate should be just a short way further," she said as she put her makeup stuff back in her purse and adjusted the green tipped ear rings while smiling broadly.

"Come on James, we've come this far, let's keep going," said Nicole. "Besides you're enjoying yourself, I can tell."

"You're right, there's nothing to complain about the car is a dream to drive and the scenery, outside and inside, is beautiful," I said as I drove back onto the pavement and adjusted the rear view mirror for a better look at the earrings.

"Isn't he a charmer?" Nicole offered.

I decided to speed up a bit just to see how the car would handle the challenging road, but as we whizzed around the third curve Camille gripped my shoulder so I brought the car to a quick stop.

"This is it right there," Camille said as she gestured toward the entrance to a narrow dirt road partially hidden by several large Yucca plants. The dilapidated wood gate was propped open by a large stone.

I turned onto the road and used only the idle speed to creep the car forward taking care not to scrape the side panels with the sharp thorns of the Yucca or Sage and not to bottom the car out on the deep ruts and large rocks that comprised most of the road. I couldn't help but think of how different this road and environment were compared to Doheny Drive in Beverly Hills.

"Boy this is a far cry from where Jon came from," I said out loud and regretted immediately, but decided to push forward with anyway. "I'll bet there's no mansion at the end of this 'Private Drive'."

"Please don't say that to Jon. He hates any talk about Beverly Hills and all the society stuff," Camille said with real concern and anxiety in her voice and on her face.

"OK, don't worry. How far is it to the house?" I said in an upbeat manner.

"I told you I can't tell how long things are."

Nicole and I laughed out loud, but I resisted making a brash or blue riposte.

"And there is no house, it's more like something you'd see at a museum or in an old movie," Camille added.

As I eased the car around some deep ruts and up a steep rise all we could see was its cream colored hood and an azure sky. We held our breaths as the hood came slowly back down revealing an expansive view of the entire coast line including much of the surf at Leo Carrillo Beach.

"Isn't it beautiful," Camille said. "I've really missed this place. Jon is so lucky to be able to come here anytime he wants."

I drove on through a small grove of Scrub Oaks and another stand of large yuccas and more sage. When we emerged a complex of puzzling looking structures dotted the landscape.

"This is it," Camille said with glee. "Wow, he's added a lot of new sculptures."

"It's certainly not what I expected to see from Jon, for sure," I said as I got out of the car.

"Oh please, please don't say anything bad about his artwork," Camille pleaded.

"Don't worry, James will be real nice, won't you James," Nicole implored as she gave me her 'don't you dare' stare.

Each of the large biomorphic sculptures had been fabricated of adobe and several of them had cool dark interiors, some with window like openings and others with only a walk-in alcove niche with a bench inside. As I strolled around I was mesmerized and fascinated by realizing the entire setting was created by Jon Doh of copulating teapot fame.

Camille was leading Nicole on a tour of her favorite pieces, so I decided to find Jon. The property sloped on the southwest side and had a slender meandering foot path leading downhill so I followed it. At the bottom near some house sized boulders was another structure, it was made of very old adobe bricks and except for the solar panels mounted above its red ceramic tiled roof, looked like it was from the 1800s or even earlier. Jon was sitting in a rocking chair on the front porch with a cooler at his side.

"How about a cold one? It must be noon by now."

"Thanks man, after traversing your defiant driveway I need one."

"I could have sworn I heard kids' voices after you stopped the car," he said.

"Well, whatever you say when they get here don't call them kids or we'll both be in big trouble," I said quickly.

"Ah, it must be pussy then, huh?"

"Dang don't use that one either, I'll end up having to walk home."

"Right, that definitely didn't sound like your old car. So who is it?"

"Mrs. Nicole Volkov and Mrs. Camille Mazor," I said as I took a long swig of beer.

"What? Camille you brought Camille, damn James, I don't even have a clean shirt to put on." Jon yelped as he finished his beer in one long gulp. "How does she look?"

"Like a vision, now just dust yourself off and make her feel good she came."

Jon dashed into the house and I assumed it was to clean himself up a bit. As I approached the cooler I noticed the book *The California I Love* by Leo Carrillo was laying on top of an old wooden orange crate. I had read this book when I first arrived in LA after it had been recommended to me by Cisco.

Carrillo was Castillian and traced his ancestry back to the 1200s and I believe it was his great-great grandfather who arrived in California around 1760. His great-grandfather was governor of Alta California, his great uncle mayor of LA three times and his father Juan Jose Carrillo was police chief and the first mayor of Santa Monica.

It was intriguing to find Jon interested in the history of the area. Including some of it in the CALog would make for a fuller, richer, and more meaningful story.

Carrillo himself was a fascinating person. He was a recognized newspaper cartoonist, Broadway actor, and appeared in about 100 films, but is best remembered for the television series The Cisco Kid. He even has two stars on the Hollywood Walk of Fame.

I picked the book up to see which section Jon had dog-eared. It was the chapter about Carrillo's activities as a preservationist and conservationist, how he served on the California Beach and Parks commission for eighteen years and played a key role in the state's acquisition of Hearst Castle, LA Arboretum, and Anza-Borrego Desert State Park and was eventually made a goodwill ambassador by the governor at the time. Leo Carrillo State Park, better known as Leo Carrillo Beach, was named in his honor, as are several other places in the state.

Jon emerged from the house and immediately reached for another beer just as Nicole and Camille appeared at the end of the trail carrying the picnic basket between them.

"Hey, go easy of that stuff. You need to have your wits about you right now," I said under my breath. Jon returned the beer to the cooler.

As soon as Camille got a glimpse of him the picnic basket fell from her hand and she ran to him with her arms wide open. Within seconds tears were filling their eyes and Nicole motioned for me to join her over by a life size ceramic sculpture of a howling coyote perched on top of a nearby boulder. I did and we left them alone for about an hour.

Nicole and I sat on the boulder and soaked in the view. There's always something almost surrealistic about southern California with clouds in the sky, especially on a striking, sunny November day like this. It's more than just picturesque. It's uplifting and reassuring. I envisioned Carrillo smiling at us.

After the picnic lunch our visit concluded with a tour of the compound while Jon told us about the area's early history as a Chumash Indian settlement; Spanish land grant; and as a location shoot for several old Hollywood films. He finished with his philosophy about "slow art" and his hope his compound be preserved as it is. I promised him I would make a special CALog about it immediately.

"What have you learned while living up here?" I said.

"Well, you know I told you I was having difficulty being true to myself in LA. I felt like I was just mimicking others which led me to frustration and probably depression too," he said as he looked sideways at Camille. "Being up here has cleared my mind and helped me to create from the heart. In the beginning I didn't really know what the work might be, but in time it came. The work now has a connection to who I am and to this place which I love."

"I love it too," Camille said with a sincere smile as she twirled around in the bright sun light.

"Are you striving for a Turrell kind of experience?" I said, thinking of light and space artist James Turrell and his epic Roden Crater earthwork in Arizona.

"I can understand how you might come to such a conclusion, but no it's not what I'm aiming for. This work is more about creating art to help you be calm and more mindful of the self. Art you can get close to and mind-meld with," Jon replied forthrightly. "Hopefully the setting will entice each visitor to sit inside one of my Neurohuts, select a view opening which speaks to them and feel relaxed enough to allow the magic to caress them, to travel past the natural enchantment of the place to reach their personal conception of what is possible in a life of peace."

Nicole stood up and extended her arms skyward, "Sort of an exercise to stretch your mental muscle and to know yourself better. There's nothing to buy, nothing to take home and hang on the wall or to set in your parlor. But if you've sufficiently relaxed while here you'll open yourself enough to carry the experience with you forever."

"Yes, that's it exactly," Jon said with a big smile. "I'm so happy you get it." He then turned to me and said "Sketchy this one is a keeper, you better hold on to her."

"Neurohuts will make a great title for the CALog," I said as Nicole and I left Jon and Camille under the trees in the oak grove. We walked back to the car and loaded up the picnic basket then turned the car around so it would be ready to head back up the hypothetical driveway and over the top of the hill.

"He makes no attempt to dispel the myth of Jon Doh, but those brush style ear rings raise lots of questions," I said to Nicole. "I wonder how good an alibi he has for the murder dates." Nicole raised her eyebrows with surprise.

We drove a short distance and Camille joined us. Jon stayed in sight waving until I managed to get the car back over the crest of the hill. The drive down to the main road was even more challenging than the drive in. Camille curled herself up in the back seat and was very quiet as we headed back toward Santa Monica.

"Are you glad to have seen Jon again?" Nicole asked her.

"It was lovely and I want to thank you both for being so kind," Camille said as she sat up and leaned her head between Nicole and me. "You've both also been very open about not hiding your feelings for one another which has given me the strength to make some decisions."

"Such as?" Nicole said.

"I'm going to divorce Brian. I should never have married him. He offered me security and a home and I know he loves me but, he's smothering me and I can't take it any longer. He's just going to have to accept we both need to move on." Camille spoke with forthright determination and it was the first time I sensed some real maturity in her.

"Wow, all this from just a lunch with Jon," I said.

"It's more than just having seen him again. It's everything. Life is so different here than in Boston and I belong here. This place is a major part of who I am. Brian doesn't like it here. I want to keep my aunt's house and her art collection. He hates them both. He tries to control everything I do, everybody I associate with, just everything. You don't do that to Nicole, do you Sketchy?" she said as we made eye contact in the rear view mirror and ran her finger tips along the edge of one of the brush ear rings.

"More importantly James wouldn't think of doing it," Nicole said. "He appreciates a free spirited woman. Don't you honey?"

"Yes I do, but right now we all need to be realistic," I said as I pulled the car into the parking lot at the Malibu Bluffs State Recreation Area. "When do you plan to tell Brian about this major change in your life?"

"Right away, why?"

"I suggest you take it a step at a time," I said reassuringly.

"OK, what should I do first?"

"Well, what do you think will happen when you tell him? I mean will he take it like a man or will he get intense and explode?"

"You're right, he can get very intense and threatening."

"Has he ever physically hurt you?" Nicole asked.

"I'm not sure."

"What do you mean?"

"Well, when I was going to him for counseling he'd give me a pill or sometimes a shot to help me relax and when I'd wake up sometimes I'd feel pain."

"What kind of pain?"

"Like having been pinched or something and my skin would feel kind of irritated in certain places."

"What places and what do mean by irritated?

"Uhm, well in very personal places, you know and the skin felt sort of chafed. You know, the way it does if you overuse your exfoliator brush to tone your skin while in the bath or something. It's not really important."

"I see," said Nicole as she raised her eyebrows at me. "Did you question him about it?"

"Uh ya sorta, he just said I was having flashbacks from when I used drugs and stuff, but he was probably just trying to keep me from knowing about what he likes to do to me. You know, all guys have things they like to do to get off," she said as she smiled at me in the rear view mirror again. "He's just too embarrassed to tell me while I'm awake, that's all."

"Did you use a lot of drugs when you were young?"

"Yeah, I guess I did after my folks' accident my life was just one big blur of sex, drugs, and rock and roll and Brian got me out of that world," Camille said as she dabbed her eyes with a tissue. "In such a flurry of constant temptations I felt like a shadow of myself. It was like looking for peace of mind while simultaneously being swept up in a turbulent hurricane of missteps and bad decisions. Brian actually helped me change my dangerous momentum."

"Did he have a lot of patients like you in Boston?" Nicole continued.

"Not really, but the ones he had were pretty hard-core druggies. I was glad when he moved out of his old offices and started having me and his other clean patients come to his apartment instead," Camille said.

"He didn't have a house?"

"No just two small apartments. He said that he wanted to stop seeing a lot of his old patients. He even let his secretary go."

"Why did he have two apartments?"

"He used one for his office and lived in the other one which was right next door."

"I see. Does he have any real money?" Nicole queried.

"I'm not sure. Sometimes I think he does, like when he buys clothes, but probably not. I don't know. I mean, he keeps trying to get me to have his name put on everything Aunt Harriet left me. You know, the house and the investments," Camille said as she climbed out of the car and started walking toward the cliff.

Nicole and I watched her for a moment, but as she got close to the edge we both felt compelled to join her.

"Are you going to tell her or not?" Nicole whispered.

"Let's wait and see what happens when she tells him about wanting a divorce," I said quietly.

Nicole wrapped her arm around Camille and said, "The wind is a little chilly out here."

"Oh is it, I hadn't noticed," Camille replied as she stopped to look down at the surf pounding the rocks at the bottom of the rugged windswept precipice.

"We should get going. We've all got things to do when we get back," I said as I gestured toward the car.

"Have you delayed signing the business and banking papers because you've been thinking about a divorce?" asked Nicole.

"Oh not really. It's because of Aunt Harriet's financial advisor. He wants me to wait until he finishes checking on Brian's background and he said he needs to unravel the securities and other stuff my parents left me from what came from Aunt Harriet. You know she was trustee of what I got from my parents."

"Aren't you old enough now to take control of everything yourself?"

"No, my parents had in their Will that I would have to be 30 before I could take control of everything," she said with a shrug.

"So now that Harriet is gone, who controls everything?" I said.

"My financial advisor. He's in his 80s so he knows a lot about all my business stuff."

"Has he found out anything troublesome about Brian?" I said as I opened the car door.

"I haven't heard from him yet and Brian doesn't like him because of the pre-nup he made him sign so I haven't called," Camille said with another shrug. "I guess I haven't really wanted to know what he found."

"If Brian doesn't have any real money, how does he afford his expensive office suite in the Beverly Palms building?" I asked as I put the car in reverse and looked at the rear camera image on the computer screen in the dash. I'm still not comfortable relying on a camera while backing up especially in the dark near a cliff.

"Oh he doesn't pay for it. Aunt Harriet owned the building and now it's mine. I had fun redecorating the front lobby and Brian's reception area," Camille said with a smile. "Did you see the cool Peter Alexander painting I had put up near Brian's office door? He hates it, but I think it's great. Ha ha."

"Yes I did and you are right it is a good one," I said as I raised my right eyebrow at Nicole.

"He also hates the carpet, but I love it. It's one of my favorite colors. It reminds me of a big lawn of new spring grass and makes you feel good all over," Camille said with a grin.

"There doesn't seem to be much on the plus side for staying married," Nicole said. "Can you think of anything?"

"Well Brian really did help me at a time when I was in desperate need of finding answers and meaning in my life. I'll always be grateful to him for his compassion."

"But is there any emotional sustenance to the marriage?" Nicole reiterated.

"No I guess not. I just hate causing anyone agony or anguish, not even him," Camille said in a soft mumble as she bowed her head. "One of the great things about using drugs was I always was able to bring happiness into people's lives."

"You mean the guys you dated," Nicole said in a terse manner.

"Yeah I guess I do mean them," Camille said softly as her head drooped even further.

"What about Harriet? How did she feel about your behavior?" I said as I turned south onto PCH.

"She seemed to be ok with most things at least until I graduated from high school, but when I decided to leave LA she got upset and real mean too."

"Did she know you were doing lots of drugs?" I said as I got the car up to speed.

"Yeah, she gave most of it to me."

Nicole's head crooked as she spoke with a snap. "Really, I'm surprised. What was she thinking?"

"Well she didn't want me to get it from the streets and she had a stash of it she took from Uncle Herschel's dental offices when he died. He had a chain of offices you know, even some in San Diego, so he had a lot of different kinds of stuff to get people mellow before he drilled into their teeth," she said as she finally raised her head back up.

"I see, that made everything real expeditious," Nicole clipped.

"And frugal," I said. "So she would give you something and let you go out of the house on a date?"

"Not exactly, my date and I would spend the day around the pool or in the cabana listening to music or watching movies and stuff on the big TV screen. She never cared what we did in there."

"Is the cabana decorated in a tropical theme," I said casually.

"Yeah, it is, how did you know?"

"Oh, I was just thinking about how Harriet's generation liked to decorate cabanas that way."

Nicole gave me a dismayed look after the comment.

"Did she make lots of dates for you?" I continued.

"Yeah, she did, but the only guy I liked from her list was Jon," Camille said with a giddy smile. "I hope to see him again as soon as I've straightened all this stuff out with Brian. I enjoyed Rollie too, but he was only interested in sex, drugs and rock 'n roll, not a real relationship. You know? He was real good at the sex stuff though. I don't really remember everything cause Uncle Herschel's stuff sometimes caused me to forget things, but Brian says it's normal and not harmful. Funny thing is those memories come back when you least expect them to," she said with a cackle.

"Did Harriet set you up on a date with Rollie?" Nicole said as she turned to look into Camille's eyes.

"No, he was a friend of Jeffrey's so I invited them over to the cabana one day when she was gone and we had a party. It was lots of fun. I danced around and around with each one of them." she said with another nervous giggle. "I outlasted all of them. It was a blast. Aunt Harriet came home early and really got mad at Jeffrey about it. She could be real erratic and temperamental at times, especially if I dated someone without her permission. She even got mad at that photographer guy cause he was supposed to shoot some new painting for her, but he joined our party instead."

"Were you high?" Nicole said. "And how old were you then?"

"Yeah I was high and drinking too. I just needed to escape. You know, I was 19 and wanted to feel free and young again."

She was wiping tears from around her puffy cheeks again, and I felt a mixture of sorrow and incensed anger. No doubt the loss of her parents when she was only

14 and having to adjust to a whole new way of life had scarred her deeply. She seem to be wandering on a mental precipice balanced somewhere between imaginative reverie and dangerous fantasy while anxiously searching for a safe portal.

"Young again. Right. Listen Camille, under the circumstances, maybe you shouldn't go back to your house tonight," I said as I looked at Nicole. "I think you should stay at my place with Nicole and me. That way you can explain everything to Brian on the phone and if he explodes he can chill without you being in harm's way as it were."

"Oh gosh, that would be great. You guys are so cool."

Nicole took a long deep stare into my eyes and reached over and took hold of my hand. "Yes, let's stop and pick something up for dinner and we can talk about what you're going to say to Brian," She suggested as she turned to face Camille. "What time will he get home from his office?"

"He's kind-a funny about that, he comes home every day by 6, but sometimes he goes back after he thinks I'm asleep."

"What do you mean?" I said.

"He says as part of my recovery therapy I need to get some deep sleep occasionally so he insists I take a pill to knock me out, but I just fake it and pretend to go to sleep," Camille said with a half grin. "After he thinks I'm sleeping I flush the thing as soon as he drives away in my aunt's car."

"Where does he go?"

"Well I assume he goes back to his office to meet with a VIP patient. He had some patients like that in Boston. They would only meet him at night cause they didn't want to be seen going to a psychiatrist, but I'm just guessing, I don't really know where he goes. It would be great if he has another woman somewhere," she said with a silly sick-like laugh.

"Why does he take Harriet's car, doesn't he have his own car?" I said.

"You feel it's necessary to ask that question?" Nicole snapped. "You have your own car, but you drive my 560 every chance you get."

That 'my 560' crack didn't settle well with me, but I didn't let it derail my effort to get more info out of Camille. "And Harriet's 560 is metallic blue isn't it," I said.

"Yeah, why do you ask?"

"Oh, just wondering that's all," I said as Nicole gave me a look of affirmation and polite apology.

"He did say once he liked the 560 because it's bigger than his Ford Escort, but I don't know why he would need a bigger car. I mean it's not as though he drives his patients around or needs a place for golf clubs or anything," Camille concluded.

As we drove along PCH the sunset was fabulous and fit the optimistic mood of Nicole and Camille's conversation. They covered everything from setting up a meeting with Nicole's lawyer aiming at kick-starting Camille's filing for a divorce to legally forcing Mazor out of her house and stopping the auctioning of her aunt's art collection.

As we came into town I drove up the California Incline to Ocean Avenue, turned right, then made a quick left through the infamous intersection where the flatbed truck and silver-streak motorcycle almost wrote my epitaph, onto Wilshire Boulevard and then right at Lincoln and stopped at Bay Cities Italian Deli to pick-up a variety of things for dinner.

It was well past 7pm when we finished eating and Camille's cell played a jingle I didn't recognize. She reluctantly answered it after the third cycle of music, if that's what it was.

"Hello, no, no," she said as she chewed the inside of her mouth and bit into her lower lip strong enough to make it bleed. "I'm not coming home I, NO, Brian I want a divorce and I'll have my lawyer call you tomorrow. NO. Don't say things like that, I ..."

We all could still hear Mazor yelling when Camille's shaking finger hit the off button.

"Are you all right?" Nicole whispered as she embraced Camille.

"Yeah, I'll be OK, he's just upset that's all," she said as she wiped more tears from her eyes and leaned against Nicole. "Maybe I should go see him tomorrow?"

"I wouldn't advise it, but if you do I'll go with you," Nicole insisted. "You didn't tell him where you are?"

"I didn't want him to know I'm here. I wouldn't want him to bother you guys especially while he's fuming with rage."

Under the pretense of taking Duie outside, I phoned Cisco to fill him in on everything I had learned. He said he would make a presentation to the prosecutor in the morning and see if he can get an arrest warrant. When I came back inside Nicole and Camille were still talking so I suggested they take the bedroom upstairs and I would sleep on the La-Z-Boy. Duie looked confused by everything so he slept at the foot of the stairs on an old pillow he uses when I paint for hours.

Nicole and Camille continued talking well into the night, but both of them managed to get up, shower, and dress before I crawled my contorted body off the La-Z-Boy. By the time I had showered and dressed they were heading out to meet with Nicole's lawyer. I really needed to hear some live music, but Nicole felt we shouldn't be too obvious in displaying our relationship in public until all of her divorce papers were signed, sealed and delivered. She suggested I go to the club on my own. In the meantime, Duie and I went for our regular fast walk and stopped for a long break when we got near Brice's studio. It felt good to be back into our routine, except knowing I would never again be able to talk with Brice, David or Collier was still weighing heavy on my mind.

As I approached Front Street, Mac was sitting near a dumpster at the entrance to the alley. I was thinking we should get a bite to eat at the vendor vans nearby.

"How have you been doing, Mac? Are you staying warm at night?"

"Uh, I'm fine thanks for asking," he said slowly.

"I was just thinking of getting a bite to eat, how about joining me, my treat?"

He paused and finally turned to look at me when he spoke again. "Yeah, sure I'd enjoy sharing a meal with you Mr. Terra."

"Please call me James."

As we walked toward the food vendors, Mac stopped at the drinking fountain near the bike path to wash his hands and face. I could tell he enjoyed it causing me to wonder why he didn't do it more often. Perhaps he thought people wouldn't give him handouts if he looked to clean. Appearances still mean a lot in this town.

"You look like you lost something James. What's troubling you?"

"Yes, you're right I have, three bright lights to be exact and there isn't anything I can do to bring them back. The whole thing leaves a dark feeling in one's heart."

Mac squinted and sheltered his eyes from the midday sun as he tried to watch a young bikini clad girl on skates do some kind of dance around a hat she had placed in the middle of the boardwalk. "People used to believe the sun would keep sinking lower and lower in the sky every winter and the world would turn dark if they didn't do a ritual dance to implore the sky mother to give birth to a new sun. Today we know the sun just continues on and will rise higher and higher starting on the winter solstice no matter what we do. Perhaps that is what has happened to your three lights, they went down, but will rise brightly elsewhere no matter what we do here."

He then took another peep at the graceful skater and swallowed a big chomp of his Turkish Spinach Pide which he obviously was enjoying. Duie danced about impatiently hoping for a morsel to fall. I tossed a fiver into the girl's hat.

"Mmm maybe so, but it still feels like a terrible unnatural loss," I mused as Mac shrugged and took a gulp of Dr. Pepper.

"Walk with me for a while Mac," I suggested as we finished our fast food. "How long have you lived down here?"

"Long enough to know what it was like before the Henna-tattoo parlors, sunglass shops, and Segway rentals," he said with deliberate emphasis on each item as we both quickly stepped aside for a pedi-cab that rang its bell behind us.

"Yeah, this new breed of silicon beach creatives have deep pockets which are affecting the area's real estate market and ability to house my fellow artists," I said as a tall willowy woman in her 50s and dressed like a Las Vegas showgirl walked past us with two Russian wolfhounds leading the way. I was convinced it wouldn't be long before we encountered some guy wearing a holographic spandex onesie or a woman in sparkling translucent booty-shorts.

Cosplay and role playing in general was the main event in this part of LaLaLand, even more than on Hollywood Boulevard.

By the time I had realized I had forgotten to take my cell with me it was after 2pm so Duie and I scurried back to the studio. There were two missed calls listed. I clicked on Cisco's first in hopes of hearing he had arrested Mazor, but the bottom line was the prosecutor felt there was no real evidence against the man. The other message was from Nicole letting me know she and Camille had met with the divorce attorney and everything was moving forward on that front.

After sitting out on the deck for another 20 minutes or so I decided to make a couple of suggestions to Cisco. Luckily he was still in his office. My first suggestion was for him to check with Camille's financial advisor to see if he had turned up anything on Mazor. To my surprise Cisco had already talked with the advisor when he looked into ownership of Camille's 560. It seems the previous owner was a company Harriet had owned and the advisor was listed as one of the co-owners. I was doubly surprised to hear the advisor had told him Mazor has money of his own from a couple of investments in Boston that are just barely covering their expenses as well as one in LA. So my second proposal was we somehow make Mazor boil over to see what he does. Cisco didn't like the idea at all because of the investment advisor had told him about Mazor's personal background. It seems the advisor had been a close personal friend of Harriet Wagner so he wanted to make sure Camille was going to be taken care of properly. Consequently he hired a Boston based P.I. to look into Mazor's history and discovered Mazor's parents divorced when he was 13 and his mother was arrested for solicitation and public intoxication several times before being found dead in an alley in the Roxbury Crossing district. His father couldn't be found so Mazor was put into foster care and because of his severe belligerence had to attend compulsory psychological counseling until he was 18. At 19, he inherited a small house and a little money from his long lost farther who had committed suicide while doing missionary work in the Philippines. Mazor then entered college as a psych major, but was kicked out of two colleges very quickly for aggressive behavior toward female students and a female professor of art. He ended up graduating from a questionable private college in South Carolina with a doctorate in the psychological disorders of substance abusers. I didn't know they gave degrees for that. Once again I found myself wondering why Camille married a man with such a troubled past and so many obvious peculiar personal glitches.

Cisco also said he would keep the 24/7 surveillance on Mazor.

After I made a call to Liz and filled her in on Jon's Neurohuts project. She agreed it would be perfect for a special edition of CALog and expressed her amazement at how I could come up with it so quickly. I heard her "oy veh" as I reminded her again of my famous resources. At that point there didn't seem to be anything to do but paint or sketch and I just wasn't up for either so I sat out in my favorite deck chair and watched the sun start its slow slid toward the Far East.

I awoke when Duie began whimpering at my side. It was dark and the air was chilled. It was time to go inside. As I opened the door the scent of cooking surrounded me and I was surprised to find Nicole and Camille hovered around the stove.

"Mmm sure smells good," I said with my arms wide open and a smile as big as a gators on my face. "When did you two get here?"

"You were snoring so loudly you didn't hear us tiptoe past you a couple of hours ago. We knew as soon as you woke your first thought would be about food, so we decided to beat you to the punch," Nicole said as she danced into my arms. "Camille suggested jambalaya."

"Did you make a side trip to New Orleans on your way to Boston?" I suggested. "I mean, where did you learn to cook like this?"

"A guy Jeffery introduced me and I'd see at the gym. He taught me."

"You met him at the gym here? What's his name again?"

"Rollie, he's Creole," Camille said as she began to serve.

"Ah as in Roland or something?"

"Sort of. His real name is Raimond, but he changed it for his work."

I looked at Nicole who was frowning, but decided to respond anyway. "I seem to remember reading something about a weight lifter dude by a name of Rollie."

"Yeah, that's the guy," Camille said as we all sat down to eat.

"Is he a chef?"

"Ha ha ha no, he's one of those extras for the movies. But he doesn't get much work cause he's typecast, you know, being a Creole and all."

"I see, well he must have some way of making a living if he lives around here and can afford gym membership."

"He used to work with Jeffrey," Camille said as she took a mouthful of spicy rice and fish followed by a quick, dainty swallow of wine.

"Did you know Jeffrey well?" Nicole asked.

"Not really we dated only a couple of times, but I'd see him at the house when he'd come over to meet with Aunt Harriet."

"What did they meet about?" I asked.

"Oh Aunt Harriet was an investor in his printing business."

"Have you seen Rollie since you returned?" Nicole asked.

"Only once, he was working for the company that delivered Brian's new office furniture."

"Wow, that's a step down from doing acting for a living. He must not have been a very good actor," Nicole added.

"Well, I don't know, but the films I saw him in certainly showed off his build and the things he knows how to do best, that's for sure," Camille said with a little girl giggle and slight blush. She took a larger sip of wine.

Her redden glow made the gang bang party art photos flash back into my visual cortex and I could tell the same had happened to Nicole.

"Did you talk to him while he was delivering the furniture?"

"Just a little. Brian deliberately interrupted us and he ended up talking to him more than I did," Camille continued. "I was kinda surprised at Brian cause he never seems to like any of my friends, especially the guys."

"Nothing more? You didn't exchange phone numbers or anything else?" Nicole said with an edge of disbelief in her voice.

"I wanted to, but I didn't get a chance. Besides I think he did with Brian."

"What? Why do you think so?" I said as calmly as I could.

"I saw Brian give him a business card."

"Why would Brian do that?"

"He always does when he meets someone he thinks is a druggie," she said with a little too much bitterness.

I opened another bottle of my favorite Italian dry red wine and we finished the jambalaya then gathered around the coffee table to talk more, but Camille's cell started jingling. She took one look at the incoming number and a complete veil of consternation descended across her delicate face.

"Speak of the devil, its Brian again. Damn I don't won't to talk to him," she said with dismay.

"Turn the thing off," I said.

"Yes, damn it," she said as she regained her composure and fiddled with the phone. "I need to get a new number so he can't keep hounding me."

"Did he call earlier?" I said.

"Several times while we were out and about," Nicole said with a look of concern.

"I see, did you speak to him at all?" I asked Camille.

"Only once. He's still incensed so I just hung up on him."

"Did he threaten you in any way?"

"Not really. He never does. It's the tone of his voice that is so frightening and I feel so bullied afterward."

"Well you're safe here," Nicole said with a maternal smile.

"He always seems so calm and controlled to me," I said in hopes she would provide a key to causing Mazor to make a wrong move.

"Oh he's controlled alright, but calm he's not. Most guys are domineering and controlling, but he gets so jealous, he turns into a green-eyed monster just like my dad was."

"Hookers green," I mumbled to myself.

"What?" asked Camille.

"Nothing, ah you said green-eyed monster?"

"Yeah, my dad used to call mom all sorts of bad names when he was mad at her and she'd say he's a green-eyed monster and now I've ended up with one too."

"I hope he remembers to take care of Fido."

"Who? Who is he?"

"He's our dog," Camille said as she picked up Duie and petted him.

"Did you bring him with you from Boston?"

"Oh, no, one of Brian's new VIP patients gave him to us."

"When?"

"Just a couple of weeks ago. Brian doesn't want to keep him, but doesn't want to take him to the animal shelter either. He didn't even bother to ask his patient what the dog's real name is. Isn't that silly? Why do you call Duie, Duie?"

"It's short for Duchamp."

"What kind of name is that for a dog?"

"He's named after Marcel Duchamp, a famous artist."

"Oh, did he make paintings about dogs?"

I wanted to suggest she try the name Ruff for her dog, but finished the bottle of wine instead and decided to make it an early night, so Nicole straighten up the kitchen and I took Duie for his last outing of the night. When I came back in, Camille was all curled up in a blanket on the La-Z-Boy so I headed up the stairs to Nicole while Duie stayed on the small pillow beneath the stairs. When I entered the bedroom Nicole was just walking out of the bathroom wearing my pajamas which I took as a signal we might talk some before calling it a night, but we wouldn't be doing anything further.

I tossed and turned constantly throughout the night while visions of Duie playing chess with Duchamp swirled in and out of my consciousness. Each chess piece on their oversized board looked like a ready-made sculpture put together in an unorthodox manner raising endless puzzling suggestions fought by the three-piece suit I felt I was wearing. Also sitting at the table were the Mona Lisa sporting a mustache and Dr. Mazor disguised as Salvador Dali groping a melting clock. At the center of the chess board was a strappingly handsome Creole guy stirring a steaming pot of jambalaya.

Around dawn I opened one eye, gazed at Nicole and rolled over and saw Dr. Mazor sticking a limp needle into Camille as she emerged from the steaming pot eating a mauve coated chocolate s560. The images were still vividly floating at the edges of my consciousness as I sleep walked to the toilet and relieved myself. Hopefully I aimed at the right piece of porcelain because everything seemed like a blur even after I emerged from a cold shower, finished breakfast, wished Nicole and Camille a good workout at the gym, and speed-walked Duie on a very much abridged route.

When Duie and I returned my mind was still in a wine induced fugue as he raced passed me up the stairs. He obviously wanted to charge the roof gulls into flight. So I followed him up, opened the sliding glass door and walked out onto the upper deck. The gulls were waiting for him and he didn't disappoint them. I stretched out on one of the deck chairs and closed my eyes to take a quiet nap, but the image of frightened birds jolted my mind back to the painting and prints I'd seen in Mazor's office and revived queries I'd had of how he came into ownership of those works in the first place. Did he buy them from Jeffery before he died or were they part of Camille's heritance from Harriet?

Nellie seemed like the most likely person capable of answering such a question, but she had made it very clear she did not want to talk about Jeffery. That left only Camille to fill in some of the gaps about the business relationship between her Aunt and Jeffery. I decided a visit to the gym was in order, besides I was real curious about the place for lots of reasons.

Finding parking near the gym was impossible so I left my car on an adjacent residential street where spaces are limited to those with a local permit. Knowing how locals feel about having their streets annexed by outsiders I fully expected I'd find a ticket or a terse note on the windshield when I returned.

I hadn't been in a gym since graduating from high school. Even in college I managed to fulfill the P.E. requirement by taking archery, which didn't require me to sweat or change my clothes.

As I entered the ultra-contemporary building I was greeted at the reception desk by two healthy looking young ladies who eyeballed me with skepticism as I explained I only wanted a day pass to do a light workout not a full club membership. After filling out and signing a liability waver I was politely escorted to the men's locker room.

Having brought no gym bag or special clothes to change into I wasn't sure what I was expected to do in there so I passed quickly through it and emerged into a large L shaped room filled with an endless array of hi-tech looking machines and a motley group of people comprised mostly of woman in their 30s to 50s and a few men over 55. I surmised the younger crowd were at work and probably wouldn't show up until evening.

Sheepishly I wandered around, stopping here and there to do one or two reps of exercise on apparatuses I thought I understood at least until I tried them. I made a sincere effort to comprehend the fundamentals of gym etiquette as I civilly scrutinized the variety of diminutive outfits the ladies were barely wearing and nodded to each gent I encountered who I could tell were also scrutinizing them. I was hoping to spot Nicole and Camille quickly.

The more I ventured about the more I felt as though there were a hundred pairs of eyes focused on me, but more likely nobody actually cared about me as I had learned long ago everybody else is also self-conscious of how they look in such situations. In fact, I once read in a men's health magazine that over 90% of the gym-going population doesn't know how to exercise properly or dress correctly to do it.

The more I wandered around the more I came to believe Nicole and Camille had already left or they had never been there. As I pondered the question a shapely brunette walked up to me and said "Hi, would you like to join me on the tandem treadmill?"

I could feel sweat forming on my back and we hadn't even started yet. I resisted the urge to yell out Nicole's name at the top of my lungs when the brunette wrapped her arm around mine.

"Sure, lead the way," I said apprehensively.

"I'm Karissa," she said as she weaved us through the room toward a line of treadmills that were facing a wall of glass which overlooked the pool.

"James Terra," I said in my most professional voice.

"I thought so. I recognized you the moment you entered the room," she said with a seductive smile and provocative twist to her engaging feminine figure.

As we walked along the row of treadmills I couldn't help but notice everyone on them was running, not speed walking. That thought made the sweat on my back increase with each sprinter we passed.

"The tandem mill is against the side wall at the end," Karissa said as she moved in front of me and began to work her hips more. "Do you like the front position or the back?" she said as she turned her head and gave me a wonderfully inviting smile.

Between watching Karissa's enticing hip action and scanning the walls for the nearest exit sign I was hoping my cell would sing out and rescue me. When we reached the end of the row and turned I couldn't seem to raise my eyes above Karissa's posterior even though it had stopped moving and had stepped aside revealing another set of beautiful legs.

"Hello darling. How wonderful you could join me," Nicole said as she leaned against the tandem treadmill. "Thanks, Karissa."

"No problem. I'm always happy to help a friend. Byyee sweet James," Karissa said with a wink.

The look on my face must have been too good to resist because Nicole gave me a kiss more passionate than any other she'd given me before.

"Did you really come for a workout or is there something else on your mind," she said as her eyes assessed by general appearance then gave me a full-frame survey, down then up.

"Well, well I, I would like to be able to join you in some kind of exercise, but I had also hoped to have an opportunity to talk with Camille."

"I see, well neither will be possible right now. Camille left early to meet with our attorney again and you're not really dressed correctly for exercising. Let's go over to the club shop and see if we can find an outfit and some shoes you will be comfortable in," she said as she took my arm and walked me through the maze of equipment and her fellow workout ladies.

As we proceeded I felt like all the women in the place were watching every move we made and they all seemed way too happy. So happy in fact I had to ask Nicole what was going on. "Does exercising always make women this cheerful or is there something going on I'm missing?"

"You missed it big time, but it's a good thing and that's why you've made them and especially me very happy and proud."

"Mmm I don't get it and what's wrong with the way I'm dressed?"

"You mean besides the 501 jeans, long sleeved polo, and leather ankle boots nothing. Maybe you just need a haircut," she said with a jovial laugh.

I was beginning to feel there was more than just a few years of age difference between us. There was obviously a major lifestyle disparity as well.

In the process of trying on and buying several gym outfits I learned functionality was top priority, closely followed by style, and accepting female feedback about fashion faux pas was essential but, I still felt the need to understand what I had done in the gym to garner such female adulation.

As I stepped out of the dressing room wearing the outfit Nicole thought would best serve for a light workout I felt I needed to readdress the major topic she had let slip away. "OK, so now I'm dressed appropriately to re-enter the gym, tell me what I missed you and your friends are so pleased about."

Nicole smiled broadly and looked directly into my eyes as she fiddled with the tie string on my new workout hoodie. "You didn't ogle or say anything even mildly insulting or suggestive to any of the hot chicks who were wearing practically nothing as you walked by and you resisted touching or even chatting up Karissa, whom we all agree is the most erotic looking of all of us. It takes a real man to pass such a test of fire."

"Mmm, well, to be honest, I think you are being a little too generous with your praise. I did notice, uhm, how attractive the ladies looked, but remember I'm an artist and as such I've seen many female bodies before so I don't ogle, I just appreciate. As for Karissa, this will sound perhaps strange to you, but admiring her obvious attributes did make me want to find you right away."

At that moment, I received another wonderfully passionate kiss.

When we left the gym, Nicole said she had arranged for us to meet Camille at the Rose Café. Parking there wasn't any better even though the building had recently been completely renovated and the name shortened to simply the Rose. Nicole insisted we sit in the outdoor patio section because 'the weather is still nice'. The ladies both ordered a salad, while I devoured some veggie samosas. As we ordered another round of raspberry ice tea I was racking my brain on how to redirect the conversation away from divorce settlements toward what Camille might know about Jeffery's death and his fine art printing business.

"You know, this place has been here for as long as I can remember. It used to be the midday hangout for most of the artists in the area, but it's too pricey for them now," I said as I looked around at the upscale crowd and furnishings filling my old haunting grounds.

"I am glad they kept the rose mural at the front door. It's a nice touch."

"Yeah, Brice brought me here a couple of times back then," Camille added. "He liked it because it was relaxed and easy. Back in his Elvis days," she said with her little girl giggle.

"What does that mean," Nicole inquired. "Was he a big fan?"

"Absolutely, especially after his surfing accident," Camille continued.

"Surfing," I said. "I didn't know he was a surfer or that he liked Elvis. What happened?"

"He told me he was surfing at Trancas, got caught in a rip tide and ended up smashing into the rocks at the south end. He broke his nose, both cheek bones and got some deep gashes on his head. He even had to have all his hair shaved off so he started wearing the Elvis wig. He didn't want people to see the stitches."

A flash streaked across my little grey cells as the camera at the center of my brain lit up and projected a rerun at the back of my eyeballs of the guy in the gang bang photos who sported Elvis style sideburns and the broken nose and cheek bones explained why I didn't realize before it was Brice.

"Yes, those Elvis wigs are popular. Nicole and I were looking at some old photos the other day of a guy wearing one. Weren't we?"

It took Nicole a moment, but when she made the connection she instantly went into action mode. "So you dated Brice during that time?"

"Well, Jon didn't invite me to move in with him and Brice's studio is or I mean was near the beach. Plus he was a friend of Rollie's too. So yeah, I dated him a little, but not long. He was too much of a druggie too. That's the real reason why he hit the rocks, he was surfing while high. His accident didn't have anything to do with a riptide. Besides, the lifeguards won't let you in the water if there's a riptide so he lied. He probably just got beat up by some gang guys or something."

That bit of information completed the gang bang trio ... Jeffery, Rollie and Brice. Two are dead and Rollie is missing plus the cameraman, Collier, is also dead. Rollie had worked for Jeffery and Collier had worked for Harriet. Neat packages always bother me and this one seemed way too tidy and tightly wrapped. I was beginning to feel Nicole was right. There had to be a stronger reason for straight-laced Dr. Mazor to turn from a cantankerous old man suffering from self-inflicted jealousy into a determined green-eyed serial killer. A major element seemed to still be missing and as I was mulling it over a swift kick spiked my left heel.

"Was our workout too much for you, darling, or is this your usual siesta time?" Nicole said with a stern tone.

"Oh, ah speaking of Jeffery, I was thinking of maybe doing a CALog about his printing business. Is there anything you can tell me about it?" I said to Camille.

"Not much, Brian is much more interested in it than I ever was."

"How so? I mean how did he come to select the painting and prints in his office? They did come from Jeffery didn't they?"

"Oh, not exactly, he saw those last year when we came here to visit Aunt Harriet while she was sick. She had them in the den and he was so taken with them he met with Jeffery and decided to invest in the business, that's all."

"Really, that is interesting. Did Nell take over the business after Jeffery died? Is she the major owner now?"

"No, no she didn't want to have anything to do with it so Brian bought her out. Are you seriously interested in doing a show about it? Hey, are we going to have some dessert?"

"Let's walk over to FreezWiz Yogurt and get something there," Nicole suggested as she flashed her eyelashes at me in a manner which unequivocally said don't argue.

The sun was so bright and the sky so clear and blue it felt more like mid-summer than late fall as we strolled along the sidewalk. There was even a beach themed Thanksgiving display in the window at the yogurt shop.

"I like three flavors together with nuts on top," Camille disclosed.

Everyone on the street must have thought I was a nut as I laughed out loud, waved and headed toward my car. I'm not sure what excuse Nicole came up with for my behavior and quick departure, but it probably didn't matter to Camille anyway because she was so enthralled by the endless selections available at FreezWiz she seemed completely mesmerized. Her enchanting childlike behavior seemed anything but like the adult images of her stored in the X file in my brain. In many ways, everything about her was hard to believe. I didn't know whether to take her at face value, or were there dark currents running beneath that sunny exterior, damages that might have led her to do, who knows what? Maybe even murder.

Either way, it was time to fill Cisco in on Elvis impersonator Brice; to see if there was anything new on Jeffery's death; and to let him know Mazor now owns the fine art printing business. So I contacted Cisco and we agreed to meet at the Club for a brew. There is a city parking structure near the club and there are usually spaces available on the top floor. As I drove up the ramp, the thought occurred to me maybe since Rollie has met Mazor, he may have asked for his old job back at the printing company.

As I entered the club, I could hear Spider playing softly on his Big River Harp from over in the far corner near the new sound system's control panel. He was listening to a song by European blues singer Amy Belle. He has often spoken about how much he enjoys attending her concerts when he performs in Europe. Everyone in the joint was quietly listening to him playing along with the tune *I Don't Want To Talk About It* so I tiptoed over to the bar, gestured for two long necks and carried them to my favorite booth. Listening to him and Belle was a real treat. By the time Cisco arrived, I had finished both bottles of brew and Spider had accompanied Belle through three really enjoyable numbers.

"Who is he singing with," Cisco whispered as a fourth song began.

"Our man Spider is scatting deep southern blues with a Scottish belle."

"Sounds good, I like it," Cisco said as he waved to have two more long necks brought to the table.

"How are things going at the station?" I inquired quietly.

"It's eased up a bit since no more artists have been brushed off. How about with you?"

"No major complaints to grumble about, just a lot of new experiences to sort through," I said with a smile. I didn't feel up to explaining the trials and tribulations I went through at the gym.

"Yeah, it seems there's been a lot of that going on amongst the art crowd lately," he said with a little too much consternation.

"What do you mean exactly?"

"I managed to get a copy of the coroner's report on Jeffery's so called accident and it looks pretty suspicious to me."

"Why?"

"Well not the accident itself, but rather what may have caused it. There are three things which seem odd, especially since they were never made public; the blood test revealed an unusual combination of drugs in his system, his bladder was self-destructing, and some parts of his brain were festering while other parts were drying up."

"What the hell was causing all that," I said with wide eyes and an alarming volume to my voice.

"The best the lab came up with is some kind of synthetic drug cocktail, but to determine anything further they'd have to re-examine the body which requires major paperwork to convince the prosecutor and a judge, and of course the Meyerhoffs to exhume the body. Chances of doing such are less than slim," he said as he finished his beer.

"Right, feels like a dead end, ah, no pun intended."

"Well, not entirely. On a hunch, I had the lab take another look at all the vics and guess what they found?"

"Not the same thing?"

"Damn close. Both Brice and David show signs of bladder and brain damage."

"Wow, this is beginning to sound like we may have found our missing link," I said with even wider eyes. "What about Collier?"

"No, apparently he didn't use drugs of any kind, let alone exotics. The only thing in his system was some residue from one of those little blue pills," he said with a grin.

I didn't feel up to responding to those pills so I moved forward. "So this means Jeffery's use of this unknown drug destroyed his bladder and parts of his brain which probably caused him to fall into the rollers of the big printing press at his company. Brice and David used the same drug, but were murdered with an injection of a Benzo popular with dentists, Collier was also killed by a Benzo injection, but didn't use any drugs. Drugs seem to be all over this case."

"You got it, but none of it tells us why they were killed or gives an inkling as to who did it," Cisco said with a sense of dismay. "Plus these drugs are all illegal in this country, but they are readily available fairly cheap in Asia."

"Where in Asia?"

"China and Thailand."

"Well I'm not surprised to hear about China, but Thailand seems a bit odd."

"Well, since the military toppled the elected government the place is not considered a beacon of democracy anymore. In fact, it has been sliding toward dictatorship, replete with tightened restrictions on freedom of expression and the press, but no restriction on the manufacturing or selling of synthetic drugs."

"Synthetic marijuana is called K2, Spice and even Green Giant, and I understand it can be bought for as little as a fiver. What is this new stuff called on the street?" I asked.

"Don't know. Even the guys in Vice aren't sure. It can be made from dozens of different chemicals which are often sprayed onto common shredded plant material like oregano and inhaling the smoke affects the same receptor in the brain as natural marijuana, but it can be hundreds of times stronger. It's a killer."

"So the attraction is the kick it gives, its cheap price and easy availability."

"I suppose so plus its aftereffects last longer. But, its use can also cause gross confusion and violence to the point the user will require general anesthesia and intubation to protect them from hurting themselves. Obviously, like all idiots, the users think they can control the stuff at least until they get chest pains and bladder failure. Plus the rehab center says anxiety, vomiting, tremors, seizures, hallucinations and paranoia are also common among synthetic drug users. And now this new batch of junk has been shown to cause the brain and genitalia to shrivel."

"I see, this might explain why Rollies' porn agent hasn't seen him in some time. He's addicted to this crap and it shrunk his dick."

"Well the worst part might be there is no antidote for it and no way to repair the damage it does. Plus its effect varies among its users. It may have no violent effect on you and cause another user to behave in a way landing them in prison or even lead to their death," Cisco said as he concentrated on peeling the label off his beer bottle.

The music had stopped, we had finished our drinks, and Spider moseyed over and joined us.

"That was great man, when are you going to invite Belle over to perform with you live?" I suggested.

"Ah, she's too big of a star to play in this little place and I can't pay those kinds of greenbacks," Spider said as he cleaned out his harp. "Besides being in this place would be like going back to the start for her. Why would she want to do that?"

The sound of a small bell rang in my head. "You know Cis, that's a good idea. Let's go back to the beginning, the real beginning. Let's take a hard look at Jeffery, his business, and his death. After all, since his death was thought of as an accident, it was never fully investigated by Homicide, was it?" I said as I slid out of the booth.

"No it wasn't. Where are you off to?"

"I'll see what I can find out about the art side of his business, Ok?"

"Just don't do anything to spook Mazor."

"Right and Spider, thanks for being you man and don't give up on Belle, you should contact her. You never know what she may say. Maybe she'd like to visit L.A.." I suggested as I headed out the door.

As I huffed and puffed my way toward the top of the parking garage stairs I was trying to think of who in the art community would be familiar with the kind of printing Jeffery's company did. Real fine art printmakers and publishers stay as far away as they can from the cheap offset reproductions most so-called art publishers like Jeffery made, so I was struggling to come up with who to approach.

As I got to the top of the stairwell I saw a cat in the nearby tree trying to sneak up on a couple of unsuspecting pigeons. That little drama reminded me of the hunting scene painting and prints I'd seen in Mazor's office suite. I don't remember getting into my car, but as I sat there staring at the weathered concrete wall with its faux brick pattern it made me realize why the painting had looked so familiar. I'd not seen it before as I had originally thought: it was the pattern of its texture I had seen before. It isn't a painting at all. It is a print made in the new 3-D process that mimics the appearance of thick impasto paint on canvas. It's the process I'd seen before in countless decorator shops, furniture stores, and in the waiting rooms of businesses too cheap and shortsighted to buy original art. I hadn't realized Jeffery's company was capable of making large scale embossed prints.

Solving this bit of confusion felt good, but didn't get me any closer to learning about Jeffery's company. I needed to find a decorator who had done business with him, but no names jumped forth immediately. All the decorators I knew dealt only with original art acquired directly from artists and art dealers. It was time to consult with Stephanie again. I recalled her telling me she had dealt with some decorators before moving into gallery directing and high end art auctions. Perhaps she still maintained a link to the commercial end of the art world. I decided to go home and e-mail her rather than have another face-to-face tightrope pirouette.

Arriving home I was surprised to find Nicole already there. She was doing laundry, which was an even bigger surprise.

"Hi beautiful, what's up," I said as Duie jumped against me. "Yes, yes, how are you boy?"

"Just taking care of some housekeeping chores. I haven't done things like this since before I married Patterson and I know how touchy artists can be about bringing outsiders, like housekeepers, into their private domains so I'm doing it for us. Is it OK? I won't disturb anything in the studio area," she said in an unusually quiet manner.

"What can I do to help?"

"Just tell me again how happy you are we're together."

"Absolutely, but would it be alright if I send an e-mail first?"

"Sure, what's so important?

"Oh, after I left you and Camille in the goodies shop I met with Cisco and we determined we should know more about Jeffery's printing business."

"I see, so who are you e-mailing?"

"Stephanie. She used to deal with decorators and probably knows someone who did business with Jeffery."

"Oh ah, there's no need to contact her. I know lots of decorators."

"Mmm, but probably not the low end kind who handle cheap reproductions like those Jeffery's company specialized in."

"Right, low end and cheap so you immediately thought of Stephanie."

Oops, I was feeling a little cornered and needed to nip this sprouting weed right away. I turned away from the computer, took Nicole's hand and led her to the La-Z-Boy and guided her onto my lap. The look on her face was of a school girl about to be reprimanded.

"Now beautiful, such an attitude doesn't look becoming on you. It's true Stephanie and I used to date and we are still friends, but there isn't anything else between us."

"But this is the third time in the past week or so you've mentioned her. You don't need to contact her. I can find you a low end decorator."

"Nicole, what is going on? Did something happen after FreezWiz that shook your world?" I said as easy as I could.

"Well, yes I guess it did and maybe I'm overreacting about Stephanie, it's just Nellie told me you and Stephanie had been very close."

"Yes, had been, is the key part of the statement. Tell me what occurred and maybe by talking it out together we can find a way to deal with whatever it is," I said calmly.

"Patterson changed his mind about several things we'd already agreed to and I'm concerned he might decide to challenge everything else too and I will lose the whole enchiladas."

"What specifically does he want?"

"He wants the Big Sur house back and the New York apartment plus complete control of both planes."

Wow, I felt run over by a steamroller. I hadn't really given any thought to the scale of the settlement Nicole had been hoping to get from Patterson. I was at a loss as what to recommend.

"Let's go for a walk on the beach, things always look better when you're outside in the fresh air," I said as I lifted her up into my arms and hugged her tight.

"Yeah, Camille said something like that too, she's already out there."

"Mmm, you know I don't mind her being here and under the circumstances she definitely needs our help, but perhaps we should think about getting something nicer for her to sleep on than the La-Z-Boy?"

"We talked about it already and she really wants to get her own place just in case our attorneys can't get Brian out of her house. She'll only stay here until she finds something. Just give her a few more days, OK?"

The beach walk was wonderful, but didn't seem to resolve any of Camille, Nicole or my major concerns about divorce or our future together.

CHAPTER 15

By the time I had showered, shaved, dressed and came down for breakfast Nicole had completed all of the housekeeping and prepared my favorite morning yogurt/blueberry/walnut pick-me-up and even fed Duie, who was looking especially content.

"Good morning beautiful. Based on how great this place looks you must have got up at dawn."

"I had a lot to think about and you seemed more restless than usual so..."

"Right, so what's on your agenda today and where is Camille?"

"She's out and about working on her problems and the first thing I'm going to do is find you a low end decorator," she said with a sheepish grin. "It should be pretty easy, you and I will just walk into one of those big box furniture stores near the freeway which feature ready-made room setups. They always have a decorator on staff."

"Yeah, I was thinking about the whole thing and instead of starting with a decorator I've decided to start with Harriet's financial advisor. Since she was part owner of the business he should be able to tell me something," I said with an even bigger grin.

"Great idea," replied Nicole. "Thank you, this means I can invite Patterson to join me for lunch and maybe I can persuade him to be reasonable."

"Also a great idea, especially the reasonable part, if it means as in evenhanded, equitable, and rational and if I may say, if it's practical to our future life style together."

"Yes, you are right again. I will keep that in mind," she said as she snuggled up against me.

I got the financial advisor's name and contact info from Cisco who was bogged down with investigating an assault and attempted murder case of a local gang member.

After arranging to meet with the advisor at 10am in his office I called Jon Doh to finalize which day would be good to shoot the Neurohuts CALog. We both agreed it should be before the holidays and before the weather turned cloudy or the local council decided to bulldoze.

As I drove east on Santa Monica Boulevard toward Beverly Glen I refreshed my memory as to what little I knew about financial advisors. Obviously the title alone implied they advise their clients on how best to invest and grow their money, but Harriet's guy, Bernard Levy of Levy & Holliston, seems to have gone much further. Or maybe it was only because he was now working for Camille, who probably doesn't understand the interplay of her various assets to the extent her aunt Harriet did.

Anyone can hang out a shingle as a financial planner, but that doesn't mean they really know what's best for each client. Many of them tack on an alphabet soup of letters after their names, but according to what I found online before leaving the studio the only letters which are really significant are CFP (short for certified financial planner). Which means they passed a rigorous test plus take mandatory updating classes regularly.

As I drove through the upscale neighborhood of Westwood I wondered if Bernard earned his living from commissions or by charging hourly or flat rates for his services. Advisers of all kinds are not always the most unbiased source of advice if they work on an hourly basis. However, from the way Camille talked about him I had the feeling he probably got a percentage of all the assets he was minding for her. Then there's the fact his office is in Century City which implies he caters exclusively to the rich or the one percent or whatever they're referred to now.

Perhaps the best thing about an advisor is as your plan gets more complicated they can help you remain disciplined about your financial strategies. They'll make the moves for you or badger you until you make them yourself. As I understand from some of the well-heeled art collectors I know, procrastination can cause all sorts of money problems, so it pays to have someone riding you to stay on track and my fatherly feelings for Camille were telling me she needed just such a level of help.

By the time I arrived at Levy & Holliston, CFP I had paid a twenty spot for the privilege of parking my own car and hoofing it some distance to their offices.

However, since I had skipped my regular morning fast walk with Duie I was happy about getting some exercise.

When I entered the foyer I was doubly happy to see an enchanting George Rickey sculpture near the center of the room. It was over 10 ft. tall and its gentle kinetic movements were whimsical and a joy to watch.

The lead receptionist for the offices used an ear mounted intercom system to notify Levy she had directed me down the hall toward his office. He opened the door before I reached it and extended his right hand. It was round, soft and comfortable to shake, like wearing an old glove.

"It's a pleasure to finally meet you Mr. Terra, though I had thought it would have been sooner than this," he said as he continued to hold my hand and guide me toward two plush chairs facing a large picture window on the west side of the office. He looked to be in his late 70s or early 80s, had grey-white hair on both sides of his shinny spherical shaped head and his fleshy, rose colored face contrasted sharply with his bright lime-green tie which I was convinced had been selected for him by someone much younger.

"It's good to meet you too, Mr. Levy, but what makes you think our meeting should have been sooner?"

"Oh, well Missy Camille and Lieutenant Rivas speak so highly of you I assumed you must care about both of them a great deal."

Mr. Levy was fast making himself a likeable fellow in my eyes, for only time and wisdom enables a man to make such an observation.

"You're right and to continue doing so I need to know all you can tell me about the printing business Dr. Mazor bought from Camille and Nell Meyerhoff."

"The lion's share actually came from Camille, or should I say from her aunt Harriet," he said with a twinkle in his eyes.

"Right, but I didn't realize Harriet was the majority owner."

"Yes she was, but first let me say I'm surprised it is you and not Lieutenant Rivas who is asking about this particular investment."

"What do you mean?"

"Well, as you probably know I had advised Missy Camille not to sign over any of her business interests to Dr. Mazor before I could do my fiduciary duty to check him out as they say," he said with another twinkle.

"It's good to know you exercised your option to do so, but why do you think Cisco, ah I mean, Lieutenant Rivas, should be involved?"

"Well, maybe not him, but at least someone associated with him perhaps in the Prosecutors Office."

"So you found something illegal going on?"

"Let's just say there are some very unusual business dealings going on which don't match up with what should be normal for a business of this kind."

I was feeling a little exasperated by Levy's slow paced conversation skills, but it was good for me to slow down and relax. "Like what?" I said.

"For example, a large percentage of their products, specifically the most expensive prints they offer are made in Thailand, not here. Plus most, if not all of the buyers of those prints are located in the largest cities in the U.S. and Europe. Not in any medium or small ones, and the buyers are not what I would call customary or even typical customers."

"In what way are they not conventional?"

"They aren't interior decorators or decorator type businesses or galleries of any kind?"

"Mmm, so what are they?"

"That's a good question, and I had it investigated in only one city, New York."

"OK and?"

"Let's just say all the purchases were made by curious businesses like meat-packing plants, a private trash disposal service, and a building demolition company."

"You are right, those don't seem like normal customers for reproduction prints of 18th century hunting scene paintings," I said as we both stared at the Santa Monica Mountain skyline for a minute or so. "Was there anything else to strike you as odd or strange?"

"Well, keep in mind my expertise is in financial planning, not fine art printing, so what may look offbeat to me may be perfectly normal to folks in the art business such as yourself."

"Like what for instance?"

"Jeffery had ultra-high resolution photographs made of the paintings he inherited from his grandmother as well as a dozen or so others he purchased with assistance from Harriet at an antiques shop in San Francisco. Then he shipped those photos and the real paintings to the company in Thailand specializing in 3D scanning and art replication of heavy impasto paintings," Levy said with a look of puzzlement. "What do you make of such a sequence of actions?"

"Ah, well, 18th century paintings of hunting scenes are not made with heavy impasto paint. In fact, there is rarely any visible texture in them at all."

"Exactly," he said with a firm jaw. "But Jeffery had several full scale 3D embossed type reproduction prints made of each painting which makes them appear to have originally been rendered in heavy impasto paint. Why would he have done so, why did Harriet agree to pay for them and why does Mazor continue to order more of them and believe it or not, why do so many 'non-normal' customers pay a high price for them?"

"What are you considering a high price?"

"Over five grand for each print," he said as his eyelids widened and amplified his expression of concern. "Would you like to have a drink or something Mr. Terra? You look as though you might need one."

"Ah, well my throat does feel somewhat dry," I said as I stood up and moved about a bit to concentrate on all Levy had said and what it might mean.

I was still sifting through the conversation when I heard a faint buzzing sound. A moment or so later a young lady entered the office carrying a tray of drinks which she sat on a small table near our chairs.

"Please help yourself," Levy said as he gestured toward the assorted bottles of colorful sodas and juices. I selected the natural Ginger Ale and had finished most of it before resuming my seat.

"So what do you think is actually going on Mr. Terra? Does it really have anything to do with fine art reproductions?"

"Well if it does, no one in the art world knows about it but, what's more important is Mazor does which could impact on Camille or most likely Cisco and other law enforcement agencies."

"Exactly again and this is why I made sure Missy Camille was completely divested of any legal connection to the business. I must add I'm very happy you are assisting her in dissociating herself from Dr. Mazor as well."

It was time to move on and to meet with Cisco. "Thank you, Mr. Levy, for everything you've done for Camille and for generously sharing your discovery with me. I can assure you Cisco will know what to do next just keep all of this under your hat for now."

Levy tapped his forefinger against the side of his nose, shook my hand again and walked me toward the foyer. I complimented him on the Rickey sculpture and he told me it had been in Harriet's collection and was only recently installed as a long term loan from Missy Camille.

"Why do you call her Missy?"

"I've known her since she was a child and she's always been Missy to me," he said with his biggest twinkle ever. "My wife and I have no children of our own."

"I see. Oh, by the way, how did you manage to acquire such detailed information about the print company? I mean, surely a private investigator couldn't have found such details. And what is the name of the company?" I said as I admired the Rickey swirling about in the refracted sunlight.

"It's called Paragon Apex Prints and the info was provided by Nell," he said as his eyes widened again.

I saluted him and smiled at the ladies behind the front counter as I exited the building and headed toward my car. It was lunch time so on a hunch I headed to a little taco place on Pico Boulevard Cisco often stops at. He and I used to spend time there when we were students at Santa Monica Community College. They make great chicken enchiladas and I wanted a draft of Dos Equis XX too.

Yep, as soon as I got past Gloverfield Boulevard I spotted his car so I pulled in behind it and walked into the small café. Cisco was in the last booth facing the front door so he saw me instantly.

"Hey, I didn't know this was old home week," he said with a smile. "What's brought you to the hood?"

"I've always loved the smell in here. It reminds me of good times," I said as I sat across from him and the waitress approached. "Dos enchiladas de pollo y una cerveza Dos Equis por favor," I said with great hesitancy.

Cisco's eyebrows rose and his smile filled his awe-struck face. Even the waitress seemed somewhat stunned and nodded with amusement.

It took a solid hour to convey everything I'd learned about the history and business practices of Paragon Apex Prints especially since Cisco asked an endless array of questions, including, if I could manage to get one of the 3-D embossed prints for the crime lab to check out. Plus the surveillance on Mazor had already led his men to PAP which is located in an industrial park near LAX, and they noted the building had security fencing with dogs and razor wire plus laser beam activated alarms and an armed guard so he advised I not try breaking into the place to steal a print. Why he thought I might pursue such a plan, eluded me.

Cisco also stated the surveillance hadn't revealed anything else really worthwhile and there was no sign of Rollie anywhere, so his budget wasn't going to allow for the shadowing much longer. His cell blipped and he had to leave so I had another Dos Equis and pondered how to get an embossed print from PAP without paying for it. It was time to go home.

"Ve con dios," said the waitress as I took a long look around the small café and enjoyed finding it hadn't change much since my last visit there.

When I arrived home I could hear Nicole and Camille talking up on the upper deck, but when I opened the front door Duie was sitting right there waiting for me.

"Good boy, Duie, it's great to see you too. Did anyone let you out for a walk?" Duie barked and ran up and down the stairs a couple of times which made my two ladies sashay down, so I let Duie out to do his business and the three of us watched him run over to the lamp pole in the cul-de-sac and relieve himself.

"Well ladies, are we making dinner or driving to it?"

"You really thought it was necessary to ask?"

"Right, so where shall we go, serious, dark and romantic or entertaining, light and fun?"

They both looked me up and down and said 'entertaining'. I wasn't sure whether to laugh or yell 'hey'. "Ok, let's walk over to the pier, there's lots of fun food available there."

"Great, I feel like riding around in a circle with no destination in mind. Oh, or better yet, shooting something and watching it fall over then spring right back up," Camille said with a small sneer.

As I locked the door and the four of us headed toward our objective Camille's cell jingled. She answered it cautiously. "Yes, what? I don't know, why? OK, maybe tomorrow if I have time. No. Good bye."

"Is everything OK?" Nicole said as she put her arm around Camille and studied her distressed expression and posture.

"It was Brian again," she said with a gesture of sheer exhaustion.

"What did he want this time?" Nicole questioned.

"One of those dumb hunting prints."

"What? Ah, do you mean a hunting print from Jeffery's company?" I said probably too quickly. "Do you have one? Where is it?"

"He thinks he left one in the trunk of my car. It's probably just one of his stupid schemes to get me to meet him," Camille added with revulsion.

"In your 560? Where is it?" I was feeling real hopeful.

"It's parked up there somewhere, there weren't any empty spaces around here," she said as she gestured toward the dark end of the street.

"Come on, let's go see," I said as I gave Nicole a nod.

"No it can wait until tomorrow. I'll check it then, I'm not going to jump just because he says so and besides I'm not even sure it's there. I mean after all I don't ever look in the trunk," Camille said as she continued to walk toward the pier.

"How about if you give me the keys and I'll go check and if it is there I'll put it in the studio and deliver it to him tomorrow. You won't have to see Brian at all," I said forthrightly as Nicole crinkled her forehead at me.

"Gee, that would be great, you guys are really, really, cool," Camille said as a smile returned to her youthful face.

"How about if Camille and I walk over to the UBakeIt and pick up two large veggie deep dish pizzas and meet you back here?" Nicole said as she snuggled up against Camille and smiled knowingly at me. "And since you're being such a good guy we'll get you one of those apple strudel things you like too."

"Perfect."

Camille tossed her key fob to me and Duie ran toward me too. As he and I hustled to spot the car in the dark I was keeping everything I had crossed in hopes the print would be there and it was one of the embossed ones not just a regular paper one mounted on illustration board. When we got to the corner I couldn't see the car in any direction so I clicked the key fob and a chirp sounded to my left. I could see the cars lights flashing behind a large SUV at about the middle of the block. Duie took off in that direction. As I approached the car I noticed again the street lamp there also made it look mauve instead blue. As I walked toward the back a folded piece of paper tucked under the windshield wiper on the driver's side got my attention, but I decided to check the trunk first. Luckily the 550 has a strong trunk light so it was easy to see inside the large space, but at first glance it looked empty until I realized the entire trunk floor was taken up by a large flat object wrapped in a black plastic bag. In fact, the color of the plastic almost made it disappear on the dark rubber matt. I impulsively ran my hands across the top and along its sides which confirmed there was an ornate picture frame inside. When I placed both hands directly in the middle and pressed down the breath I had been holding finally escaped. There was definitely an embossed, impasto print inside.

As the glare from the headlights of an oncoming car flashed across me, I immediately removed the package from the trunk, secured the lid and started walking back toward the studio. It took only a few steps before I remembered the folded paper under the windshield wiper. To retrieve it without scratching the 550, I carefully sat the print down and leaned it against the SUV which instantly set off its alarm. My first thought was to grab the package and run, but better judgement prevailed. I reached across the 550, grabbed the folded paper which intuition and its general feel told me was a parking ticket. I then told Duie to sit by my side. It didn't take but a moment for a big fellow, looking weary and very annoyed, to emerge from the nearby house and head straight toward me. I noted immediately his arms were completely covered with tattoos and his knuckles were enormous.

I endeavored to convince him I wasn't trying to steal his SUV, the package in my arms or the 550, but his wife insisted she had phoned the police and he had better keep me there until they arrived. It took well over 45 minutes before the two patrol officers and everyone else on the block were satisfied I wasn't a crook and could go on my way with the package. The older of the two young looking officers assured me he would convey my regards to Lieutenant Rivas right away.

As I got to the corner, Duie took off running at full speed toward the studio and when he disappeared into the darkness I could hear Nicole calling to him. No doubt she had become concerned at what had delayed our return and had gone searching for us.

We walked slowly back to the studio while I explained why Cisco and I wanted a PAP print and everything I had learned from Mr. Levy. She was real happy to hear I felt Levy was a good guy and Cisco had told me not to try breaking into PAP. When we got to the studio Camille had already baked both of the pizzas, opened another bottle of my favorite red wine, and set the table.

The three of us devoured all of the pizza and Duie got most of the thick crust parts. As we sat around sipping wine I wanted to find out more about the print before Camille took off in the morning.

"Why did Brian put a print in the back of your car?" I said in a casual manner.

"Oh, he's done it before. They're too big to fit into the trunk of his car so he sometimes uses mine to deliver the special ones to local clients. Especially if it's a new client he wants to impress."

"If we open this one, would you be able to tell me if it's a special one? I'd like to learn more about them so I can decide on whether to feature them in a CALog."

"Ah, I mean I've seen them a couple of times so I can probably tell."

"Great," I said as I untied the package and slid the print out of the plastic bag and stood it up on the easel.

"It looks like a special one. Turn it around that's how you can really tell," Camille said as she ran her fingers across the front of the print.

I turned it around and carefully placed it back on the easel.

"Yes, this a special one. See how the entire back is shiny just like the front? That means it's completely sealed all the way around to protect it from dust and stuff. You can wipe the front with a damp cloth and it won't hurt it at all."

"So there are other prints embossed like this which are not sealed?"

"Yes, those are the cheaper ones."

"How much cheaper are they?" I asked.

"That I don't know. I don't know how much the sealed ones are either. The whole business doesn't interest me because those artists are all dead and the subjects are all boring and stupid looking. It's amazing to me Brian believes you can actually make money selling these things.

He really is as weird as they are."

"Do you know how much he paid for the business?" I said as I put the print back inside the bag.

"No, Uncle Bernie handled all of the selling stuff for me. He said it was a good deal so I just signed the papers."

"Uncle Bernie? Do you mean Bernard Levy your financial advisor? I didn't know he was a relative of yours," I said without sounding too snoopy.

"Oh, he's not a real uncle, I just call him one because I've known him my entire life. I thought the deal was kind of odd, I mean here I am married to Brian and I have to sign a bunch of legal stuff in order to sell a business to him. I don't really understand why I couldn't just give it to him. I mean after all, I didn't want it, but Uncle Bernie insisted."

"He was probably taking precautions in your best interest," Nicole said.

"Yeah, that's what he said too. I'm tired, let's go to bed."

CHAPTER 16

Wanting to get an early start, I managed to shower, shave, dress and leave before both Nicole and Camille. Duie, however, wasn't happy when I left without him again.

I drove directly to the police lab which is in one of those city owned renovated buildings near Bergamot Station. Cisco met me in the parking lot and I didn't give him the print until I was completely satisfied he understood how important it was the thing didn't look messed with when I delivered it to Mazor.

"Yes sir Leonardo," he said through clenched teeth.

It was no surprise when he refused to allow me to be in the lab when the examination took place. So considering how early it was, I couldn't go to one of the big-box furniture stores to see if they had one of the cheap prints available to buy cause they don't open until 9 or 10am. I couldn't even go talk to Stephanie because her gallery, like most of the others, doesn't open until 11am. So I went to Fromin's and had a leisurely breakfast.

By 8:30am I was back in the studio reading a note from Nicole, which informed me she and Camille would check in with me around lunch time.

At 11am, Cisco texted to meet him at Clover Park on Ocean Avenue, so once again I took off without Duie and again he was not pleased so I gave him a bone to keep him occupied.

Cisco was obviously concerned if we met at the lab it wouldn't have looked right to anyone passing by to see him take something large, wrapped in black plastic, from his trunk and putting it into mine, but in a park it's natural to see people take things out of their car. So we did and there was no problem. From this particular park you can watch small private planes take off and land at Santa Monica Airport so we sat on a bench beneath some trees to talk and observe.

"So what's the verdict?" I said when we finally got settled.

"The lab confirms the print and the sculptured frame were both made of a synthetic drug paste. All you have to do is peel the clear plastic film off both sides of the print and immerse it and the frame in hot water. They will both dissolve into a pudding type consistency."

"What about the gold leaf on the frame?"

"It's a water based imitation," he said with raised eyebrows. "So it will dissolve as well."

"Then what? I mean you can't sell pudding very easily."

Cisco just stared at me and shook his head. "Right genius, you dry the pudding and pulverize it into a fine powder. Then sell it in any amount size you want."

"And so how much in total quantity are we talking about here?" I said as a new looking Cessna took off over our heads with a loud reverberation.

"About 250 ounces, which is approximately 2 gallons."

"And I assume on the street it would be worth more than 5 grand."

"Yes, but its real value is being able to move it through customs and around the world using legal shipping services. Even our dogs can't smell the stuff. The plastic seal encasing the print and the imitation gold leaf on the frame do not allow any fumes to escape, especially since synthetics don't have as strong an odor as natural drugs do to begin with."

"To say nothing about the fact a framed print just doesn't look like it could be drugs. So what do we do now?" I said as I leaned forward to look at another plane taking off.

"Well, unfortunately we can't bust him as a drug dealer," he said with a maddened look.

"You mean you want to get him for murder instead, right?"

"Yes and no. It seems the Feds have been keeping an eye on our Dr. Mazor's drug dealing activities and they don't want to bust him until they have determined who all of the participants internationally are. How do you like those apples?"

"They're full of worms," I said as a nifty homemade looking small plane attempted a precarious landing.

"The only way we are going to be able to get past the Feds is to get Mazor riled up enough to do something dumb. So we can catch him in the act."

"Ok, how about this, I won't return the print to him right away and maybe it will make him do something rash," I said as I continued watching the funny plane bounce its way down the runway.

Cisco took a deep breath and stared off down the street before turning to face me. He looked me hard in the eye. "Yeah, I guess it's worth a try, but it's probably time to tell Camille we suspect her husband ... unless you still feel she may be in on the murders."

"No, she's just too sweet to be a killer. I'll tell her today or tonight. I'm not sure when I'll see her. By the way, how did you find out the Feds were watching Mazor?"

"It seems they've been tailing him too and our surveillance team bumped into theirs. Which reminds me, do you have a gun?" Cisco asked as he gave me another hard look.

"No man, you know how I feel about guns. Beside, Mazor may be greedy and he's probably wacko, but he doesn't seem like the kind to use a gun. I mean after all, so far all the murders have been by cold needle, not hot lead."

"Right, well, stay in public places and lock all your doors and windows tight."

"Si el senor lo hara," I said nonchalantly hoping it would sound natural.

As I headed back toward Lincoln Boulevard I texted Nicole to see if we could meet for lunch. She responded instantly and told me to meet her at the Tastemaker Café on the Santa Monica Mall near Arizona Avenue. They specialize in artisan energy bars and hot-butter-and-coffee drinks. I really didn't feel very hungry by the time I got there. Perhaps it was the thought of having to select something from their limited menu, but I reminded myself I was just starting a new relationship which hopefully would be a long term one and therefore I needed to be open to new things, especially if they were being suggested to me by my new significant other.

The place looked and felt more like a tech incubator than a site to relax and eat so I don't remember what I ordered, but I do recall by evening I didn't feel like having dinner. In fact, all three of us were tired and turned in early.

It was shortly after 4am when I heard Duie scratching furiously on the sliding glass door downstairs which was his regular way of letting me know he needed to go. Not being surprised, given how early we had last let him out, I got up and carefully made my way down the dark stairs trying not to make any sound which might wake Camille. There was a pale shaft of moon light cutting across the center of the studio and I could see she was still snuggled-up on the Lazy Boy. Her silent charm stirred paternal feelings in me again. It must be your age I said to myself. Duie was nowhere in sight.

It was unusually cold in the studio and when I reached the glass door the reason was obvious. The door had been jimmied open. As I attempted to close it there was a faint sound near the painting storage racks behind me so I turned and stepped in that direction. It was Duie. His back legs weren't working, his head was bleeding, and he was trying to drag himself toward me.

As I bent down to help him a silhouetted figure of a large man holding something in his hand charged out of the darkness and lunged at me. I shoved his hand aside and walloped the side of his head hard. He gave out with a deep groan then swung around and stormed at me again. I grabbed his wrist with both my hands and pushed him mercilessly backwards onto my work table. Paint containers, brushes and a wide assortment of art supplies flew in all directions as the table collapsed under our weight and Camille let out with a terrified scream. I saw her dart through the moonlight into the kitchen nook area as the attacker and I rolled around on top of the scattered art supplies. He continuously jabbed his hand at me as I picked up anything I could find in the darkness and threw it at him. Despite the mayhem I managed to belt his face a couple of times more and when he stumbled back he slipped on the paint soaked floor and fell on his back so I sank my knee into his neck, pinned his hand down with my other foot and dumped an opened container of turpentine and waste paint all over his head hoping it would blind him. I stepped back to look for a weapon when he mopped his face quickly with his open hand then grabbed hold of the easel and pulled himself up. As I bent to pick up my metal T-square to use as a weapon he pushed the easel over. I spun to get out of its way, but I wasn't fast enough. Its upper crossbar bounced off the back of my head and hit the concrete floor with a tremendous metal thud which reverberated like the whole place had been hit by a giant sledge hammer. As I reached my hand up to feel if my surgery scar had been ripped open he was on me again. I was amazed at the man's continued strength and grit. We hurtled and collided with everything until we were both exhausted, but he stormed at me again and then a loud crash boomed throughout the studio. I turned and saw through the darkness Cisco and a uniformed officer smashing through the front door. Cisco had his gun in hand. The attacker twisted out from under a pile of broken paintings and rose up gasping and snorting to clear his nose and lungs of turpentine, then charged his hand at me again. I crouched and threw a heavy container of modeling paste at him just as a shot rang out. The bullet grazed along the left side of my head, leaving a bleeding furrow through my hair just above my ear, then it tore a hole through the attacker's leg. He froze for a moment as his leg went out from under him and he fell onto one knee. The studio's track lights flashed on, blinding everybody. As my eyes adjusted I realized I was almost face to face with the assailant.

He looked like some kind of alien creature with paint and turpentine caked on his face and oozing from his eyes, nostrils and mouth. But I could tell he was Raimond Hortense Puissant. He was holding a large hypodermic needle in his hand and the wound in his leg was bleeding profusely. I turned to see Nicole at the bottom of the stairs with one hand on the light switch and her other holding a broken wine bottle like a weapon. Camille was hiding under the stairs and holding a large kitchen knife with both her hands. She looked totally traumatized. Cisco still with his gun aimed directly at Rollie told the other officer to call for backup, paramedics and an ambulance. Everyone gasped as Rollie raised the hypodermic up to his throat and took a drawn-out look at each of us. He then focused on Camille, strained to clear his throat and spoke with a rasping high pitched slur. "I didn't want to hurt you, it was just the drugs I needed and he wouldn't give them to me unless I ... I ..." He then plunged the needle deep into his right main neck artery, injected its deadly toxin and slowly collapsed face down in an eerie pile of paint, blood and brushes. He was obviously dead before his head hit the floor.

We all felt stunned and shaky, but relieved. As I pressed my left hand against my head wound I turned and nodded to Cisco and walked toward Nicole, but she disappeared into darkness when the lights suddenly went out again and a gun fired from somewhere back in the storage racks. I felt a hot searing pain erupt in my left shoulder. I sprang forward to where I had last seen Nicole standing and happily landed on top of her as a second shot raced over our heads and hit the wall. Two quick shots came from Cisco and streaked into the storage racks, which collapsed in a thunderous gladder.

It was eerily quiet for a moment as the room filled with the smell of gun powder and Duie started whimpering. I rolled off Nicole and started crawling toward him when an ugly groan came from under the pile of rubble at the back of the studio.

"Are you all right?" I whispered to Nicole.

"Yes, I'm fine."

"How about you Camille?"

"I'm ok," she said sniffling.

"Cisco, I'm going to get the flashlight?"

"Right, I've got him covered," he replied.

I scampered over to the sink while struggling to believe Rollie was still alive. Remarkably I found the flashlight still standing upright beneath the sink. But the cabinet surrounding it was destroyed, as was the one above. Broken glasses and dishes were scattered everywhere.

"Find the breaker switch and turn it on," Cisco commanded.

I aimed the light toward the electrical box and could see it was open and had blood smeared across it and the adjacent wall. I looked down and was surprised to see Rollie hadn't moved. He was definitely dead. I was suddenly conscious of another body under the rumble at the far back of the studio. I reached up and flipped the main power switch back on. The studio filled with light and the rubble moved a bit. I could see it was Mazor on his back, trying to hide beneath several broken paintings. He was breathing, but just barely. Cisco came forward as the uniformed officer dashed in with gun in hand stating backup and paramedics were on their way. Cisco told him to wait outside to direct them to the right condo. Nicole helped Camille up and they came to my side as I lifted a large painting off of Mazor. Cisco picked up Mazor's gun and checked his pulse. Mazor opened his eyes, looked at Camille, took a short breath and said, "All I wanted was to be the only man to have you." His last breath was silent and wet with blood. Cisco had shot him twice in the chest. I'm not sure what happened then. All I remember are the sharp pains at the back of my head and in my shoulder as blood was running down my arm from both. I blacked out.

EPILOGUE

It was 3pm over a week later when I was being pushed out of St. Johns Hospital in a wheel chair. I felt older than ever and longed to be surrounded by salty sea air and to sink my feet into some beach sand. Nicole and Duie were waiting at the curb in the 560. Duie looked as dog-tired as I felt and we both had bandages on our head and shoulder. I insisted we go home despite Nicole's reluctance to take us there. Duie tried to sit up in his usual place on the center console between us but he just couldn't balance so I held him on my lap as Nicole drove to the studio and parked under the street lamp with that eerie ochre glow.

The condo wasn't looking good. The front door and its frame were completely missing replaced by a sheet of bolted plywood. I sat down on the small front door landing, removed my shoes and socks, dug my toes into the temperate sand and took a deep breath. Duie glanced at the nearby gulls, but made no effort to move from my lap. Nicole suggested we try the back entrance. It felt good to walk around to the back deck. The sliding glass door frame was still there, but the broken glass hadn't been replaced so it too had plywood bolted to it. It took Nicole a few frustrating minutes of fiddling with the mangled lock before she could slide the door open enough for us to squeeze in. Upon entering I immediately had a flashback of Brice's wrecked studio. The destruction in the studio was far beyond what I had imagined it would be. Most of the furniture was demolished, many of my paintings were damaged, everything including the walls was either cracked, shattered or smashed and all were splattered with paint and dried blood. If I didn't know better I would have thought the fight had lasted all night and involved at least six men, not just three. I started to sit Duie down, but he didn't want me to. I handed him to Nicole and started picking up some of my brushes and other art supplies. Each painting was either obliterated or beyond repair, except the one on the easel ... the yellow scalene painting I had favored and held on to for so long. It looked unscathed, which made me laugh and inhale an overwhelming amount of turpentine and paint fouled air. I stepped forward and felt sharp bits of broken glass under my bare feet.

"We can't stay here. Let's get a room somewhere," I said as I took Duie back from Nicole.

"Come on, I know a place you'll enjoy," she said.

She drove south on Neilson Way and went only a short distance then turned toward the beach.

"I didn't know there was a hotel in here."

"Well it's a very special one. It's only for invited VIPs like you," she said with a wonderful flash of her eyes as the car came to a stop in front of an ultra-modern beach house.

"Whose place is this?"

"It's ours now, darling," she said with pride.

During my stay at St. Johns, Nicole had concluded her divorce negotiations, which resulted in her getting most of what she wanted including the beach house, a generous monthly alimony payment, and most of Patterson's art collection, plus a warehouse in the airport district to keep it in. I was very happy for her and somewhat intimidated by her arbitration skills.

The first thing I saw as we walked in the front door was one of my paintings hanging on the facing wall and glimpses of others were visible as I looked in all directions. Nicole had taken them from the destroyed studio and had them cleaned and mounted on new stretcher bars. There was even one of my very early expressionistic figure paintings mounted near a door labeled Studio. I couldn't resist opening the door and taking a look around. She even managed to retrieve my computer and Sally's old hard copy files. I felt completely at home as we walked out onto the deck with Duie to watch the sunset.

Camille of course retained her aunt's Beverly Hills mansion, art collection, investment portfolio and properties, and also inherited Mazor's apartments in Boston which she was looking forward to renovating. However, his bank account was being retained by the FBI until it could be determined how much of it came from selling drugs. Nell had agreed to help Camille develop themed traveling exhibitions from her aunt's collection. Plus Camille's efforts to reignite her relationship with Jon was moving forward. It was a good feeling to know she was enthusiastic about life again, but none of us were able to convince her to see a new therapist, not even a female one. She insisted she was going to enroll in philosophy classes at UC Santa Monica. I was reluctant to explain to her she would probably have to start with basic remedial courses. When you're young, the future seems infinite, but at a certain age, you start thinking about how the future is finite. Regardless, maybe, just maybe studying the great thinkers from the dawn of humanity might help her recover her complete sense of self.

Cisco got kudos from all the bigwigs on the force, City Hall and the Arts Council. It wasn't long before he suggested we get together at the club for some brews and blues. I told him I'd come only if he made sure we didn't have any of that reconstituted stuff, because it was worse than Montezuma's revenge. The FBI weren't overly happy about having to curtail their hopes of finding all of the individuals Mazor had sold the dangerous synthetic drugs to, but they were pleased he was dead, his entire operation was shut down, and no one would have to suffer through a long costly trial. Short of starting a war, there didn't seem to be much anyone could do to stop the manufacturing of the lethal drugs in Asia.

Liz was very happy we had not made a CALog with Mazor and wanted to know if I had any resources in the music and theatre industries, because the name of the program was being changed to California Arts Log.

As I ran a finger slowly along a still enflamed new raw scar, which almost reached the re-opened old one at the base of my skull, its visceral-ness immediately made me think of Spider Washington and Zimmee Chan. What a great CAsLog that would make.

"All things considered, you don't look half bad. You're still 5'11" or so, still have mostly dark hair, your brown eyes are not blood shot and your hospital stay didn't put any weight on your 160 lb. frame. We just need to get you shaved and bring a smile back to your face," said Nicole as she slowing began disrobing.

Maybe she just wanted to put me in a holiday state-of-mind.

"Jingle, jingle all the way."

ABOUT THE AUTHOR

Originally from Australia, M. Lee Musgrave holds a Master of Art degree from CSU, Los Angeles. He is the recipient of a National Endowment for Arts Fellowship. His artwork has been in solo and group exhibitions world-wide. As a Professor of Art and curator he organized hundreds of exhibitions involving artists, collectors and a variety of related enthusiast. Those many experiences and his ongoing personal art activities inform his writing about LA's exciting art community.

NOTE FROM THE AUTHOR

Word-of-mouth is crucial for any author to succeed. If you enjoyed *Brushed Off*, please leave a review online—anywhere you are able. Even if it's just a sentence or two. It would make all the difference and would be very much appreciated.

Thanks!
M. Lee Musgrave

Thank you so much for reading one of our **Mystery** novels.

If you enjoyed our book, please check out our recommendation
for your next great read!

K-Town Confidential by Brad Chisholm and Claire Kim

"An enjoyable zigzagging plot."

–Kirkus Reviews

"If you are a fan of crime stories and legal dramas that have a noir
flavor, you won't be disappointed with *K-Town Confidential*."

–Authors Reading

View other Black Rose Writing titles at
<u>www.blackrosewriting.com/books</u> and use promo code
PRINT to receive a **20% discount** when purchasing.

Made in the USA
Monee, IL
07 April 2021